His First Wife

Also by Grace Octavia

TAKE HER MAN

Published by Dafina Books

His First Wife

GRACE OCTAVIA

Dafina
Books

KENSINGTON PUBLISHING CORP.
www.kensingtonbooks.com

DAFINA BOOKS are published by

Kensington Publishing Corp.
850 Third Avenue
New York, NY 10022

All Kensington titles, imprints, and distributed lines are available at special quantity discounts for bulk purchases for sales promotion, premiums, fund-raising, educational, or institutional use.

Special book excerpts or customized printings can also be created to fit specific needs. For details, write or phone the office of the Kensington Special Sales Manager: Attn. Special Sales Department. Kensington Publishing Corp., 850 Third Avenue, New York, NY 10022. Phone: 1-800-221-2647.

ISBN-13: 978-0-7582-1849-0
ISBN-10: 0-7582-1849-4

First Printing: October 2008
10 9 8 7 6 5 4 3 2

Printed in the United States of America

For the women and men of
historically Black colleges and universities,
who lift as they climb and
pray along the way

and

Georgia,
on my mind . . .

ACKNOWLEDGMENTS

First, I have to thank God for all the love I have received when I thought that maybe I'd already asked for too much. The greatest thing about God's grace is that it is abundant for those who pray and ask that it is granted. My journey in publishing has been assisted by God's angels, who have opened their hearts, homes, and sometimes . . . their wallets to support my passion. Second, one established writer told me not to be surprised if my family doesn't support my work. This could not have been farther from the truth when my first novel, *Take Her Man*, was published in 2007. My book sales are a direct reflection of everyone I know making it their personal business to go out and support. From my line sister in California ordering it before anyone else had it, to my blood sister in Maryland making everyone in her office read it, my family and friends inspired me to keep doing this writing thing. Third, to my sister Cynthia Renee Williams. You called me every day to find out when *Take Her Man* was coming out and then every day after to let me know who'd bought the book. Your voice was a bright spot on many mornings and I thank you being there for me (even when I don't answer the phone). I guess that's what big sisters are for. My grandmother Julia Reid, who continues to prove that a real woman is rare and precious. Thanks for making this possible.

Thank you to my agent Tracy Sherrod and editor Rakia Clark for being patient with me as I grow. Kensington Publishing and Adeola Saul for believing in my work. My first readers Bobby Jean Wooten Bryant (how many names do you have?), Jurgen Grandt (for staying up for two days with me), Natasha O'Dell, Chika Carter, and Daheli Hall.

My sincere supporters Erskine Roberts (you boosted book sales, dude! . . . lol), Dr. Alma Vinyard and the English department at Clark Atlanta University, Steve Faulkner and Shorter College, Munson Steed, Yvette Caslin, Michele Fling, and Melinda Johnson at *Rolling Out* (thanks *ro* for always putting action behind words to support artists—many meals were paid for by your checks).

To the family: Eric, Kenyair, and Jacala, Jaimie for always trying to lead me in the right direction, Aunt Tina, Gina, Kayla, Trinity, Mikie, and Aaron. My aunts and uncles—Lucielle and Alfred (who made me answer all of their questions), Sam, Nancy, Gerrie and Nadine, Thirjane. Cousins and close family friends Tamika, Tony, Jumari, Jayquan and Little Toni Grace, Lemuel and Gwen, Ray and Chiv (and your multiplying family), Madeline, Lil Madeline, Tony and Antionette, Nan "Paul" Adesegun (for always looking for jobs for me) and his family, Alfred Johnson, Jr., and Gracie.

To the reviewers and organizations who have supported me, *Essence* magazine, *Romantic Times*, RAWSISTAZ, *Urban Reviewers*, APOOO, *Deltareviewer*, the Zora Neale Hurston Literary Conference in Okalahoma, John Holman and the other professors at Georgia State University, Rodney Carmichael at *Creative Loafing*, Tasha Martin and Sistahfriend.com, Shennice Cleckley, Professor Sonja Lanehart and the African American Women's Language Conference (had a great time!), Elizabeth Fields and the *Mandala Literary Journal* at UGA, the Links, all black sororities and fraternities, Professor Grandt and his students at Georgia Tech, KBMS in Vancouver, the *Westbury Times*, and UGA Press.

The readers and readers' groups: Phyllis Street, Tulsa Sisters Sipping Tea, Lynette Barclay and Between the Lines of GA, Donnica Copeland and the ladies of Sista Talk in GA, Eugenia Holloman and Cover 2 Cover of Columbia SC, Kenae Danley and Real Ladies Read, Allison and Impressions Book Club in DC, Overbooked, my myspace.com blog readers!

To my Sorors of Delta Sigma Theta, who—as always—showed up and showed out. The ladies of Epsilon Tau, Atlanta Suburban Alumnae, Columbia (SC) Alumnae, Tuscaloosa Alumnae, Queens Alumnae and all others I may not mention, thanks for putting a sister on the agenda! Lakeisha Scott and the Arts and Letters Commission at National Office. My line sisters—ten years strong! Khanya, Frankie, Sadiqa and Tanya. Roslin Spigner for always checking in with me. My spec Naima and her line sisters of Spring '99! Aretha, thanks for putting the reading group together, the supportive "babies" Sasha, Carinda, Tabora, Yery, Tiki, Satonja, Tabitha, Danny!!! Love ya!

My dear friends who put up with me hiding in holes and living in coffee shops when all you wanted to do was just "talk." Thanks for your patience and understanding. Orpheus Malik Williams, Renita Ward, Billie Jo, Felicia and the NEW Nickerson!, Shamita, Crystal, Braylon, the South Carolina Crew—Essence, Cari, Mr. B, Tinisha, Carolyn Hall, Glenda Gooden, and Tamalyn Peterson, Earle Hall, James Tolliver, Jermaine Smith, Kamal, Lou M., Omar, Richard "Freedom", Lav C., the Mayor of Night Life in Atlanta Russell Hopson, Valesia, Tyre and Just Loafin (free food!).

To my composition students at Clark Atlanta University. You are the new scholars. Keep reading and writing. I'll see you when you get to the top. Don't forget, Ms. Reid.

The artist friends. Abyss, the hardest-working poet in the

world (I think you were in Alaska one day when we spoke), whose lovely poem, "God Sent," inspired the closing of this book. Yes, sometimes love is so divine, we must find it in our next lifetime. Askia at *Compound*, Lenny M., Ronda P., my classmates at GSU, and others out there.

Finally, to YOU, the reader whose name is not here. To YOU, the reader that I may never meet. May you experience in these pages the love I have for my people and my desire to portray us as we are, in our own beauty. Know that I gladly take the journey into the pages with you. Thanks for the love. Keep supporting black writers.

Peace.

PART ONE

Birth

"You got to say, you need to say,
you better say, you oughta say . . .
Hell, hell, hell, hell, hell, hell,
HELL NO!"

—Ms. Sophia and Her Sisters,
The Color Purple: The Musical

EMAIL TRANSMISSION

TO: Jamison.Taylor@rakeitup.net
FROM: duane.carter@hotmail.com
DATE: 3/15/07
TIME: 9:57 PM

Hello. If this e-mail works and it's Jamison Taylor, I think I found your PalmPilot in front of my house this morning. All I could find was the name Jamison Taylor inside and I Googled it and found this e-mail address. If it's you, I have it.

EMAIL TRANSMISSION

TO: duane.carter@hotmail.com
FROM: Jamison.Taylor@rakeitup.net
DATE: 3/16/07
TIME: 5:03 AM

You don't know how happy I was to get this e-mail. I had my assistants running around all day looking for that thing. Where are you located? Can I come pick it up?

Jamison

Foolish

It was 5:35 in the morning. I was doing 107 on the highway, pushing the gas pedal down so far with my foot that my already-swollen toes were beginning to burn. It was dark, so dark that the only way I knew that I wasn't in bed with my eyes closed was the baby inside of me kicking nervously at my belly button and the slither of light the headlights managed to cast on the road in front of me.

I-85 South was eerily silent at this time. I knew that. I'd been in my car, making this same drive, once before. I kept wiping hot tears from my eyes so I could see out of the window. I should've been looking for police, other cars on the road, a deer, a stray dog that had managed to find its way to the highway in the dewy hours of the morning, but I couldn't. I couldn't see anything but where I was going, feel anything but what I didn't want to feel, think anything but what had gotten me out of my bed in the first place. My husband.

Jamison hadn't come home. I sat in the dining room and ate dinner by myself as I tried not to look at the clock. Tried not to notice that the tall taper candles had melted to shapeless clumps in front me. Knowing the time would only make me call.

And calling didn't show trust. We'd talked about trust. Jamison said I needed to trust him more. Be patient. Understanding. All of the things we'd vowed to be on our wedding day, he reminded me. My pregnancy had made me emotional, he said. And I was adding things up and accusing him of things he hadn't done, thoughts he hadn't thought. But I was no fool. I knew what I knew.

Jamison's patterns had changed over the past few months. And while he kept begging me to be more trusting and understanding, my self-control was growing thin. The shapeless clumps on the table in front of me resembled my heart—bent out of shape with hot wax in the center, ready to spill out and burn the surface. Jamison had never stayed out this late. And with a baby on the way? I was hot with anger. Resentful. I was ready to spill out, to spin out, but I held it in.

I helped our maid, Isabella, clear the table, told her she was excused for the night. Then I moved to the bedroom, and while I still hadn't peeked at the clock, the credits at the end of the recorded edition of *Ten O'Clock News* proved that any place my husband could be . . . should be . . . was closed. I wanted to believe I was being emotional, but that would've been easier if I didn't know what I knew. Maybe he'd been in an accident. Maybe he was at a hospital. Yeah . . . but maybe he wasn't.

I laid in bed for a couple of hours; my thoughts were swelling my mind as round as my pregnant stomach. I knew what was going on. I knew exactly where he was. The only question was, what was I going to do?

Then I was in my car. My white flip-flops tossed in the passenger seat. My purse left somewhere in the house. My son inside of my stomach, tossing and kicking. It was like a dream, the way everything was happening. The mile markers, exit signs, trees along the sides of my car looked blurry and almost unreal through my glazed eyes. The heat was rising. My emotions were driving me down that highway, not my mind. My mind said I was eight-and-a-half months pregnant with my first child. I didn't need the drama, the stress. I needed to be in bed.

But my emotions—my heart—were running hot like the engine in my car. I was angry and sad at the same time. Sometimes just angry though. I'd see Jamison in my mind and fill up my insides with the kind of anger that makes you shake and feel like you're about to vomit. And then, right when I was about to explode, I'd see him again in my mind, in another way, feel betrayed, and sadness would sneak in. Paralyzing sadness, so consuming that it feels like everything is dead and the only thing I can do is cry to mourn the loss. I wanted to fight someone. Get to where he was and kick in the door so he could see me. Finally see me and see what this was doing to us. To our marriage.

I didn't have an address, but I knew exactly where she lived. My friend Marcy and I followed Jamison there one night when he was supposed to be going to a fraternity function at a local hotel. But having already suspected something was going on, I called the hotel and learned that there was nothing scheduled. That night six months ago, before he left, I gave him a chance to come clean. I asked if I could go. "No one else will have their wives there; it's just frat," he said, using the same excuse he'd been using for three weeks. He slid on his jacket, kissed me on the cheek and walked out the front door. I picked up my purse and ran out the back where Marcy was waiting in a car we'd rented just for the circumstance. When Jamison finally stopped his truck, we found ourselves sitting in front of a house I knew I'd never forget. The red bricks lining the walkway, the yellow geraniums around a bush in the middle of the lawn, the outdated lace curtains in the window. It looked so small, half the size of our Tudor in Cascade where the little house might envy a backyard cabana. It was dark and seemed empty until Jamison climbed out of the bright red "near midlife crisis" truck he'd bought on his thirtieth birthday. Then, the living room light came on, my husband walked in. And through the lace I watched as he hugged her and was led farther away from me. I fell like a baby into my best friend's arms. What was I to do?

I promised myself I would never forget that house. So there was no need to look at the address. I knew every turn that had brought me there. I just couldn't figure out why.

Now, here I was nearly half a year later, dressed in a silk, vanilla nightgown at five in the morning, making the same trip, but with a different agenda. I knew why and where, and something in me said it was time to act.

I saw that red truck parked in the driveway when I turned onto the street. It looked so bold there. Like it belonged. Like nothing was a secret. *They* were the perfect family. There was no wife at home, no child on the way; our love, our love affair, was the second life he was living. *She* was his wife. I was just the woman he was sleeping with. Sad tears sat in my eyes, my anger refusing to let them roll down my cheeks. Every curse I knew was coming from my mouth as I held the steering wheel tighter and tighter the closer I got. My husband, the person I thought knew me better than anyone else in the world, had turned his back on me for another woman.

I pulled my car into the driveway behind Jamison's and turned off the ignition. The sudden silence hit me like the first touch of cold beach water on virgin feet. Without the hum of the engine, I realized I was alone. I'd gotten myself all the way there, but I didn't know what I was going to do. I knew I had to act, but what was I going to do? Burn the house down or ring the door bell and sell them cookies? And if she came to the door, what was I going to say? Ask another woman if I could see *my* husband? Curse her out? Scream? Cry? Should I hit her? I hadn't hit anyone in my life. What if Jamison answered the door? What if he was mad and told me to leave? If he said it was over?

The baby kicked again, but lightly, as if he was nudging me to go and get his father out of that house, away from that woman. Coreen Carter was her name. Marcy found it on a piece of mail she'd snatched from the mailbox when we followed Jamison. It was a simple name, but Coreen Carter couldn't be that simple. She had my husband inside of her house.

The anger let go at that thought and the sad tears began to fall again. What was I doing? What was happening with my life? I felt like I was being torn inside out. My baby was the only glue that was keeping me together. I felt so alone in that car.

I snatched my cell phone from the seat beside me and called Marcy. She picked up her phone on the first ring. She was an RN and her husband was an ER doctor, so she was a light sleeper.

"I guess little Jamison is about to make his arrival?" she assumed cheerfully, but I couldn't answer. I was sobbing now. Sadness was coming from deep inside and I was sure the only sound I could make was a scream.

"Kerry?" she called. "You okay? Where are you?"

"Here." I managed. There was no need for me to say where exactly. She knew.

"It's six in the. . . . He didn't come home?"

"No."

"Kerry, why didn't you call me? You don't need to do that right now. Not in your condition."

"I just want this to stop," I said sorrowfully.

"I understand, but right now just isn't the time. You have other things to take care of." She paused. "I know I sound crazy to you, but I just don't want anything to happen to you or the baby. You understand that, right?"

"Yes," I said, with my voice cracking. "But I'm just tired of this crap. I mean, what the hell, Marcy? Why? Why is Jamison here with this woman?"

"I don't know that. I can't answer that. Only Jamison can."

"Exactly." I felt a twist of anger wrench my gut. Again I went from feeling sorry for myself to being angry that I was there in the first place. Jamison was *my* husband and he was cheating on me and I wasn't going to just sit in a car and let it go on. I slid on my flip-flops and opened the car door.

"What are you going to do?"

"I don't know," I said. I really didn't. But, again, my emotions were driving. I was spilling out like that hot wax and before I knew it, I was charging up the walkway.

"Just don't do anything foolish," Marcy said before I hung up. Later I'd think about how crazy that sounded. How could I possibly do anything more foolish than what was already being done to me?

The little cracked doorbell seemed to ring before I even pressed it. It chimed loud and confident, like it wasn't past 6 AM and the sun hadn't already begun to rise behind me. It was quiet. The only noise I heard was my heart pounding, shaking so wildly inside of me that I couldn't stand still. I waited for another five seconds which felt like hours. My husband was on one side of the door and I was on the other. Our wedding bands and my large belly were the only signs we were connected. I looked at his truck again. It was the only piece of Jamison I could see from where I was and my heart sank a bit farther. The shine of the paint, the gloss on the wheels, it looked so happy, so free, so smug, so complete. Everything he wanted. I was tired of making this all so possible for Jamison. Making his life so comfortable, so happy. His perfect wife, carrying his perfect son. I was alone in my marriage and I was tired.

I began pounding on the door then. Ringing the bell and then pounding some more. My fist balled up and it pounded hard like a rock threatening to burst through. Someone was inside and they were coming out. If there were children inside, a mother and father, a dog, a parrot. . . . I didn't care. They were all getting up and out of that house.

A small, light brown hand pulled back the sheet of weathered lace covering the square at the top of the door. A woman's face appeared. Her eyes were squinting with the kind of tired worry anyone would have over a knock at the door at 6 AM I'd seen those eyes before, and before she widened them enough to see who I was, my fist was banging at the glass in front of her face. I was trying to break it and if I could break it, I'd grab her face and pull her through the tiny square.

"Tell my husband to come outside," I hollered, my voice sounding much bigger than I was. She looked surprised. Like she never expected to see me or hadn't known Jamison even had a wife. I pressed my face against the window to see inside. To see if Jamison was there behind her. The flap fell back down over the little window and I heard heavy footsteps. I was beside myself. Had totally let go of whoever I was. My baby grew lighter, as if he wasn't even there, and a thunderbolt inside shocked me into action.

"Jamison!" I shouted heatedly. "Jamison, come outside!" I began banging on the door again. I couldn't believe what was happening. I knew it was her. Coreen Carter. I saw her only once before in my life. But when she came to the door that time to let Jamison in, I learned her face the way a victim does her victimizer.

She was what most men would consider beautiful. She had short, curly red hair. From the car I thought it was dyed, but up close I could tell it was her natural color. Fire engine red, like the truck, from the root. She had freckles of the same color dotted around her eyes and her skin was the color of Caribbean sand. Really, she looked nothing like me. In fact, we were complete opposites. My hair was so black and long, most of my friends called me "Pocahontas" growing up. My hair wouldn't dye and most days it wouldn't hold a curl of any kind. And if the skin of the woman in the window was the color of Caribbean sand, then mine was darker than the black sand on the beaches of Hawaii. My mother didn't like to talk about it, but my grandfather on my father's side was half Sudanese, and while he died long before I was born, my father always said the one thing he left behind was his liquorice color on my skin and my perfectly shaped, curious almond eyes.

My cell phone began ringing. I opened it, certain it was Marcy making sure I hadn't killed anyone, but it was Jamison.

"Jamison," I said, looking again in the window to find him. What was this? What was going on? I felt far from him already. Now he couldn't even come to the door?

"Kerry, go home." His voice was filled with irritation.

"What?" I asked. "Are you kidding me? Jamison, come outside." I couldn't believe what I was hearing. He sounded as if I was doing something wrong, like I was out of place.

"I don't want to do this here. It's not right," he said.

"Not right? Not right to who, Jamison? Her? I'm your wife!"

"I know that."

"No, you don't because if you did, I wouldn't be standing out here in my nightgown, eight months pregnant. Or did you forget about that?" I started banging on the door again. Thinking of my child made me furious. I wanted that door down. I'd forgotten all about where I was. People were starting to come out of their houses, but I didn't care. I wanted it to stop and Jamison being on the phone from inside the house wasn't making it any better.

"Kerry, she didn't do anything to you. Just go home and I'll be right behind you." He was whispering like a schoolboy on the phone with his girlfriend late at night.

"I'm not going home. You come out here now or I swear I'll bust the windows in your car and set it on fire if I have to." I couldn't believe the things I was saying, but I felt every syllable of them. At that moment I was willing to do anything, and Jamison must've felt it too. He hung up the phone.

The door opened fast, like he'd been standing on the other side the whole time. Jamison stood there alone, dressed in a pair of boxers I'd bought him.

"Did you really think I was going away?" I asked. Through the corner of my eye, I could see an old lady standing in her doorway next door wearing bright pink foam rollers in her hair and a flowery nightgown. I wanted to lower my voice, but I was beyond caring about embarrassing myself. "What is this? What is this?" I started crying again, but I didn't bother to wipe my tears. I just wrapped my arms around my stomach and held tight. The baby felt heavy again, like he was feeling the weight of the moment.

"I can explain it—" He stopped mid-sentence and reached for me. "It's nothing. I'm just . . ."

I stepped away.

"Just what?"

"Look, Kerry, I think you should go. I'll put on something and then come too, but I need to get dressed."

"I'll be damned if I let you walk back into that house with that woman," I hollered. "Does she know you're married? That you have a son on the way? Why can't she come out here and face me? Don't be embarrassed. I'm here now." I tried to push my way through the doorway, but Jamison held me back.

"Let me in," I said, pushing my way in farther. "I just want to see her. I just want to see her. I want to see the woman you chose over me."

"Don't do this," he said, pulling my arms. "Don't do anything foolish."

I pulled back and looked my husband in the eyes. We'd known each other for twelve years. He was my first love. The only man I'd ever imagined marrying. He looked so naked standing there in front of me. So defenseless. He had pale, milky white skin, looked almost white sometimes in pictures, and the centers of his cheeks were beet red, the color they turned when he was sad or angry.

"Don't do what? *Anything foolish?*" I cried. "*Foolish?* You jerk. You fucking jerk."

I practically jumped into Jamison's arms and started pounding my fists into his face. He was 6'5", well over a foot taller than me, but I was towering above him then. Every bit of anger and frustration I felt grew me taller. I was swinging and screaming and hitting to make him feel the pain I felt. I was beat down and beat up by his lies and now I wanted him to feel the same thing. It didn't stop what I was feeling, but it felt good, like I was releasing something. Letting go, or at least loosening up my anger.

"*Foolish,*" I screamed. "I'll show you *foolish.*"

"Ma'am, stop it!" I heard an authoritative voice before I felt a hand pull at my shoulder. "Ma'am."

My body was being lifted up. I felt two hands on both of my sides.

"She's pregnant," Jamison said, reaching for me as the hands pulled me farther back. I turned to see two police officers standing beside me, while two others were holding me. Suddenly, I could see the flashing lights from their cars in the street, the flickering blues hitting small groups of people huddled in different places along the curb. There had to be at least six cars out there, and all I could think was where they'd come from and who they were there for.

"He ain't worth it," one woman said in the crowd.

I turned to look at Jamison. There were so many people

there, so many people I didn't know, and I felt like adding Jamison to the list. He seemed a part of this place, farther and farther away from me than I thought.

"Do you live here, ma'am?" one of the officers asked me. She was the only woman and she was so small the blue uniform seemed to swallow her up.

"No," I said.

"That's Coreen's house," someone called from the crowd.

Then, as if the person had summoned her, Coreen Carter came shuffling out the door. Her face was streaked with tears that seemed bigger than mine. Her eyes were red and she was visibly shaken. She stepped outside and stood beside Jamison in front of the door.

Seeing the cops had brought me back to reality, but seeing Coreen stand beside my husband sent me into what I can only call an out-of-body experience. Baby and all, I twisted out of the police officers' hands and charged after her. The word "nerve" was echoing in my head and if I had my way, I wanted to cut it into her chest with my bare hands. I was filled with rage. With disbelief. My life wasn't supposed to be like this. My marriage wasn't supposed to be like this. And love wasn't supposed to feel like this. All I could do was blame her for all three.

The female cop and another tall, white cop caught me and pulled me farther down the walkway, away from Jamison and Coreen, who were standing together.

"Ma'am," the female officer said, standing in front of me. "I'm Officer Cox. What's your name?"

"Kerry . . . Kerry Taylor."

"Ms. Taylor, I can see that you're upset, but I need you to calm down, so I can talk to you and figure out what exactly is going on here." Her eyes were soft and brown like my Aunt Luchie's. The look on her face was sincere, kind, like she was the only person out there who understood what I was feeling. "Now we don't want anything to happen to your baby. You understand?"

"Yes," I said. I wiped a tear from my eye and looked over at Jamison. He was talking to two male officers, a fat white one and a black one who seemed like he was in charge. Coreen was standing beside him with her hand over her mouth.

"You don't live here?" Officer Cox asked me again.

I shook my head no.

"Were you sleeping here?"

"No," I said, looking at Jamison. He was looking back at me. Tears were in his eyes. The other officer was telling him not to come over to me.

"Is that man with you?" the other, tall officer asked me.

"He's my husband."

The weight of my words must've surprised both of them. Officer Cox stopped writing on her little pad and looked at the other officer.

"Yes," I said, confirming what they were both thinking.

"Hum," she said and looked over at Coreen. "He's here with her?"

"Yes," I said again.

"Should've told us that first," the tall cop said. "We would've given you more time on him." They both exchanged glances and a short, nervous laugh.

"I know what you're feeling. We see this all the time," Officer Cox said, writing again. "But you have to control yourself."

"And not let the cops see you hit your husband," the tall cop said.

"Cox," the officer in charge called, coming toward us as he adjusted his holster.

Jamison turned toward the house when the officer walked away, but I could tell he was crying. He punched the door so hard it sounded as if a gun had gone off.

"Ma'am, I need you to go on in the house," the white officer said to Coreen. "We'll come in and speak with you after we're done out here."

Coreen turned and looked at me quickly, her eyes still wet with confession. She went to walk into the house, reaching first for Jamison, who stepped away from her immediately.

The older officer signaled again for Cox to walk toward him.

"You just stand here, calm, and I'll be right back," she said, stepping away.

"What's going on?" I asked. I could see some trace of dread in her eyes.

"She's just talking to our captain is all," the other officer said. "Standard procedure."

"Am I in any trouble?" I watched as Officer Cox talked to the captain. Her eyes dropped and she placed her hand over her mouth just like Coreen had.

"Probably not," the officer said. "They'll probably let you go."

"Let me go?"

I looked back at Jamison.

"Baby," he tried, his voice filled with desperation.

"Sir, I'm going to need you to stay where you are," the fat officer said, putting his hand over his gun.

"Jamison?" I called. "Jamison."

"She's my wife. You can't take her." He kept coming toward us. Two other cops ran to him and held him back from either side. Suddenly, there were at least ten cops between us.

"Take me? What's going on?" I asked. I looked back to Officer Cox. She was obviously pleading now with the captain, but he kept shaking his head, and then finally she looked me right in the eye and mouthed the word "sorry."

"Just be patient, ma'am," the officer beside me said timidly. "They'll be back over in a minute."

"Can't I just speak to her before she goes?" Jamison yelled. "She's pregnant. She can't go to jail."

"Jail?" I said. The word slapped me so hard my bladder dropped and urine came flowing from between my legs, wetting the front of my nightgown. "Jamison!" I cried. "Stop them!"

The female officer came toward me, pulling handcuffs from her hip.

"Mrs. Taylor," she said, her voice deep and throaty, as if she was forcing it to be stern. "I'm going to have to place you under arrest—"

"No," I hollered. "No! I didn't do anything. I was just here to get my husband. He's my husband." I began crying again. My adrenaline was wearing thin and the thought of being arrested for the first time in my life suddenly made me feel desperate and ugly. Not who I was. Not Kerry Taylor who'd grown up privileged, on the right street, in the right part of Atlanta. Not me. Jail? I looked at Jamison, for him to do something. To stop them from taking me away. This thing wasn't for me.

"Baby," he said, still being held by the officers, "just go with them and I'll come get you. I promise."

"But I didn't do anything."

"Mrs. Taylor," Officer Cox said, "because we all saw you assault your husband, we're going to have to take you in for domestic violence."

"Domestic violence?" I couldn't trust the echoes vibrating through my ears. "But he's here with that woman cheating on me." My spine began to twitch as the baby shifted, panicking, from side to side.

"I know. But because we saw you and our captain is with us, we have to do this. If the captain wasn't with us, we could let you go, but we have to protect ourselves. You understand?" Her voice turned to reason for a second and she slid the cuffs on and began to read me my Miranda rights. The crowd, which had grown even larger, stood silent in fear and amazement.

"That ain't necessary, officer," one woman said, "She's pregnant. Just let her go."

"Yeah," other people agreed. But it was too late. My hands cuffed on top of my belly, I watched them all desperately as the officer began walking me to the car. I turned again to see Jamison still standing there, looking at me helplessly. He'd done this to us, to me. I was being sent to jail for hitting a man who had beaten my heart to a pulp.

"You'll be out quickly," the female officer said, helping me into the car. The rainbow of lights went shining again and we were off.

Inside Out

Classical piano. Ballet and tap. Etiquette. Jack and Jill. Private school for thirteen years and four years at Spelman. It seemed that my mother had spent my entire life trying to ensure that I'd never see the inside of a jail cell, yet there I was, her perfect little girl, sitting in a muggy, gray room that at once defeated all of her hard work.

I want to say the jail was like a nightmare, but really it wasn't. It was dark, musky, cheerless, and filled with every design no-no I'd ever observed in *Homes & Gardens*, but really the place wasn't anything like what I'd seen on television. Beside the fact that I was being held there against my will, it seemed like a regular office. There were computers and people on the phone. Folks eating breakfast at their desks and pictures of ugly children on the walls. Besides the "Most Wanted" signs, bars, and drunken prostitutes, you could pretend you were at a part-time job—one you never wanted to go to.

It's funny how when you're in a situation like that, when you feel you've completely lost yourself, all you can seem to do is think of who you are.

As a chubby-faced black woman with fake gold rings on every finger took my picture and fingerprints, I thought of how far I'd gone in my life, how far I thought I was from ever being booked into a jail, sitting beside prostitutes who had track marks up the insides of their starved arms, drunks who could hardly sit up, and just plain wild women who cursed and spit at their own shadows.

I was Kerry Jackson-Taylor, army brat daughter of a retired Desert Storm veteran. I'd been raised by a socialite and army wife who had old Atlanta money and a name that opened doors wherever we went. I'd had the best of everything in my life. Hadn't ever wanted for a thing. Had been taught to play by the rules: say your prayers, obey the law, love your country, and be a good citizen, wife, and mother. When I went to college, everyone called me "Black Barbie." Even my professors. Girls groaned in envy when I pulled up in front of the dorm freshman year in my black Corvette. They wanted to ride with me, borrow my designer clothes, study with me at the library, go with me to the hairdresser where my long black hair was perfectly pressed, do anything and everything I did, because they all thought I was so perfect. I could lie and say I didn't feel the same way about myself. But it was hard. Things just came to me then. I'd never had a pimple in my life, had gotten straight A's throughout prep school and college, and by the time I saw my picture plastered in *Ebony* magazine when I won Ms. Spelman, my head was so swollen I actually went out and bought a T-shirt that said "Black Barbie" across the front. The back, of course, read, "Perfect 10."

Thinking about those times, it seemed as if I was nothing like the women around me. Not even like the ones whose prisoner I'd suddenly become. But like them, I was there. Still in my nightgown and a jacket one of the officers had given me, I was there and feeling completely pitiful. A pitiful Black Barbie. No corvette or Ken in sight.

Finally in my cell alone, all I could think of was how I got there. Thick tears gathered as I thought and thought about this question. I couldn't answer it. All I could do was think it. Over and again in my mind I asked myself the same thing, but answering it just seemed so hard. Yes, Jamison was having an affair, but how did we get there? And then if we'd gotten to the place where my husband was having an affair, how did we get *there*? It didn't make any sense. I didn't make any sense. The pain of the circumstance was wearing me down and as I sat in the holding cell, searching for the courage to make my first phone call, I felt tired, and finally it seemed I was a pregnant woman who had no business being away from her bed so early in the morning.

I even grew tired of crying. I couldn't find another tear within myself, so I just sat there on a hard bench and rehearsed what I'd say to my mother. Yeah, I'd have to call my mother to come and get me.

One of the guards said that Jamison had come up to the precinct to bail me out but that they couldn't release me into his custody because I was being charged with hitting him. I asked how I was going to be charged for hitting someone who was trying to bail me out of jail, and she explained that Jamison didn't have to press charges. The state pressed charges in domestic violence cases. Apparently, it was standard procedure because most victims were afraid to press charges against their mates.

I listened to this information as if I was watching Court TV and she was talking about someone else. That Savannah beauty queen, who'd shot and killed her boyfriend. Lorena Bobbitt, who'd snipped off her husband's penis. Domestic violence? First offense? Counseling? Charges? Going before the judge? Bail? There was no way she could be talking to *me*. "Do you have anyone else who can come get you?" she asked. I didn't respond. There were only two people, besides Jamison, whom I could entrust with something so low as coming to bail me out of jail. One was Marcy, and I knew she was probably already on her way to work, and the other was my mother.

I know most people wanted to get out of jail as soon as possible, so they pick up the phone to call whomever and say whatever to get them there, but my situation with Mother was quite different.

She wasn't an overbearing or overprotective mother, like most. That would've been easy. My mother was a little more distant than other people. Shortly after my father came back from the Persian Gulf, he started showing signs of post-traumatic stress disorder. They tried to control it with counseling, but it just got worse, and soon my mother simply couldn't deal with it, so they put my father in a nursing home. While I was away in prep school when it all happened, the change affected all three of us, my mother the worst. She was so angry with my father for being sick that she seemed to pretend he was dead. She immersed herself even further into her social life, throwing these expensive parties, some even on weeknights, flying to Boca Raton for long weekends and going on monthlong cruises with groups of people she claimed were her "new" friends. "I'm alive again," she'd say when I asked what was going on. "I lived for your father and the Army for too long and now I'm alive." I knew it was a lie. My mother was simply trying to cover up the pain she was feeling inside for losing the best of the man she loved—his mind. He couldn't even recognize either of us anymore, had taken to calling her "the enemy" when she did find time to visit. I knew that had to hurt. It hurt me. So Mother kept burrowing within herself, pulling away from me, my dad, and even herself as she sipped overpriced wine and pretended everything would be okay in her "new life." Now my mother was a bit of a shell, a disconnected, empty shell that I loved for who she once was and hated for who she was becoming. Nevertheless, I hated letting her down. She'd been let down enough in her life, and I never wanted to be that person who did it again. Together, we'd carefully planned my life, and I knew this would be a blow.

I wasn't sure how she might take the call. The old Mother, before Dad went to the nursing home, would've run to my rescue and been mad that I'd gotten myself in such a predicament. She might drag me home and try to take care of me and my baby, saying we didn't have to ever go home as we both swore Jamison off forever. It wasn't what I'd wanted, but it was what most daughters expected of their mothers. We all hated it, but in the end, it was comforting to know someone could care for you like only a mother could. Yet, I expected none of that from my mother now. She simply wasn't capable of it. I just wanted her to come bail me out and drop me off at home. But could she even handle that?

E-MAIL TRANSMISSION

TO: duane.carter@hotmail.com
FROM: Jamison.Taylor@rakeitup.net
DATE: 3/17/07
TIME: 7:38 PM

Coreen:

I just wanted to say thanks again for finding my PalmPilot and taking time to contact me. By the way, I was shocked when you
answered the door this morning. I was expecting "Duane Carter"
(the name on the e-mail). But I guess you were a more pleasant surprise. Thanks again. Have a great day.

Jamison

E-MAIL TRANSMISSION

TO: Jamison.Taylor@rakeitup.net
FROM: duane.carter@hotmail.com
DATE: 3/17/07
TIME: 10:15 PM

HAHA! I knew something was wrong with you. When I opened the
door, you looked like I wasn't wearing a shirt or something. You
should've seen your eyes grow all big. Yes, I am a woman and my
name is not Duane. Duane is my husband. Well, he's deceased. He
died in 9/11 at the World Trade Center. He was a computer
programmer. Anyway, one of the last things he did was install the
Outlook on my computer so all of my e-mail has his old address on
it. I never changed it. I guess I just didn't want to. Kind of like having
a bit of him around. You know? And there's no need to thank me.
Losing a PalmPilot could happen to anyone. I'm sure people find
PalmPilots along the street every morning. LOL.

Coreen

E-MAIL TRANSMISSION

TO: duane.carter@hotmail.com
FROM: Jamison.Taylor@rakeitup.net
DATE: 3/18/07
TIME: 6:57 AM

Try telling my assistants it's normal! They say finding things I've mis-placed should be in their job description. Thank goodness they have backups for all of the data on my PalmPilot.☺

I apologize for bringing up the e-mail address thing. I can understand why you would keep your husband's address. And I'm sorry to hear he passed. I know it's probably hard on you, even after so long. My father died of leukemia when I was seven, and my mom had it pretty bad. Let me know if there's ever anything I can do for you. I do owe you one.

Thanks again!
Jamison

Not Yet Gangster

A husky cough came cracking through the phone as my mother attempted to clear the night before out of her throat when she picked up the phone.

After realizing that I had to get out of jail before I gave birth to my child in the big house and everyone started calling him Tupac, I decided to just call her and suffer whatever drama she would bring until I got home to my bed. So far, she was right on point with the drama part.

"Mother," I said sternly.

"That you, Kerry?" She coughed again. "I was wondering why anyone would be calling me so early . . . wait, is it the baby? Is the—"

"No, Mother, it's not that," I cut her off. "I need . . . I . . ." There was no simple way to put it.

"Oh, I thought the baby was here. Did you talk to Jamison yet about the name? You know I really think the whole junior thing is not necessary, considering that our family has the—"

"Mother," I said, but she kept right on going.

". . . solid name. Just name him after my father. Dean is a great name. Don't you think? My father would've been so proud and—"

"Mother!" I yelled again. "It's eight in the morning. Do you think I'm calling to discuss baby names?"

"What?" she said.

"I need your help."

"Well, you don't have to holler at me like that. Control yourself, Kerry. You know no one likes a woman with a loud mouth."

"Okay, fine," I said, lowering my voice to the level she agreed was desirable. "Look, I know this isn't going to come out right, so I'm just going to say it." I was stalling but I knew I had to get to the point. The woman waiting in line behind me looked like a cross between Big Foot and Goliath and she was staring at me like I was standing between her and a cheeseburger. It was no time to play prissy.

"Are you okay?" my mother asked. "Is there something wrong with the baby?"

"No, Mother. Just listen to me. I need you to come and get me."

"From where?"

"I'm in jail," I said finally. The baby kicked at my stomach. He must've been sleeping for a while because I hadn't felt his kick in a minute. I turned my back toward the woman behind me and whispered into the phone. "I need you to come and get me out NOW."

"Jail? Stop toying with me, Kerry," she said with a thin laugh. "I can't sit on the phone and play games with you. I have to get myself ready to go to the airport."

"Mother, I'm serious. I'm in jail."

"No, you're not. Stop playing. It's not funny. Jail? Could you imagine?" I could hear the seriousness slipping into her voice. She was whispering into the phone as if there was someone in the room with her, but I knew she was alone. This was just her way. The last bit of Southern belle left in Thirjane Jackson made it impossible for Mother to say certain words aloud, for fear that someone, even a ghost, might hear her. She was the kind of woman who still wrapped liquor bottles in brown paper before throwing them into the trash to hide them from neighbors, ordered the newspaper even though she didn't read it, because it didn't seem fitting for a house to be without a newspaper, and opened and closed the blinds promptly at dawn and dusk each day. Bailing her only daughter out of jail was certainly not on her to-do list.

"I'm not playing, Mother," I said. Big Foot tapped me on the shoulder and groaned tiredly. She wanted her cheeseburger. "Look, I don't have time. I need you to come and get me. I'm in Riverdale."

"Riverdale? Why in God's name would you be out there? Are you serious? Kerry, why are you in jail?"

"I can't explain it all. It's just me and Jamison; we had a fight and I was arrested." As soon as the words came out of my mouth, I regretted them. My mother was very cold on Jamison. Not lukewarm. Cold. She never thought he was good enough to be my husband and at my wedding (which she half-refused to come to), she actually whispered "You're her *first* husband," when he and she danced at the reception. As could be expected, hearing that we were fighting was music to Mother's ears. She'd probably be happy to hear that there was another woman involved. I'd done a good job of hiding it from her for so long, but I was worn out.

"Arrested for arguing with your husband? That seems unlikely. What happened?"

"Well, I'd gladly tell you if I had time," I said, mimicking her inexcusable properness. With a raised index finger, I signaled for one more minute to Big Foot.

"Oh, this is ridiculous. How could you be in jail? My daughter? And you expect me to come and bail you out?"

"Yes, Mother."

"And how do you expect me to come and do that? I've never been to a correction facility before. I don't even know where one is."

"Mother, I'm pregnant and tired. Just figure it out," I said. She always made things harder than they had to be. And God forbid she forgot about herself for one second.

"Why can't your husband come and get you?" she asked.

"Mother, this is not the time for you to debate the validity of my marriage. I'm in jail!"

"Ma'am, your time is up," a guard said. She looked like a little plump Ewok, standing with Big Foot. I signaled for one more second again.

"Oh, God. I just don't understand how you could be in jail, Kerry. I taught you better than that, didn't I?"

"Mother, I need you to stop and come and get me now. We can talk about it when you get here. Okay?"

"I suppose so," she said as if I was asking her for a kidney. I was her daughter, who was about to give birth in a jail with Big Foot and an Ewok looking on and my mother was only thinking of a bad headline.

After I gave her the precinct information, I was led back to my holding cell by the same gold-clad guard who took my fingerprints. As we walked down the hallway, which had cells on either side, kind of like a hallway in a dorm (but with bars instead of doors) I thought back to Jamison and how I'd ended up behind bars. I felt so humiliated, so stupid for what was happening to me. I loved Jamison with all of my heart. I tried my best to be a good wife, a good companion to him. I had left my job, a job I loved, so I could help him out with his company. I believed in him. I was there for him when he needed me, even put up with his crazy ghetto mama and her constant judgments about me.

I'd been crying all morning so my eyes were already swollen

to the size of golf balls, but still tears managed to fall as I walked down that hallway, a prisoner with her belly protruding so far in front of her that she couldn't see her feet. I wanted my bed, I wanted my husband, I wanted last night to be a bad dream I was about to wake up from.

I needed to curl up in a corner and be by myself, alone with my tears and my baby until my mother showed up. But when the guard and I stopped at my cell, I realized that *alone* was now impossible. While I was away, I'd gained a roommate. A cell mate. There she was, sitting on a wooden bench with her legs far enough apart that you'd think she was a man. Her face toward the floor, she had a head full of blond weave that was completely matted. It looked like a little cocker spaniel was stapled to her skull. She was wearing a soiled wifebeater, and tattoos mapped both of her arms. If the rest of my jail experience hadn't been real thus far, I was confident that she was about to make it all a reality. That was clear. I felt like a nervous kindergartener walking into her first day of school, and when the guard opened the door for me to walk into the cell, I wanted to cling to her arm for dear life. I was big and bad at Coreen's, but I was no fool and I wasn't trying to have a real girl fight.

I stepped inside and the woman didn't move to say hello.

"Um . . . do I get another call?" I asked, turning to the guard. I rubbed my stomach and flashed a *"Don't leave me in here with this woman!"* look across my face, thinking maybe the guard would have mercy.

She didn't even respond. She just pointed into the cell with the golden pyramid ring atop her index finger like I was the escaped cocker spaniel hanging from the woman's head.

"Well, I need to use the bathroom. Is there one I could use?" I asked, stepping into the cell. The guard grinned and returned the petrified look I had with a "Lady, please" eye roll. She pointed again, but this time it was to a little commode that was in the far left corner of the cell. I'd seen it earlier, but thought for sure it was for something other than using the restroom.

"Okay," I said glumly. She slammed the door and smiled, showing a gold tooth for the first time.

"Anything else?" she asked mockingly.

"Well, I could use a magazine or something. Maybe a book?"

"A magazine?" She started laughing and turned to walk away. "A magazine . . ."

I stood at the cell door, afraid to move. I'd been holding in pee, but standing between me and the toilet was the lack of a door and a woman I was sure had been a man once. While she was sitting down, I was certain she was at least six foot tall and about 200 pounds. I'd gained twenty pounds of baby weight, but I was still no challenge for her.

"A magazine?" I heard, but it wasn't coming from the guard anymore. She was long gone.

It was the woman, but I didn't respond. I was too busy trying to figure out how long I could hold off going to the toilet.

She started laughing and I turned to look at her to see that she was now looking at me.

"You in prison, lady," she said loudly. "Ain't no damn magazines."

Suddenly, laughs came echoing down the hall, crescendoing around me and slapping me upside the forehead. They'd all heard her.

"I know," I said.

"McKenzie," she said, reaching out to shake my hand.

"I'm Kerry. . . . Hi."

McKenzie didn't look as bad in the face as I'd imagined. There were no cuts in her eyebrows, no bullet wounds, no tears beneath her eyes. In fact, oddly enough, she had what most people would consider a sweet face. While her hair was a five-alarm mess, her nutmeg-colored skin was as smooth as a baby's and her eyes were gentle and clear, nothing like someone who'd spent a life on the streets. Her eyes were comforting, in fact. They allowed something in me to loosen, and while she'd made everyone in the jail laugh at me, my ankles were about to implode if me and my extra twenty pounds didn't sit down, so I walked past her and sat on a bench near the commode—I still wasn't brave enough to use the toilet just yet. I'd have to hold it.

"These fucking crackers picked me up this morning on some old bullshit," she said. Her voice was scruffy, nearly baritone.

"Okay," I said. What else could I say? I wasn't privy to jailhouse chat, but I knew I shouldn't ask too many questions.

"You a damn lie, McKenzie," someone shouted from down the hall. "You know you was selling that bent-up pussy of yours."

Everyone started laughing again. Some people yelled similar sentiments. I was sure she was about to get up and kick through the bars like Superman to go beat up the girl, but McKenzie just laughed.

"Fuck you, Pepper," she said, getting up from the bench. She walked to the bars. "I was doing that shit, but they didn't have to arrest me. Got to feed my damn kids."

The baby kicked me hard three times when the word *kid* fell from McKenzie's mouth. Perhaps he was just as surprised to hear that news. Two things I might have never thought about my cellmate were now true—she was a woman and she had children. I'd believe that George Bush was taking a pilgrimage to Mecca before I ever connected those two things to McKenzie. But my disbelief didn't stop me from laughing. I rubbed my stomach to let my son know I heard his kick and laughed about the ridiculous prospects of the news—I laughed inside, of course. It was crazy, but it was just the kind of news I needed to get my mind off of Jamison so I could stop crying long enough to let the swelling in my eyes go down.

"Fucking crackers," McKenzie said.

I had so many questions to ask her. . . . Like why was she a prostitute? Who would have sex with her? And who had sex with her to make her get pregnant? But all I could say was, "Yeah."

"So, what you in for?" she asked, leaning against the bars toward me.

"Me?" I asked a stupid question and she looked at me the same way. "Oh," I continued, "I . . ." Before I could try to make up something cool, the truth came barreling from my overfull gut, ". . . I caught my husband with a woman."

"What?"

"Yeah, he was at her house. And I just hit him. I hit him and I hit him and . . ." I didn't know where all of the emotions were coming from, but the anger I felt at five that morning was restoring itself in my mind. McKenzie was the first person I was really able to tell what happened.

"Hell, yeah," she said, swinging her fists at some invisible foe in the room. I was getting her all riled up. I guessed we were bonding. I wondered how she might fit in at the next book club meeting. "Yoooo, rich lady beat her husband's ass," she yelled down the hall.

"Word?" someone said who sounded like Pepper, the woman who was speaking to McKenzie before. "Why she do that?"

"Caught that fool in bed with some ho!" someone else said. I got up and walked to the bars. Had the woman seen me? Was she there?

"I would've beat that clown's ass too. Him and the trick and then the cops for trying to stop me," someone said. They started laughing again and I laughed too. The thought of my turning crazy on everyone was a picture I'd love to send to my mother in the mail. Let her hang that in the den with the pictures of me at my debutante ball.

"You go, lady!" someone said.

"That's right, rich lady. Fuck men!"

"Tired of them doing us wrong. That's why I'm in here in the first place. My man don't know how to act either. Got me out in these streets. I'm too old to be in these streets. My pussy 'bout to retire!"

We all started laughing and McKenzie patted me on the back.

"Shit, we all in here because of some negro in some kind of way," she said. "That's how it starts."

I caught myself nodding my head like I knew anything about what she was saying. Besides my current situation, the only time I even knew anyone who'd gone to jail, it was a girl in my first-year dorm at Spelman who was arrested for allowing her boyfriend to hide drugs in her room. Apparently, while she'd never handled or distributed the drugs, they put her in jail and threw the key into Lake Lanier.

"Well, I'm off the streets when I get out this time," Pepper said. "Don't make no sense. I don't even know who got my babies. Think my mama got them, but she tired of my shit. I got to get myself together. For them anyway. I don't want them to go through what I done been through. They need better."

"How you gone give them better?" someone asked. "You like the rest of us in here. No education. Ain't got shit. Yo' man don't act right. And the government ain't doing shit either."

"That's why you in the streets anyway," someone else said.

"It don't matter," Pepper said. "I don't know how I'm going to do it, but I am. And that's all." Her voice cracked and she was silent.

Her words must've been a rude taste of reality for everyone, because they all stopped laughing and I watched as one by one they turned and stepped away from the discussion in the hall.

"Go on and use the bathroom, if you have to. Ain't nobody

looking at you," McKenzie said, walking back to the bench. "I know when I was pregnant, I was going every ten minutes. I don't know how you lasted that long."

After I went to the bathroom, I laid down on the only cot in the room and took a nap. I was exhausted, and while I was sure at least ten people had died on that cot, I wasn't feeling particularly choosey about anything after using the way-too-public toilet. McKenzie tried to wake me up when someone came down the hall giving out breakfast, but I decided I'd wait for my mother. If the jail food was anything like the accommodations, I wanted no part of it. I told her she could have my share.

Later, a male guard came down the hall, calling my name. He explained that someone had posted my bail and that I was free to go. While I'd made an odd, new friend in McKenzie, I was happy to hear my name and wasted no time getting to my feet. She was a decent woman once you got to know her, but I was no inmate. As I walked out of the cell, we exchanged nods. "Rich lady," she said, "I'll see you next time you get locked up."

I smiled uneasily and walked behind the guard down the hall. I peeked into each of the cells to see the faces of the women I'd come to know for a few hours. They looked a little less unfriendly on my way out. Some waved. Some smiled. Others shook their heads, making it clear they'd wished the guard had called their names instead of mine. But, no, it was time for me to go, and I wasn't missing my chance to bust out of the big house—even if it was in my mother's Mercedes.

E-MAIL TRANSMISSION

TO: Jamison.Taylor@rakeitup.net
FROM: duane.carter@hotmail.com
DATE: 4/01/07
TIME: 9:45 AM

Hey Jamison:

How are you? It's Coreen from like a month ago. You remember, with the PalmPilot? Anyway, I'm sure I'm far from your thoughts, but I was just in a meeting at work and your name came to my mind. Management is looking for a new company to handle the lawn care at the firm I work for (I'm a paralegal at Stein and Muck downtown) and they were asking if we had any suggestions. You came to mind! I didn't remember the name of your company, but I said I had a "friend" who would be great. You know a sister has to hook the brothers up. LOL. Well, if you're interested, give me a buzz and we can set up a presentation or something with the senior manager. Of course, I'd be there to back you up.

Coreen
555-673-0254

Busting Out

A year after I graduated from Spelman (with full honors—just as my mother and her mother did), I went through some hard times. It was what my mother called a small depression, but really it seemed to me as if my world was dissolving into sand. While everything was near picture perfect with Jamison and me, my career just wasn't taking off in the way I'd planned. Before I even enrolled at Spelman, my mother and I had sat down at the dining room table where all important decisions were made and put together a schedule for my career on a rose-colored piece of stationery with butterflies playing tag at the top. I was only sixteen and knew little of what to put beneath the butterflies' flapping wings, but the first thing my mother wrote down was *Doctor*. I shrugged my shoulders in the way that she hated and sat back in my seat. I didn't know the first thing about what it meant to be a doctor and had little interest in science in school. "It would be great for you, all of the girls are doing it now," my mother said. "Now, when I was at Spelman, we didn't even have the courses to prepare us to go into medicine, and no one wanted to be a doctor anyway; that was for our husbands," my mother said. "But not now. I hear lots of girls are doing it, just taking classes at Morehouse and heading off to medical school. It's a good thing really. Times have changed. Men like women of substance. Women who help people. Don't you want to help people, Kerry?" Helping people was exactly what I'd wanted to do. Since I was six years old, I'd been recording the names of each girl who had won Miss America in my diary. I'd trace their goals and try my best to align my own with theirs. I admired how strong and secure in their lives they appeared. Especially Vanessa Williams—when she won that year, I was sitting in the living room with my mother and thinking she didn't look anything like me, but she was beautiful and everything my mother said a black woman should be. But they were all beautiful and smart and kind and it seemed that everyone liked them. And what seemed to be consistent in all of these women's stories when they described their goals was that they wanted to help "mankind" or "serve those less fortunate." This was what I wanted out of life. To be beautiful, liked, and to help people. To be like Miss America. So, that afternoon at the dining room table when my mother said being a doctor would get me closer to doing just that, I signed up willingly. She smiled her happy smile, and even the butterflies seemed to flicker their wings and float off the page.

We decided that a focus in biology with classes at Morehouse would be most appropriate for me to prepare for medical school—at a tier one, Ivy school, of course. I'd focus on trying to get into pediatrics. It was an area men would find "sweet," my mother assured my sixteen-year-old ears. It would attract the attention of a wealthy and successful suitor looking to mate with a smart and successful, yet also caring, wife. A great career choice for a Spelman woman. I wasn't really thinking about marriage and suitors just yet, but I didn't want to take that smile off my mother's face, so I agreed and smiled, hoping it would all pan out.

Our plan worked just fine until the rejection letters from every Ivy I'd applied to started rolling in before graduation.

Thin envelope after thinner envelope, I opened them all to find that I was either rejected or worse—wait-listed (which Mother said meant they thought someone was better than me). My adviser explained that while my application was no doubt stellar, the top schools may have felt I lacked personality or diversity. "They like round students," she'd said, patting me on the shoulder with her awkwardly tiny hands. I was heartbroken and embarrassed. "I thought we agreed you'd apply to more than just the top five. What about those schools?" she'd asked. I just shook my head. I was Kerry Jackson. Black Barbie on campus. The perfect daughter at home. Miss Kerry America in my diary. I was supposed to get into any school I selected. I had the grades. I didn't think I needed a backup plan for anything. Apparently, I was wrong and I had a stack of tear-soaked envelopes to prove it.

When my mother got the news, she went into action. Swung her black, patent leather purse over her shoulder and dragged me around the city to all of her connections to see how she could change the result. But we eventually found ourselves with a specialist who'd gotten a bunch of kids into Ivy League medical schools. He assured her that her Southern connections would not get me into schools up North. She clutched her pearls and asked what we could do. "Reapply," he said frankly. "Get her a little life experience, and do it again. She also needs to pull her MCAT scores up a bit if she wants to get into a top school." My mother shot me a look of disdain and turned her back. They then agreed on a new plan with no rose-colored stationery and butterflies. To save face and the family name, I was to tell everyone at school (they were all expecting a Harvard-destined departure) that I was taking a year off to help take care of my father. I'd reapply to the same schools after I got a few months of experience doing community service and assisting a doctor in a medical office.

This plan worked with perfect precision, just as my mother had promised. One of her best friends got her husband to let me work at his office and I volunteered at my church, packing toiletries and Bibles to give away to the homeless. It felt good. I was making my own money (it wasn't a lot) and I honestly felt smarter, more experienced, and more mature than I did the year before. I was ready to be accepted and take the next step in my life. I was a grown woman and I could stand on my own two feet. I'd show them that in my statement of purpose. I'd have the grades, raise my MCAT scores, and have some life experience. While the MCAT scores didn't go up that much, I was still confident. In fact, I was so confident that once again, I only applied to the top five schools. Surely, they'd see me differently this time, surely they'd give me a chance to contribute to their schools all that I had to offer. . . . Surely, I was dead wrong.

It seemed like it took about a day for the schools to start rejecting me again. I wasn't exactly hurt when I got the first letter. It was a fluke. Some hate-filled receptionist had sent me the wrong letter by mistake. . . . But by the time I got the last letter, I was a wreck. No one even bothered to wait-list and then reject me this time. There were five no's and one sad me.

I showed up at a romantic dinner Jamison had been planning for months (anticipating an acceptance) with my eyes so swollen that one of my contacts popped out onto the table. I couldn't stop crying and Jamison, who'd already gotten his acceptance to Cornell Medical School but had decided to put it off to stay in Atlanta with me until I left for med school, was trying his best to cheer me up. "Are you sure being a doctor is what you want?" he asked uneasily. "I'm just saying, I believe in you, that you can do it, I really believe that, baby, but sometimes the universe has a way of showing us what we really want." I wanted so badly to scream at him and tell him he'd had some nerve saying that. I was meant to be a doctor. It was my dream. It was written on the piece of stationery. I wanted to say all of this, but I was tired and kind of feeling like he was right. I wanted med school, but sometimes, late at night when I was lying silent in my old bedroom that my mother had turned into her gift-wrapping room when I left for college, I'd wonder how it was going to help me get closer to what I wanted to really do . . . whatever that was. I enjoyed being with the patients at the medical office, but the doctor seemed so tired all the time, worn out and stretched in so many directions. I wondered if I could do that. If I wanted to do that with my life.

"I don't know," I said to Jamison that night. I just kept crying and shaking my head.

"Maybe that's someone else's dream," he said, his eyes moving quickly from me to his plate.

"Whose?" I asked.

There were two things Jamison and I tried not to speak about in our relationship. The first was his mother. She hated me because Jamison put off medical school to stay in Atlanta with me. And the second was my mother. She hated Jamison because he wasn't from any Georgia name she could recognize. He'd gone to Morehouse, but it was on a full scholarship. And while he was clearly a smart man destined for success, this just wasn't enough for my mother. "Title entitles," she'd always say, advising me to find a man whose last name carried weight in the traditional Georgia movers-and-shakers circle.

"Maybe you're so stuck on the doctor dream because of your mother," Jamison added. I was speechless. Of course, I'd toyed with the idea of this before. My mother was somewhat of a control freak. She was a master manipulator and since my father got ill, I was her project. It could be overwhelming sometimes, but mostly it felt good. She was usually right about the advice she gave me and thus far my life had been perfect because of it. It was a lot of pressure, but the way people looked at me, the way I felt about myself, made it all worth it in the end. "We're the winning team," she'd always say. "The best pearls of the dive."

That night when Jamison and I got back to his place, he made me promise that I'd get some real help to work through all of the emotions I was feeling. I'd never been rejected before, and it had to be hard. If he couldn't help me, I needed to talk to someone (besides my mother) who could help me get things into perspective. While I wasn't exactly excited about what he was suggesting, I felt so down I was sure something was really wrong with me that I couldn't fix, and I wasn't about to ignore it. So, instead of telling my mother about the new set of rejections, the next morning I called a random number in the yellow pages and went to see a psychologist.

Like Jamison, my psychologist seemed to keep coming back to my mother whenever we started getting to the root of what he called my "obsession with perfection."

"You carry too much weight," he'd say, pushing back in his old, sweat-stained leather office chair. "No one can breathe under all that weight. Lighten the load."

After three months of biweekly therapy sessions, Dr. Bellinger gave me the best advice I've ever received concerning my mother. His words would get me through the next eleven years as my mother continued to try to rule my life and allow her own to spin out of control.

"Stop letting her surprise you," he had said. "Stop setting yourself up to be hurt by her disappointment and letdowns. Accept your mother for who she is and expect nothing from her other than what she commonly gives."

It was like the *Daughterhood Bible* had finally been translated into my language. Something in me slowed down, while something else sped up. For the first time in my life, I was able to tune out my mother and tune in myself. While most of my thoughts sounded like hers, at least they were coming from my own mind. I could hear her, but I fought with everything I had not to let her drown me out.

I supposed I should've heard Dr. Bellinger's wise words in my ear when I was walking toward the waiting area of the jail. While I'd stopped seeing him years ago, "Stop letting her surprise you" might have come in handy when I expected my mother to be there on the one day of my life when I needed her most. I was about to give birth and had just gone to jail for hitting my husband in front of a home that belonged to the woman he was having an affair with. I wanted my mother to be there for me. Therefore, "Stop letting her surprise you" would've been the perfect phrase to have pinned to my brain when I walked into the waiting area and this was not the case. Sitting in a little, red, plastic chair was . . .

"Marcy?" I called, fruitlessly scanning the room for my mother. My heart sank in shame.

"Kerry!" She jumped up and ran toward me with her arms wide open, concern on her face. I was a bit perturbed that she wasn't my mother but also very happy to see my best friend. Marcy had the kind of "girl-next-door" beauty that was hard for most people to see. She had soft, delicate features like a baby. A little button nose, chubby cheeks, and perfect pouty lips. Her complexion was clear and her skin was the light brown of a perfectly toasted croissant.

"My mother . . . I thought she was coming," I said, accepting Marcy's embrace with the little bit of arm space I had due to the baby.

"She called me at my job."

"Your job?"

"She said she was on her way out of town and that she needed me to get you," Marcy said. I was beginning to feel

angry, but my body was so drained that I was just happy someone had come to get me.

"I'm sorry—" I started.

"No," Marcy said, clasping my hand in hers to stop me. "This
is not about that. You needed me and I'm here. You don't need
to be any more upset than you already are, so let's let that go."
She took the small bag that held my belongings and led me to
the car. She said Jamison called her too and said he'd be waiting
at the house.

"He's there?" I asked, standing beside Marcy's car.

"Yes," she said. "But you don't have to go there. You can
come home with me. Whatever you want to do, I'm here."

I sat back in the seat and covered my face with my hands. I
didn't want to see Jamison. I wasn't ready. I started crying again
and this time the tears were coming from a place of fear I hadn't
yet felt. I was literally falling apart. Everything I knew to be
true about the world and the life I was planning was about to
topple over and I had not one unswollen leg to stand on. I wanted
everything to disappear and to have my life back. If I couldn't
have Jamison, then I didn't want his baby. And if I couldn't have
my baby, I didn't want to live. It was too much and I couldn't
keep pretending I was strong enough to make it. I was afraid of
being a single mother. I didn't have whatever those women in
jail had. I wasn't raised to be strong alone. I needed my husband.
I wanted my husband.

"Kerry, I know it's hard. And I'm here for you for as long as
you need me. You hear me?" She was crying now too. "Neither
of us expected this from Jamison, but it's here and we'll get
through it together."

Marcy started the car and because I didn't want to go home
to see Jamison, we decided to go back to her place, so I could
freshen up and get some sleep before her daughter Milicent
came home from school.

"I meant what I said before," Marcy said, turning onto her street after listening to me sob the entire way there, crying about how stupid I felt for being married to and impregnated by an adulterer. "You're not stupid because no one would've ever thought this would happen between you and Jamison. Not the way you two began. . . . I was there and it was like the two of you were meant to be together. He was crazy about you."

I nodded yes as I wiped tears from my cheeks, forcing a chuckle. Marcy was right. Jamison adored me and treated me like the best pearl. I waited for a long time for him to come into my life. But when he arrived, it was like he'd been there all along and I hadn't waited a day, because my life was finally beginning.

Barbie Meets Ken

February 1995

The day after my debutante ball, my mother made it clear that in her eyes, it was time for me to begin the search for a suitable mate. My father was her escort to her debutante ball, and while she was only fifteen, she claimed she knew he was to be her husband and planned the rest of her life accordingly. My father was from a long line of military men, beginning with my great-great grandfather who fought with the Louisiana Native Guards in the Union Army's first regiment of black soldiers in the Civil War. Dad had gone to college, as my grandmother made him promise, but after that, it was off to the Army. Love-struck, my mother prepared herself to be an army wife, ready to travel by his side and face the possibility of being a stay-at-home wife if it was clear he needed her there for support—which she did, even though she had a B.A. in Music and graduated at the top of her class.

Her goal was for me to do the same. But because it was clear that none of the "play dates" she'd arranged for me were working, she'd resolved that my match would be made in college. "A Spelman and Morehouse wedding!" I remember hearing her say time and again after asking had I met so-and-so's son from her church on campus yet, or had I called a Morehouse boy's number that she'd slipped into a care package. The worst part was her visits. Then she'd manage to finagle some senator's son or judge's nephew to escort us to lunch as she painfully gave him reasons to like me. "Well, my Kerry speaks French," she'd say if he was a French major. "Well, my Kerry eats ice cream," she'd say if he ordered the banana split for dessert. My mother's efforts were well organized and I felt so bad that they never worked out, because I was tired of being single, but things just never seemed to fit between me and the fellows who came knocking on my door after they survived her inquisition.

Either they'd be too stuck-up and highbrow or they'd turn out to be be classless or completely barbaric. And some were just a mixture of both. My first year, through one of my mother's sorority connections, I ended up on a date with Preston Allcott. He was a third-year at Morehouse, who'd already taken the MCAT and was no doubt on his way to Morehouse Medical School, where both his father and uncle had received their M.D.s. Preston was a beautiful thing to look at. He had chiseled, Grecian features, smooth olive skin, and piercing blue eyes you would swear he stole from a white man. I was a bit excited to be going on a date with a junior when Preston picked me up in his BMW. All the men picked up their dates in front of the big iron gates at Spelman, where everyone could see who was getting into what car—it was quite a "who's who" parade of door opening. And when Preston pulled up in his car and opened the door for me, I distinctly remembered hearing someone say, "There's Black Barbie's Ken!" But a "Ken" Preston was not. He was crass and mean to everyone we came in contact with. He told the waitress at the restaurant that she needed to go back to "waitress school" to learn how to serve food (she had reached over his arm) and refused to tip her.

I was stunned. But that wasn't it. After laughing about the

incident in the car (with himself), Preston decided to "advise" me about how to date a man like him. "You need to let me call you," he said with not one hint of irony in his voice. "And don't ever ask me when I'll call, or miss my call. I'm a busy man and I can't be expected to hold a routine with a woman or be left waiting." I was laughing inside. I knew his kind too well. He wanted his cake . . . he wanted to eat it too. "And please don't ever ask me what I'm doing on this night or the other. I don't tolerate that. My business is my business and it'll always be that way." I couldn't get back to my room fast enough. And while the car was still shiny, Preston was looking mighty dull. By the time we stopped in front of the school, I was completely ignoring him. "But I do like you," he said. "I could see myself marrying you. You come from good people and while you're a little dark for my taste, you have nice features and we can make a beautiful baby." He ran his hand down my cheek. I wanted to vomit. "Now, the only thing we will need to do to seal the deal is sample the goods." "Sample?" I asked. "Yeah, we have to have sex, so I know if it's good." I was flabbergasted. Not only was I a seventeen-year-old virgin, but that kind of speech was never used by any of the other duds I'd been out with. He then reached over the middle console and dug his little pasty hand so far down into my crotch that I swear he scratched the seat beneath me. I got out of that car so fast I had no time to curse him out. I was afraid he'd come after me to "seal the deal."

Over the next years, it was pretty much the same thing. Shiny cars. Dull men. I wasn't matching up with anyone, and while I was sure I didn't want to settle for just anyone—I was never at a loss for offers—I was getting a bit scared. It seemed like everyone was hooking up and Spelman and Morehouse wedding bells were floating in the air everywhere I turned. Some girls had even hooked up with those fine, rugged men at Clark, and the brothers at Morris Brown had planted a few

rings on excited fingers. But I was a dead woman walking . . .
the perfect Spelman woman living a perfectly solo life.

When the annual Valentine's dance came around my senior
year, I'd put together a strategic plan to ensure optimal
success—I was staying locked up in the apartment I was sharing with Marcy. My date would be a bucket of ice cream and
my big dance would be to the music of the commercials on television. But, as usual, Marcy wouldn't have it. I was rolled up in
bed, happy and content with my solitude, and in she came completely overdressed in a red satin gown and diamond earrings
that couldn't possibly be real. Marcy was from a middle-class
family in New York. Her mother was a former hairdresser who
now owned two shops and her father managed a limousine service. When Marcy arrived at Spelman, she knew little of the
Southern way of things. She was New York flashy and usually
New York loud. But she had a great sense of style and could
make anyone laugh. That was why I liked her so much. She
wasn't like most of the girls I'd grown up with. She put on no
airs and had no rules. Most of the girls I went to prep school
with were what I called pretenders—the Southern lady way of
being mean meant you were sweet and kind on the outside, but
evil and envious on the inside. Not Marcy. She was very
forward with her feelings and if she didn't like someone, they
knew it fast. While this caused her to stumble a bit when it
came time to fit in with the rest of the women on campus,
Marcy's humor and style (as it toned down) eventually led to
her falling into favor with most of the girls and she'd grown
into the true social butterfly of our twosome since we'd met
freshmen year. Marcy knew everyone on campus and seemed
to know everyone's business. If it was important, Marcy knew
it, and if it wasn't, she knew it too. Often her gossiping led to
bumps in our relationship, specifically when the gossip was
about me, but we always worked through it and she was my

biggest supporter. After begging me to go with her to the Valentine's dance so Damien (who she'd later marry) wouldn't think she was only going to the dance to see him, she literally dragged me out of bed and forced me into a black dress my mother had dropped off for the dance the day before.

"I'm only going because you're begging me," I said lazily. I fully intended to sit in that bed all night with my ice cream and television. "I won't have any fun, and I'll end up sitting alone looking stupid."

"Kerry, please. You know those brothers can never get enough of you. You just act so funny they're afraid to ask you to dance. They think you're stuck-up."

"Well, I am stuck-up," I said, hoping this wouldn't be a re-peat of all of the other dances where men would ask me to dance and then take me back to my seat when it was clear I wasn't about to let them gyrate on my backside.

"I guess you have a point. You can be a little stuck-up," Marcy said. "But if you're ever going to meet the right man, you're going to have to unstick yourself. So, he can stick you." She forced her left index finger through a tight hole she created with her other hand to symbolize my virginity. Marcy always said that because I was waiting to save myself for Mr. Right, she was sure I'd lose my mind the minute I finally lost my virginity.

"Whatever," I said, laughing. "I'll go with you to the dance, but if some pervert tries to grope me, he's going to get my 'go to hell' stare."

We both stopped and gave each other the icy, top-to-bottom stare we gave to random men who'd found themselves wander-ing around campus in search of female company. When they'd start moseying in our direction, we'd pause, step back, and give them the "go to hell" stare. It was a guaranteed deterrent.

* * *

Those college dances were all the same. Ill-placed balloons and unfortunate streamers combined with poor lighting and cheap refreshments. One year I was actually served nacho chips. Better still, it seemed as if no one even wanted to be there. The dejected or distracted professors and administrators either looked sad that it was no longer their turn to be on the dance floor, or as if they'd rather stayed locked up in their offices to drink whiskey and remember days gone by. And the students looked anxious at first, but as soon as they realized the DJ wasn't going to be allowed to play any of the nasty, sexually explicit music they were used to hearing on the radio and no strippers were going to come shooting out of the ceiling, they seemed to wish they were old enough to go to a real club and ditch this glorified high school scene altogether—which the older ones usually did.

For these reasons, the balloon-and-streamer dance became more of a who's who at Spelman College competition than a dance. While there were a few couples and soon-to-be couples on the dance floor at the beginning of the night, most of the attention was on who was walking into the room with what date and what they were wearing. At the top this list were the Greeks and rich kids. While I never felt a desire to pledge (as a legacy of pink and green, this was against my mother's best wishes, of course), I fell into the latter category, and every time I entered a campus function, it was as if the Red Sea was dividing in the form of tasteless red, chiffon dresses and crimson sequin gowns as people pretended not to stare, but couldn't help but whisper to their neighbors that once again, Black Barbie was alone.

As Marcy and I struggled up the steps in our heels and shared a few fake, forced hellos with her sorority sisters who were outside posing on the front steps as they awaited their grand entrance, I prayed things would be different this year. I hadn't shared it with Marcy, but part of the reason I hadn't wanted to go was because of all of the pressure I felt at the dances. It was OK . . . even easy . . . for me to put on my perfect exterior around campus and at other functions where a date wasn't necessarily required. There I was the Kerry they all expected. I was together and full of smiles. But at the dances they expected more from a senior who'd had years to find at the very least a handsome escort. And while people still spoke to me and smiled with envy heavy in their eyes as they admired my new dress, I knew inside they were wondering where my Morehouse man was and what was wrong with me that I didn't have one yet. What Halle couldn't do. What Oprah couldn't do. What Kerry couldn't do. Keep a man. I didn't want to have to face those accusations in their eyes again.

When the French doors swung open as dramatically as Marcy's gold gloves had pushed them, I saw that my mother's Methodist God had answered my silent prayers in his normal low-key fashion. People were everywhere. Laughing and talking, chatting and dancing. The room was so packed it looked as if we'd sneaked off to one of those loud nightclubs off campus. It wasn't even a dance; it was a real party. There were no streamers or balloons and no one seemed to notice me.

"I know Damien is in here somewhere already," Marcy screamed in my ear over the music. "Let's find him." She pulled my hand and we tunneled through the crowd, stopping every once in a while so Marcy could crane her neck to see if she could spot Damien. They'd been dating a few months now and Marcy was determined that he was the man she was going to marry. She'd later prove herself right, but it took a lot to get him there. Damien was what women on campus called "top breed." The type of man I was sure my mother wanted me to marry; he was rich, from a prestigious family, had been educated in Europe, handsome, and Greek. He was a top pick

at Morehouse, and the women at Spelman were competing like
track stars at the Olympics for a place in his heart. They were
gaining way until Marcy met him at a Greek party. While
Marcy was beautiful, her roots made her a little less than what
people would expect him to end up with. She had no prestige
and a little less polish than the rest of the girls lining up at his
door. But this difference served her well, because the lack of
polish and prestige was defeated by her blunt style and bold
demeanor that kept Damien's eyes bright and fixed on her,
while the other girls must have seemed normal and a bit bor-
ing. He was obviously taken with her. But it seemed that when
things got serious between them, Damien got nervous. He
liked hanging out with Marcy, but marriage was a whole separate issue. His family hadn't quite accepted the idea of Damien
marrying an outsider. They had big society page wedding
plans, and Marcy wasn't . . . society. I knew it hurt her to realize this; she'd broken all of the other barriers on sheer personality, had even pledged a sorority and was accepted wholly, but
the guard wouldn't budge. Didn't even want to see her. Yet she
was in love with Damien and he was in love with her. So, they
played this game until finally something gave. She got
pregnant a year after graduation. Needless to say, there was a
wedding.

"There he is," Marcy said, pointing toward a small group of
men in black suits. She drew me close to her and pulled a tiny
compact mirror from her clutch. "Do I look okay?" she asked.

"Yes, lovely. Perfect."

"Makeup is soft? Not too makeup-y?" She was never worried about being overdone before she'd met Damien, but now
everything was toned down.

"Yes."

"Too makeup-y?" she whined.

"No, I mean it's fine. Soft and not too much. Just right."

"Okay." She stashed the mirror and straightened her dress. "Now, we're going to walk over there really calm-like and say hello. But let's not look like we're going over there, but just kind of end up there. Okay?"

"We?"

"Yes, we! You have to come with me."

"Why?" I asked. "He'll see me over here. Isn't that enough?"

"Kerry ... I need to look casual and I told him I was coming with you. I don't want to seem like I'm alone and came here just for him—"

"Okay, fine," I said.

"Do you promise to be nice to his friends too?" she begged.

"I'm always nice to his friends."

She shook her head.

"I'm not?" I wasn't.

"They call you Killer Kerry," she said and gave me the "go to hell" stare.

"I do not give them the stare!"

"Look, just promise to be nice today. Please! I really need this." She was pleading as if the future of the relationship depended upon that one night. It was so cute seeing people in love ... even if I wasn't.

"I'll be nice," I said. I knew why she was so anxious. We were about two months from graduation and Marcy had to make some strong leeway with Damien. After he left the confines of campus, there was no telling where he was going or who he'd meet there. His parents might even have had someone handpicked for him.

"Hello, Damien," Marcy said casually when we made our way over to the group.

"Marce," he said, turning to her. I'll admit I wasn't the biggest Damien fan, but he was quite a handsome man. Just a few shades lighter than a bit of cocoa butter, he had a friendly

face that looked like he was always flirting, thick brown eyebrows with thin, secretive eyes that smiled with his lips. He
had the kind of confidence in his eyes that made you wonder
what he'd seen and where he'd been in his life, even though he
was only twenty years old. "You ladies look lovely tonight," he
added, kissing both of us on our cheeks.

"Thank you," Marcy said, digging into my arm with her nails.

"Fellas, you all know Kerry, right?" Damien asked the guys
behind him. "Marcy's roommate?" In usual Morehouse fashion,
all of Damien's friends were just as handsome as he was.
Drones of each other, they all had the same laugh, the same
gait, and the same privileged, confident demeanor. I was sure
I'd seen them all before, met three or two at a dorm room
party, probably even went on a bad date with one, but then, as
they all nodded their heads in agreement that they knew me,
one came pushing to the front of the group and smiled at me.

"I don't think we've met," he said. He put his hand out for
me to shake it, but I was too busy looking into his eyes to return the sentiment.

Marcy nudged me hard in the side.

"Oh, I'm Kerry," I finally said, extending my hand. "But you
probably already know that. I mean, he just said it and that's
my name. Kerry. That's me." It would be short to say I
sounded like a mad woman. Both Damien and Marcy were
looking at me like I was insane. But there was something about
the face in front of me. It was fine . . . yes. It was friendly . . .
yes. But there was something else there. Something promising.
Something real. Something familiar in a haunting way. Something that made me wonder what his name was.

"I'm Jamison Taylor," he said as I noticed that a twinkle of
the strobe light was dancing in his eyes, hypnotizing me. "And
you probably don't know that because no one said it, but now
you do because I said it."

Both he and I laughed at his little joke in response to my nervous blunder, but no one else seemed to get it.

Damien rolled his eyes and looked back at Marcy.

"Well, great then," Damien said dryly, "Marce, you want to dance?" Before she could answer, he snatched her hand and began pulling her to the dance floor.

"Hold this," she said, handing me her clutch.

I watched her walk away, nervously wishing I was escaping too. But not because I wanted to leave. I was standing there alone with Jamison, this beautiful man, and had nothing to say. It was like one of those dances in prep school where I'd be standing right beside the one guy I liked and butterflies rose and fluttered in my stomach until I did the only thing my body would allow: walk to the punch bowl. Only I didn't want to do this. I wanted to talk. To say something. To grab his hand and take him to the dance floor too. But I couldn't, so I just watched Marcy and Damien find their place in the crowd. The other guys began chatting amongst themselves, and a few found partners and were also headed to the dance floor. Time was ticking fiercely in my ear. Just say something.

"You want to dance?" Jamison asked.

"Me?" I asked.

"You're the only you there is," he joked.

"Very funny."

"Well . . . do you?" He was confident, but not self-important. The question was really a question.

"I don't really dance a lot here," I said, turning him down. I wasn't quite sure why I was doing it this time. I wanted to dance with Jamison. Shoot, I even wanted him to gyrate on me. Feel my butt. Kiss my cheek. All that and we'd just met. This man was making something rise, heat, inside me. But that didn't change my fear. I was so used to saying no; yes seemed hard.

"You sure?" he asked. "I mean, you look like the kind of person that wants to dance. You have on a pretty dress. Got your hair done all nice and put on makeup." He pushed a lock of loose hair behind my ear and I could see the muscles in the top of his arm tighten. He was built. Even his suit couldn't hide that. I felt weak. "You're sending out all of the signs of someone who wants to dance."

"You have no idea," I said, gasping.

"Well, maybe you want to dance, but perhaps just not with me . . ." He gave me a sad frown and shook his head. "I guess a brother just embarrassed himself, so I'll just sit down in shame and"—he turned to walk away—"pray some ugly girl will take pity on me."

"No," I grabbed his arm. "That's not it. I just don't—"

"No, don't lower your standards," he said jokingly. "I'll just sit alone and pray the brothers don't laugh at me too hard on the way home. They'll all know you turned me down. But I'll have to live with it." He wiped a fake tear from his eye.

"You're crazy," I said laughing. "Look, I'll dance with you, but just promise not to touch my butt and stuff." I couldn't believe what I was saying. I wanted him to touch my butt! I was screaming inside, but my words were quite different.

"Just one dance?" He turned to me, still wiping fake tears. "Not two?" He was so charming. He kind of reminded me of how my father used to toy with my mother when he wanted something from her. He'd put on one of his records in the den and pull her close to him as her complaining quickly turned to coos. It never took him long.

"Okay, two dances," I said, putting my hand out. "But that's it! And no butt grabbing!"

He took my hand and we walked to the dance floor. Jamison Taylor and me. Together for the first time. I was becoming unstuck and it was magical.

E-MAIL TRANSMISSION

TO: duane.carter@hotmail.com
FROM: Jamison.Taylor@rakeitup.net
DATE: 4/08/07
TIME: 11:00 AM

Coreen, you were the BOMB at that meeting yesterday! I just had to sit down and write you an e-mail to thank you for your help. I wasn't sure if they were feeling my presentation at first (I could tell that the office manager was kind of gun-shy about hiring another black company after the last one failed), but when you came through with all of that information about Rake It Up, I just sat back and let you run with it. They were floored and I knew we had it.

Thanks for everything. Stein and Muck is a major account (I didn't know you all had eight offices throughout Georgia and South Carolina). This is a big deal for Rake It Up! I promise we won't make you look too bad.☺ Again, feel free to hit me up if you ever need anything.

Thanks.

E-MAIL TRANSMISSION

TO: Jamison.Taylor@rakeitup.net
FROM: coreenissocute@yahoo.com
DATE: 4/08/07
TIME: 1:30 PM

I hope you read this e-mail! I have a new e-mail. I realized how crazy it was that I was still using Duane's e-mail account and went ahead and created a new one. You like the new handle? I thought it was fun.

No problem about the job. You seem like a professional man and I know you will do fine. I was honestly impressed when I saw your

Web site for Rake It Up and then located a story about you in *Black Enterprise* (yes, I read *Black Enterprise*). I know luck and hook-ups didn't lead to your grossing over $1 million last year. And basing the whole concept of the company on your father's love for lawn care is so thoughtful. I just had to help.

So, after the meeting you mentioned a free lunch. Is that offer still open? Can I switch it for a dinner?☺ me smiling back at you.

—Coreen's so cute

E-MAIL TRANSMISSION

TO: coreenissocute@yahoo.com
FROM: Jamison.Taylor@rakeitup.net
DATE: 4/09/07
TIME: 12:01 PM

Cute screen name. I was never bothered by the other one.

As far as dinner, I just don't think that's appropriate. I'm married. I hope you understand.

Thanks again for your help.

E-MAIL TRANSMISSION

TO: Jamison.Taylor@rakeitup.net
FROM: coreenissocute@yahoo.com
DATE: 4/09/07
TIME: 2:16 AM

I'm so embarrassed. I hope you don't think I'm some kind of crazy person. I know you're married—I peeped that Cartier band when you came to get your PalmPilot. But you seem cool and I was just hoping to be friends. I don't have many friends in Georgia. After

Duane died, I used the insurance money to move down here to buy my house, so I'm pretty much alone. And you seemed nice and safe and a great example of where I'm trying to go in my life right now. I just don't get to meet too many successful people like you. In these few weeks, you've inspired me. And I've decided to fulfill my dream of finally going back to college. At 31!

I apologize if I came off disrespectfully. No harm intended.

E-MAIL TRANSMISSION

TO: coreenissocute@yahoo.com
FROM: Jamison.Taylor@rakeitup.net
DATE: 4/09/07
TIME: 2:25 AM

See, now I feel bad for writing the things I wrote. I could imagine what you're going through having lost your husband. And I think it's great that you're working on trying to do big things with your life. You deserve it. Look, I'm here if you need help. I wouldn't be where I am today if no one helped me, so I understand what you mean.

Please accept my humble apology. I just didn't want to lead you on.

Naked for the First Time

The worst thing about being pregnant is that you have to get used to the fact that you're sharing your body with another person. Yes, it's a person you made. And it just happens to be a tiny person. But that little person that's a part of you pushes your body to the limit—first hormonally with the nausea and fatigue and then as the teeny tiny person grows, he continues pushing by stretching and kicking at your insides like he could make more space, simply by wanting it.

By the time I was eight months, the tiny person inside of me who was to be named after his father became a beautiful struggle. I was happy he was there and seeing his little body on the monitor was wonderful, but I could never get comfortable with him inside of me and sometimes I would just sit back and look at my fat black belly that had a platoon of stretch marks on it and pray that he would come out already. I felt bad, but I was getting tired of sharing my body and wanted out of the pregnancy thing. I wondered if I'd ever get my shape back and knew I'd have to jog a thousand miles before I'd wear my skinny jeans again.

Laying in bed in Marcy's guest room, I just couldn't get comfortable. If the baby wasn't turning and kicking, I was thinking about Jamison and crying. I took a long, hot shower when

Marcy and I got in from the precinct. And while Marcy dutifully found one of her old maternity sweat suits and laid it out for me, I just climbed into the bed, wet and naked as the day I was born. I wanted to feel my skin against the crisp linen, shock my body with the empty coldness waiting beneath the sheets, curl up like the little baby inside of me and cry myself to sleep in the middle of the day.

With the lights off and the curtains closed, sleep came quickly to my exhausted body, but after two hours, rest faded and I was up again, tossing and turning, trying to get comfortable with my body and the situation. I wondered if being at Marcy's was a mistake. I couldn't let Jamison run me out of my own home. It belonged to both of us. But I knew if I went home, he'd be there. I didn't want to see him. And I also kept wondering what I'd do if he wasn't there, if he never came back. I wasn't ready to face either situation—seeing Jamison or not seeing Jamison. I needed time to think. Time alone.

"Uppy, puppy?" Marcy said, pushing herself and the sunlight behind her into the room.

"Yeah," I said, squinting.

She came and sat on the bed beside me, placing a warm cup of milk on the nightstand.

"I thought you might like that," she said. "Something to calm your nerves."

"A glass of wine will do," I said.

"Um . . . We'll wait on that order!" She laughed and crawled to get into bed beside me. "So, how you doing?"

I didn't say anything. Fine would be a lie and bad hardly touched the surface. I was in disarray. I was unfurling. A disaster area. Hurricane Katrina. My father's mind. Was there a word for that? I started crying again.

"Oh, baby," she said, reaching over me to get tissue from the nightstand on my side of the bed. "I didn't mean to upset you."

"It's not that, Marce. I just, you know, just don't know what I'm going to do."

"He called."

"What?"

"While you were asleep, he called three times. Said he just wanted to make sure you were okay. He was going to come by, but I had Damien call him to calm him down. I think Damien went over there."

"Damien knows?" I asked. It was a dumb question. Of course he'd know. Did he know about Coreen too?

"Well, someone had to get your car from in front of that woman's house."

"He got my car?" I was actually relieved to hear that.

"Yeah, he brought it back over here and parked it right outside for you."

"Thanks so much, Marce, for hooking me up. For everything."

"No problem. I had to get him out of my hair anyway. He was driving me crazy about this party tonight. He's a bit nervous, I think."

"Oh, I keep forgetting about the party." Damien was finally leaving the ER and opening his own practice and they'd invited everyone in the universe to celebrate.

"Yeah, I've been downstairs working with the caterers for the last two hours. . . . We need everything to be perfect."

"Oh, no, am I in the way? I could leave and go home or to my mom's or something," I said, sitting up.

"Girl, please; this is your home. You don't have to go anywhere. Plus, it might be good for you to see some people. It'll keep your mind off things. And if both you and Jamison aren't here, people will wonder why. You know how they talk."

"I know," I said, " but I'm not ready for all that."

"Well, just think about it. You can mix and mingle or you can lock yourself in this room all night. I've got your back either way. I'll even smuggle a plate upstairs for you."

"Now, that's love!" I forced a smile.

"I can't let you starve my godson." We both laughed and I settled back into the bed.

"I know it's crazy, but for some reason, I keep thinking about when Jamison and I first met," I said after a long pause.

Marcy turned to me.

"I don't think it's crazy at all. When you go through something like this, it's natural to wonder how you got there and think about how things began, the good times you never thought would end.

"You remember the Valentine's dance?"

"Don't remind me of that fiasco." Marcy rolled her eyes and smiled. "You nearly broke that boy's heart."

"No, I didn't," I protested.

"All I remember is Jamison banging on Damien's car window, complaining about how you won't let him touch you and that he wouldn't have agreed to babysit you if he knew you were so stuck-up," she said giggling.

Days after we met, Jamison admitted that Damien made him promise to babysit Marcy's "easy" friend at the party and that's the only reason he asked me to dance. Apparently, all of the other boys declined because they knew who I was, but they left Jamison in the dark as a joke. He was looking for a quick lay, but got me instead. He was less than happy . . . at first.

"That's what he got for trying to be the Mack!" I laughed.

"Yeah, but everything changed when he had to drive you home," Marcy said. "Then he came back to Damien saying he was in love."

"We couldn't stop talking. I sat in his car in front of the Spelman gates grinning for three hours before I told him I didn't live there. Then the sun was coming up and we were both laughing," I said tearfully. "He said he didn't know why he assumed I lived on campus and I didn't know why I hadn't told him he was going the wrong way. We were in our own little world. We talked so much, I was sure we wouldn't have anything to talk about the next day, but we did."

"And then he kissed you," Marcy said.

"And then he kissed me." Even in my anger, the memory of that first kiss, the innocence, made a butterfly flutter inside.

"And then, just as I predicted before we even went to the dance, you lost your mind."

"No, I didn't," I protested.

"Please, both of you went crazy. Couldn't get enough of each other. If you two weren't together, you were on the phone, and neither of us had cell phones in '95, so I remember waiting for you to get off the damn house phone." She playfully banged her fist on the bed between us. "In fact, I do believe that somewhere in a history book it says that was when Spelman officially accepted its first male student, because that man was missing all of his classes, coming to yours."

"He sure did. We just couldn't get enough of each other . . ." I said with my voice sadly trailing off.

I rubbed my stomach and looked helplessly at Marcy.

"Then what happened? How did we get here?" I asked.

"You're going to ask yourself that same questions a million times and never get an answer until you ask him. Then you won't even be happy with that," Marcy said. I could tell she was talking about her situation. In the eleven years they'd been married, Damien had cheated many times and even managed to have a stalker. In response, Marcy developed a private life of her own. Like many of the women in the big houses in Buck-head, she had lots of romantic gifts, private dinners, and late nights at hotels when her husband was away. All of it, Damien's cheating, Marcy's way of getting back at him, made me wonder why they were even together. But for some reason, the dispute, their secret lives, only made them more determined to stay married. Neither showed signs of wanting to leave. It was an odd understanding, but somehow they both kept breathing.

"Nothing is going to make it all right in your head," she continued. "What you have to do now is focus on your baby and make some big decisions. And I can't do that for you."

The door chime rang throughout the house, getting louder and louder as it found its way to the bedroom. Marcy and I looked at each other quickly.

"Probably the decorator," Marcy said, knowing exactly what I was thinking. "The caterer will let him in." She turned and looked to the window. The chime came calling again. "Maybe it's the—"

"Kerry, I'm outside," a voice yelled far too loud for Marcy's Buckhead enclave. The sound of Jamison's voice made my heart race. "I need to see you."

"Jamison," Marcy said, jumping out of bed and running to the window. "Where's Damien?"

"Marcy, I need to see my wife," Jamison said.

I watched Marcy struggle to open the window as I took much longer than I wished to get out of bed.

"This is not the time or the place for this, Jamison. She's fine. She's resting and she's fine."

"I need to see her," Jamison hollered so loud Marcy jumped and hit her head at the top of the window. "I need to tell her what's going on . . . why I was there."

"You two can talk later when you calm down," Marcy said as I came up behind her. She held out her hand to stop me from putting my head out of the window beside her.

"Kerry, is that you?" he called to me. "Please come out here and talk to me. Please!"

"Do you want to see him?" Marcy said, turning to me.

"I don't know." I was crying again, standing there naked with tears streaming down my cheeks.

"Just come outside so we can talk," he cried.

Covering my body with the curtain, I squeezed into the window sill beside Marcy. Jamison looked really bad. His face was completely red, and even from the window I could tell his eyes were as swollen as mine.

"Why are you here?" I hollered. "I don't want to see you."

"Kerry, don't do this," he said. "Hear me out."

"Hear what? I don't want to hear anything from your lying ass. Did she know you were married? Did she know you had a baby on the way? You bastard!"

Marcy pulled me back from the window.

"Stop it, Kerry," she said, wrapping me in a sheet.

I was bawling so hard my chest was heaving like a child's and I could feel my heart beating, pounding all the way in my uterus.

"He can go . . . he can go," I kept rambling as Marcy sat me down on the bed, "go and be with her."

She got up to close the window, but we could still hear Jamison yelling for me to come out.

"I have to get rid of him before someone calls the police," Marcy said. "They're probably already on the way. Just promise me you'll stay here."

"Let them arrest him like they arrested me," I said, wiping my face with a little pink tissue she'd handed me.

"Just stay here," Marcy said. She ran to the door and I heard her flip-flops clacking down the steps.

"Kerry, I need you," Jamison hollered. His words flipped around in my gut.

I just sat there on the bed and waited to hear Marcy's voice on the other side. I slowly began to pull the sheet off my body. I needed to go back to bed.

The First Fight

"**Y**ou're going to forget all about me when you go to Harvard," Jamison said. We were wrapped around each other like two pretzel halves in the lumpy twin-sized bed in his dorm room. We'd been nesting there for two days straight. It was hot and musty and the only real air in the room came from a box fan Jamison had set up in the window—what he'd called "ghetto air conditioning." It wasn't the best of accommodations: I had to sneak in and out and Jamison insisted on playing OutKast on continuous loop in his CD changer.

"Whatever." I laughed and repositioned my arm because it was falling asleep, scrunched between the poster of Janet Jackson on the wall beside the bed and Jamison's back. "You'll forget me long before I forget you!"

"So you admit you'll forget me!"

"No, I didn't mean that," I said, laughing again. He had a way of keeping me laughing as he twisted my words. We'd been dating for about a month and Jamison seemed to know me better than anyone in the world. He anticipated what I'd say, how I'd feel, and was careful to be sure I was happy. I was a long way from vagina-grabbing Preston Allcott. It was more than refreshing. Enough so that I was able to put up with the music and his long-lost lover, Janet Jackson, looking over us.

"It's okay; I can take it. I'm a big boy," he playfully said. "Leave me woman; leave me be!"

"Please, you won't be too far away when you go off to Cornell for med school . . . and you already have your acceptance letter, so stop jinxing mine."

"I can't jinx fate. You were born to go to Harvard Med," he said. "And everyone knows that a wait-list means that you're practically in."

"You think?"

"Yeah, girl, they accept half of the people on the list each year," he said reassuringly. "And when you get finished . . . if you haven't forgotten about little old me . . . I'll come up to Boston and sweep you off your feet."

"Even if I'm working on a cadaver?"

"I'd hug the dead dude too!"

"How romantic."

"Then we'll get married and have eight boys."

"Eight? Boys?" I laughed.

"I'm not a girl maker. Only boys will come from my nuts. Soldiers."

"Ill; don't be crass." I plunked him on the head with my only free hand.

"Yep, all boys and they'll all be Morehouse men like their father and then be doctors too . . . like their father. I'm building a legacy, baby." He jumped up and began tickling me. "I need an army and you're going to give it to me."

"Not out of my stomach!" I playfully wrapped my arms around my stomach as he wrestled with me. We hadn't had sex yet. I hadn't built up the nerve and Jamison seemed determined not to rush things.

"Do you really think we'll be together then?" I asked out of breath. "Like that far from now."

"I can't imagine myself with anyone else." His voice was serious. Not one crack. He was still. Stopped and looked into my eyes. "I love you, Kerry. You're the best thing that's happened to me. I'll come there every weekend if that's what it takes to keep you."

"You're gonna come to class with me there too?"

"Hell, yeah!" He grinned. "I have to know what these folks are putting in my lady's head."

"Very funny."

"But whether I'm going to want to be with you isn't the question," he started, circling the inside of my navel with his index finger. "It's if you'll have me."

"If I'll have you?" I asked.

"It's no secret that you weren't exactly happy about dating me in the first place. . . . Not after you found out my past. How I got here," he said. "I was surprised you even called. Being funny can only get a brother so far with a woman like you."

Jamison was at Morehouse on a full scholarship. His mother, who hadn't gone to college, couldn't afford to send him and his father died the year before Jamison graduated from high school. His parents made ends meet before Jamison's father's kidneys gave out to a lifelong bout of diabetes, but they were by all accounts poor. He was raised in one of the toughest neighborhoods in southwest Atlanta, but his grades and penchant for science led to him receiving attention from a local doctor who went to Morehouse. The man liked Jamison so much that he and a few of his colleagues agreed to pay his tuition for four years if he got into their alma mater.

"Where you came from doesn't matter to me," I said. "You're here now."

"But it *does* matter," he replied.

"In some circles, yes. It'll always matter. This is the South."

"Yeah—home of the uppity negro . . . the Talented Tenth," he said, sitting up. "Where I'm from will always matter here. I noticed it my sophomore year when I pledged APhi and my own line brothers shut me out of certain things—Damien included. You all segment and separate people based on things they can't even help or change . . . and for what?"

He was quiet then, but I had nothing to say. I realized that I was part of the "you" he was speaking of.

"The worst part," he went on, "is that I've lived here all my life, not five miles from Morehouse, and I didn't even know it was going on. I mean, I knew people like you looked down on people like me when I was a kid, but I always thought it was just because I was poor or didn't have the right clothes. I thought that would change once I got to college, put on the right shirt and pledged the right fraternity. Then I'd be one of you."

"It's not that serious, Jamison," I said.

"It's serious to your mother. It matters to her. I saw how she looked at me when she came to visit last week." He scrunched up his face to mimic the bitter frown my mother had permanently plastered on her face when I introduced them at my apartment. She didn't even have to talk to Jamison to know who and what he was. She saw his car in the parking lot. His sneakers. His clothing. And knew the story. She wasted no time talking to him. She just sat on the edge of my sofa as if his sitting beside her was offensive and spoke to me like he wasn't in the room.

"My mother is a different story. That's just where she's from. History means everything to her," I said. This all seemed bizarre to Jamison, but in my world it was just how things were done. Our kind just married our kind and that was how it was. It was how they protected one another. Ensured that we were all going someplace. And had the same ideas. The same past. My granduncle had ties to Atlanta Life, the country's most wealthy African-American insurance company. My mom grew up in Cascade Heights and was a third-generation Spelman girl. There were rules that women with my mother's past had to follow. Rules that she'd passed on to me.

"If history means everything to her," Jamison said, "then it must mean everything to you too." He looked at me; the look in his eyes was far from what it had been just minutes earlier.

"No."

"Why not?"

"Because I know you now," I sat up beside him. "I know that you have a future. You're going to be a doctor, Jamison. And that has to count for something. Right?"

"But what if I'm not a doctor? Then will it count for something?" he asked.

"You will be." I kissed him on the cheek reassuringly. "I know it. And my mother will just have to be happy about it."

After we snacked on boxed macaroni and cheese he'd made in the microwave, Jamison fell asleep, and against the backdrop of his senseless snoring I was awake and thinking about everything we'd just talked about. I'd meant everything I said to him. I believed in Jamison. Believed in who he was and who he would be. I had the name and the money. But he'd be great one day. So what if he hadn't been in Jack and Jill and gone to the right prep school. He was going to be a doctor. We'd be okay, and I didn't need an elite Atlanta stamp to prove it.

But still, looking at the blue macaroni and cheese box in the trash, hearing rap on the radio, and realizing that I was a senior, sneaking around in a dorm room when most upperclassmen had the money to move off campus, a little part of me, one

I'd wished was a bit quieter, did want Jamison to be more like
me. More like the first boyfriend I'd imagined. He had caviar
and fine wine and cheese in the fridge, an apartment in Buck-
head and a last name that made other girls jealous. While in
my heart I knew that Jamison was better than any of the men
who could give me any of those things, Jamison was nothing
like that man . . . and really, nothing like me. I looked at him
lying in the bed and imagined how that could be—that the man
who made me laugh so hard my cheeks would ache, with whom
I never ran out of things to talk to about, was from the same
city but a whole world away from mine.

My thoughts about our differences didn't exactly dissipate
when I finally met Jamison's mother. If my mother hated Jamison, then Jamison's mother despised me. And unlike my
mother, she wasn't quiet about it.

After quizzing me for thirty minutes about why I didn't
know how to cook, she asked how I paid my bills and who paid
my rent. It was obvious that she was trying to paint me out to
be a spoiled little rich girl, and that wouldn't have been so bad
if it wasn't for the fact that she did it in front of Jamison's entire family.

To celebrate our one-month anniversary, he'd taken me to
what he called Sunday dinner to meet his mother. Assuming it
was anything like the Sunday dinners my mother hosted, I
wore a sweet, floral print dress and carried with me a flan I'd
purchased for dessert.

When we got there, it was clear that Sunday dinner looked
a little different in the SWATS than it did in Cascade. First,
there were children all over the yard and they were frying fish
on the front steps in a metal machine I'd never seen in any
store. I could smell fish as soon as we got out of the car. And
while my empty stomach made me want to stick my hand in

the hot grease to pick out a piece, I knew the entire scene would've sent my mother into shock.

When we walked inside, Jamison's mother was sitting in the kitchen, directly in front of the only fan in what I had to assume was an un-air-conditioned house full of people and screaming children. She was a short, round woman with skin that was surprisingly (because of Jamison's color) browner than mine. In fact, she was so dark that I wondered if Jamison's father was white.

She looked me up and down slowly, acknowledging what I already knew—I was overdressed.

"Mama, this is Kerry, the girl from Spelman," Jamison said.

"Hello, I'm Dottie," she said, flashing a fake smile without lifting her hand to shake mine. "You two came from church?" She was secretly trying to make fun of my outfit. I'd later learn that she was very good at these kinds of indirect insults.

"No," I said. "Excuse my attire; I just thought that it was Sunday dinner and . . ."

"She brought dessert," Jamison said, cutting me off. I was glad, because God only knows what I was about to say.

"What's that?" She finally put out her hand.

"It's flan," I said. "My favorite."

She opened the box and frowned.

"Like a cheese cake?" she asked, still frowning.

"No . . ." I said. "Like flan. It's Latin."

She looked to Jamison and slid the cake onto the table like it was uncooked fish they'd have to deep fry before anyone touched it. I'd never see that flan again.

"My baby is home," she suddenly changed her look and smiled at Jamison. "Home to see his mama." She wrapped her arms around him and kissed him on the cheek, spying me from the corner of her eye. "You know can't no woman love you like your mama, right?" she asked, still embracing him. "No woman."

By the time everyone calmed down due to full stomachs and lots of hot sauce, the crowd was thinning out and I was having a good time. Jamison's family was a lot of fun, much more fun than mine, and his aunts seemed to have advice for everything under the sun. Including some unsolicited bedroom instructions for me.

"So, Ms. Girl, who are you?" I heard someone say from behind. I was sure they weren't talking to me, but judging from everyone's eyes, I knew to turn around.

Jamison's mother was sitting in a chair with her chubby little hands wrapped around a beer.

"Ma'am?" I responded.

"Don't play with me," she said.

"Mama!" Jamison pleaded for her to stop.

"Boy, please, ain't nobody trying to scare her off. I just want to know who she is," she slurred, "and what she wants with my boy."

"I really like your son," I tried. Jamison nodded. I guessed that was good.

"You really like what about him? The money he's gonna make? I know your kind. I can smell you. Just looking to cash in."

"I don't need to cash in on anything," I said defensively. "I have—"

Jamison cut me off with his stare.

"Well then, what can you offer him?" she asked. "Can you cook? Clean? What can you do besides spend other people's money?"

The room became even more quiet. Even the babies seemed to stop cooing and crying. The men fixing the car in the driveway poked their heads in the windows.

"Mama, this isn't the time or place for this," Jamison said.

"No, let her answer," someone said. "Dottie is right."

"What can you offer?" his mother asked again.

"Well, I can offer a lot. I'm going to be a doctor too . . . and then I'll learn how to cook and clean and I'll . . ." I couldn't even believe what I was saying. I wasn't about to cook and clean for anyone. That was where I drew the line in the sand. But it sounded good. So I thought.

"Don't give me that shit about no med school. He done already told me you didn't get accepted to none of those med schools you applied to, so you can stop lying to me."

I looked at Jamison hard. He wasn't supposed to tell anyone about the letters.

"Stop putting on airs and shit," she went on after reloading by having a sip of her beer. "You ain't got nowhere to go and you thinking you about to cash in on my baby. . . . But it ain't gonna happen. My Jamison is going to Cornell Medical School, where he done already been accepted, and leaving your ass right here in Atlanta. I promise you that."

Jamison jumped up from his seat and reached for me.

"Mama, you know I'm not going to disrespect you," he said, "so I'm just going to leave. You didn't have to do this."

I didn't even wait for Jamison. I was in tears. I ran out of the house and walked right past the car, toward nowhere, I guess. I've seen and heard of humiliation, but never once in my life had it come at my expense.

"Where are you going?" Jamison called.

I stopped in my tracks but kept my back to him. While I was angry, both Jamison and I knew I wouldn't get far. I'd never been on public transportation and I was wearing two-inch heels.

"I want to go home," I said with my back still to him.

"Baby, I'm sorry. I had no idea she'd act like this," he said.

"I've brought girls home before and she was always . . . agreeable."

"I feel like crap," I said with my voice cracking. "She made me feel like crap." I could feel Jamison close behind me.

"I'm sorry," he said.

"Why did you have to tell her?" I asked. "About my letters? That was private." I turned to see that he was closer than I thought.

"I was confused. I didn't know how to comfort you, and I asked her for advice. I don't even know why she brought it up."

"I know why . . . she obviously doesn't like me. She thinks I'm a spoiled little rich girl."

Jamison was quiet.

"Is that what you think, too?" I asked, stepping away from him. "That I'm spoiled . . ."

"Well, there are some things about you that I . . . that I'm not used to." His face scrunched up so tight, I could tell he was nervous.

"Are you kidding me? Not used to?"

"You've never worked," he said, "and you have a brand-new car, you dry clean all of your clothes . . . and you can't cook . . . anything."

"How is that different? Everyone I know is like that. How is it so different? It's just me . . . and if that's not enough for you then . . ." I started crying again. I knew my points were empty. I was suddenly feeling embarrassed about the things I owned, ashamed for the things I couldn't do.

"Baby," Jamison said, cupping my face with his hands, "you are all I need, you're all I want, but we're different. You know that."

"But how can we survive, get along if everything I am you hate?" I asked.

"What if everything I am, you hate?" He held his hands

out and looked around the street. "You don't even want to be here . . ."

I was quiet this time.

"But all of that doesn't even matter, Kerry," Jamison started. "Not this place, not the differences, not even our mothers. What matters is that I love you." He wrapped his hands around my waist. "I love your dry-cleaning-for-no-reason, no-cooking-skills ass."

I could see the sincerity on Jamison's face beyond my tears. It was the first time he'd ever said I love you and it came from deep within him. It was as if I'd never heard the words before, not like that. And while love had never crossed my mind where he was concerned, the fortitude in his tone, the seriousness in his eyes awoke within my young body a flame that set me on fire. I believe it was what Marcy had said was "going crazy."

My mother had always told me that a real lady never initiates a kiss, but I heard none of this that day in the middle of the SWATS. I stepped up on my tippie toes and kissed Jamison so passionately that much of what happened after that was a blur. Suddenly I was back in his car, then in his dorm room, and then, right there on the twin-sized bed I once secretly said I would never lose my virginity on, Jamison made love to me for the first time. "I love you," I said to him so many times that night. "I love you, Jamison, and nothing will keep us apart."

TO: nicole.smith@steinandmuck.com
FROM: coreenissocute@yahoo.com
DATE: 4/16/07
TIME: 9:47 AM

Girl, where are you this morning?????? Are you even coming to work? I NEED YOU! I have to tell you what happened this weekend with my Sexy Morehouse Man! We were supposed to go for dinner on Saturday, but something happened with his wife, so he suggested we meet to watch the game on Sunday (I guess she doesn't like sports like most women—you know how that goes). Anyway, I swear I fell in love with this man. He is EVERYTHING the woman at my church said he would be . . . and more. She was right; we're perfect for each other. He's nice, funny, smart, successful, and fine as hell. What more could a woman want? I wanted to jump his bones right there at the bar! But I have to keep playing nice.☹

Speaking of which, after I got a few drinks in Jamison, he admitted that he hasn't had sex with his wife in like a month! I'm trying not to pass judgment, but what kind of woman is that? How could she re-sist his fine ass? If I had him, he'd get it like every night. And twice on Sunday! All that money he brings home and all Ms. Perfect can do is hold back in the bedroom. If she don't want him, I'll take him. Any-way, what should I do? Hit me back ASAP! I NEED YOU!!!!!

P.S. He kissed me when he walked me to my car! OK . . . he was drunk and it was on the cheek, but he did linger there for a while. Am I being trifling? I didn't make him do anything.

E-MAIL TRANSMISSION

TO: coreenissocute@yahoo.com
FROM: nicole.smith@steinandmuck.com
DATE: 4/16/07
TIME: 10:15 AM

WHAT! I can't believe I'm missing this. Dumb-ass Piper sent me to the Kennesaw office because one of the paralegals here went on maternity leave, so I'm helping them catch up. I guess I'll have to get the rest of the Sexy Morehouse Man story when I get back downtown on Monday. This might call for drinks! Sounds juicy.

And you know how I feel about the unhappily married folks. . . . If she won't treat him right, someone else will. And why not you?

There's nothing trifling about it, Coreen. It's simple mathematics. We're in our thirties and there aren't exactly millions of available black men out there. Even Oprah said it. Not ones with degrees and million-dollar businesses! The man already told you his old lady doesn't respect him. And now he's not getting any ass! They won't last. Who wants to be around all that? It's only a matter of time before he cheats anyway. You know how men do. I'm not saying you should cheat with him and be some type of one-night-stand whore, but maybe you're the kind of woman he should be with in the first place. I don't see why you should miss out on a man you really like just because he has a piece of paper connecting him to another woman from when he was like 22. I say have some fun. You deserve it, girl!

Love ya,
dablackannanicole

P.S. The real question about the kiss was whether he licked you! You know I like my men freaky.

P.P.S. Who is the woman at your church?

Ain't No Party Like a Buckhead Party . . .

It's funny how happy days can go by so quickly and sad days seem to evolve minute to minute like a perpetual Groundhog Day. By the time Marcy's house was ready for Damien's party and I was up in the guest room trying to figure out which one of Marcy's old dresses I'd put on if I decided to venture outside the room, I realized that the worst day of my life was taking forever to end. Maybe it was because it began with me in the car at 5:35 AM. Maybe it was because my heart was breaking and drama seemed to intend for this to be a slow process. Either way, I was done with Friday and praying for the same Friday one year ago, when things at least seemed perfect, to somehow find me again. This process might not have been as difficult if Marcy hadn't had most of her "big days" when she was pregnant with Milicent in the summer. Most of the dresses were pastel and the only black one had a plunging neckline. I firmly believed that pregnant women shouldn't show cleavage and my cleavage was at an all-time high.

Now if I was my regular size, I would've tried on all of the dresses and picked the best one, but putting on one dress at eight months was a hassle in and of itself. It took way too much energy to wiggle in and wiggle out.

Aside from my clothing obstacles, the other important factor slowing me down was the fact that I wasn't sure I wanted to see anyone at the party. In addition to being sad and in an utter state of shock, I just didn't feel like talking to anyone and hearing them ask, "Where's Jamison?" This question alone would send me into tears, for sure. But, a master of gossip, Marcy was right . . . appearances were everything and absence would be just as bad. While normal people might think that I was not there because of the baby coming, everyone knew that we wouldn't miss it—Damien and Marcy were our best friends. And that was enough for them. In this world, people love to contrive their own renditions of reality, and it was better to be there to catch poor gossip in the making. I learned that the hard way with Marcy in college. When we lived in the dorm our first year, I'd sit on my bed across from her and listen to people come into the room telling story after story about this girl and that girl. The stories would change several times throughout the hour and by the time Marcy got on the phone to spread the word to the next dorm, it would change again. I'd had my share of this in prep school, but Spelman was on a whole different level. Gossip shaped and shredded lives. It was the undercurrent that pushed college life along. Luckily, I had the wave maker in my dorm room.

"You gonna come out?" Marcy said, poking her head in the room.

I'd managed to pull the black dress over my head, but as I predicted my breasts looked like I was expecting an entire litter of babies to feed.

"Whoa, stripper lady!" Marcy joked.

"Very funny," I laughed. "I don't know; I'm still contemplating it. I think it might be too soon. . . . But I also need something to take my mind off of everything," I looked in the mirror at my puffy eyes, "so I can stop crying . . ."

"Well, how about you make an appearance and then come back up here? I'll tell people your feet hurt or something."

"Hum . . ." I put a dab of concealer beneath my right eye. "I guess so . . ." I started but didn't finish my thought. I wanted to say I wished none of this was happening, that I hadn't carried my behind over to that woman's house this morning, and that I still had my husband by my side, but this would only send me back into hysterics. "You think he'll come?" I asked.

"Jamison promised Damien he wouldn't come by," she said firmly. "Look, Kerry, I don't see why you should be the one hiding in this thing. You didn't do anything wrong. Let his behind sit in the house and think about the fact that he's messed up his marriage. Let him be the one forced out."

As the crowd grew, the chatter coming up the stairs escalated from a few spurts to what sounded like a mob of two hundred or so. Hiding my cleavage with a pink sash I found in the closet, I stood by the door of the bedroom practicing my entry: how I'd smile and say Jamison had a stomach virus. He really wanted to be there. But I had to come to share in our best friends' glory. I'd smile again and change the subject. Perhaps I'd bring up the new exhibit at the High Museum, that always shut up the fakers.

When I finally found the nerve to open the door and make my way down the stairs, I could see from the third step down that the foyer was full of people. Laughing and smiling as if not one person was missing, they seemed so content and full of themselves. There were men in black suits and women in knee-length cocktail dresses in the appropriate seasonal colors. Real pearls and diamonds sparkled from the women's extra-slender necks as the men held their hands in the smalls of their backs. Everything was so fixed, so on key with how things were supposed to be. They'd learned well.

But who were these people really? I couldn't help but think this as I questioned my own existence. Climbing farther down, I noticed a senator I'd been to college with. She was the first in her family to go to college. Her husband was the same. You'd never know it by how they laughed and traded secrets in the circle of spectators. They would never have been accepted at one of my mother's gatherings. They had no name, and even in politics, little money. Like most of the people there, they were new to this crowd and had no clue that they'd never be accepted elsewhere. Mixed in here and there were a few of Marcy's sorority sisters—all skinny, all light skinned, all married, all exceptionally successful in their careers. They were the girls at Spelman everyone had to know. When we were there, they ran all of the student organizations, and when I didn't run, they were nominated for homecoming titles. I'd never really clicked with these women. There was something about the competition between us, the way they seemed so surprised at my beauty that just rubbed me the wrong way. They insisted on complimenting me about my dark skin, fingered my hair but seemed surprised that it was so long and not extensions, and always seemed to follow up compliments about both with "... to be so dark" as in "You have such a nice complexion ... to be so dark" and "Your hair is so long ... to be so dark—I mean, you're not even mixed." To make matters between us worse, they knew that my great-grandmother and mother had pledged their chapter and perhaps wondered why I wasn't signing up. As one girl put it, "I was a paperwork shoo-in." But I wasn't hearing any of this. I'd grown tired of the old color thing when I was a child and my mother made it seem as if my skin, which was much darker than both hers and my father's, was some type of genetic experiment gone wrong. It was the '90s, for God's sake. We had to get over it someday.

"Is that you, Kerry Ann?" Piper Muck, one of Marcy's line sisters called when my eyes caught hers. A former big bitch on campus, she was now a big somebody in the room. She was a third-generation attorney and had just made partner at her grandfather's firm.

"Yes," I said, smiling as I wobbled down the last step.

"I thought so." She smiled and as she made her way across the foyer to me, five or six other sisters came along cooing.

"The baby," one said, touching my stomach—I hated that. "When is it coming?"

"Soon," another said who I knew was a gynecologist. "I'd say in three weeks at the most." She placed her hand on my stomach without asking and nodded her head "yes" to the other ladies.

"Well, that's it," Piper said. "When Wilma says the baby is coming, it sure is."

They all laughed and Piper, whose oddly thin body was the reason so many women became bulimic, shifted the wine glass she was holding from one hand to the other.

"A boy, I bet," she said. I could feel Jamison's name coming up in the next sentence. There was only one way to handle the attack.

"Yes," I said smiling. "His name will be Jamison. . . . Oh, you're probably wondering why he isn't here. He's sick. He sends his best."

They all sighed with a look of fake desperation. One could only wonder why in the hell they even cared.

"The poor thing has a stomach flu or something. . . ." I went on, beating them to the punch. "You know that bug has been going around up North."

"Aunt KeKe," a sweet voice called. It could only be my god-daughter.

"Milicent," I said, turning to find her cute face. A complete replica of a young Marcy, Milicent had dimples and the most adorable little bow tie nose. She was eleven and nearly taller than me, but in my eyes the girl would always be five. She was standing beside another little girl who was the same height, but she was white with blond hair and light green eyes. They were both dressed in ballet leotards.

"Look at your belly," Milicent squealed, touching my stomach with the other little girl. While most of the black families I knew insisted on connecting to their culture with a kind of shrewd militancy—attending black art shows, seeing Alvin Ailey every year and attending a small list of HBCUs—this was not the case for Damien's family. We were both of the same position, but his family was a bit "bluer" than mine. With a fourth-generation European education and a blue bloodline that led right to the front steps of a plantation, Damien still held ties in the black community, but like many in his lineage, he believed in maintaining close ties to whites. For this reason, Milicent attended a white private school where she was one of eight black students, played with mostly white children, and didn't belong to Jack and Jill or the Debutantes.

"It's a boy, right?" Milicent asked.

"Yes," I said.

"Oh, I wish it was a girl . . ." she moaned.

"We all want girls, but we all get boys," Piper said laughing with the other ladies readjusting their configuration around the two girls.

"You didn't introduce your friend," I said.

"Oh, this is Iris. She's my new best friend."

The girls smiled.

"Wonderful, how nice to meet you, Iris." I shook her hand.

"She has such beautiful blond hair," one of the other women said. "Like wheat."

"Thank you." Iris smiled and flicked her hair over her shoulders as Milicent looked on in silence. The sharp smile was fading from her face as the other women attended to Iris's golden locks.

"I wish my hair would perm this straight," another woman said.

"Please, there isn't enough lye on this earth to relax your nappy hair that straight," Piper said to another round of fake laughter. The wine glasses shifted from one hand to the other.

"And Milicent has lovely hair, too," I said to wash out their well-dated exchange. While Damien had soft, curly hair that begged to be played with, Marcy's thick, short mane was what Milicent had inherited. I'd watched as Marcy brooded over Milicent's head when she was a baby, praying it wouldn't *change* from its newborn curly state to the tightly curled naps all these women seemed to despise. Marcy even pointed out the dark circles around Milicent's fingertips and said they were even darker than hers. How could this be? She seemed to be asking. It reminded me of my mother.

These conversations grew along with Milicent and it always annoyed me. She was beautiful and I didn't want the same pain that separated me from others as a child to befall her.

"There you are, Milicent!" Marcy said, rushing over. "Why didn't you come find me? I need you to go upstairs to get changed for Daddy's party." She tugged at the little curls that had gathered around Milicent's temples.

"Okay," Milicent said. She hugged her mother. "Can Iris stay over?"

"Now is not the time," Marcy hushed her. "You see Daddy is having company."

Milicent groaned.

"Now go upstairs and clean up and I'll be up in a while to talk about Iris staying over," Marcy said.

Milicent tossed her dance bag over her shoulder and headed toward the staircase I'd just walked down.

"And do something to that head," Marcy said sharply, turning back to us. "So, are you ladies having a great time?"

"Everything is lovely," Piper said. "And Damien seems to be having a great time."

We all turned to see Damien laughing it up with a crew of men I recognized from Morehouse. They'd all grown up. Boys who'd become doctors and lawyers and politicians.

"You're so lucky, Marce," another woman, Mattie, said, that I knew from Marcy's baby shower. "The perfect husband and marriage. What more could a girl want?"

They all laughed and gazed at Damien like everyone in the circle didn't know that Damien was less than loyal to Marcy. Gossip bubbled amongst these women like boiling water. If I knew, they knew. And if they knew, the entire last statement was nothing short of an admission that Damien's behavior was perfectly acceptable to them. This was where and how I split in opinion with these women. I never expected nor accepted that my husband would cheat. It was not something I ever wanted to deal with. And this little circle they were building was not where I wanted to be.

Marcy looked over to me and smiled.

"He sure is the perfect husband," she said. "If only I could be the perfect wife!"

They all laughed.

"I know," Mattie said. "Now, that's impossible. All they have to do is bring home the money, but we have to work and take care of our homes."

"And our children," someone else said.

"And have sex with them!" another woman said who was married to a councilman that had put on about seventy-five pounds during his election.

Even I had to laugh at that one.

"Excuse me, ladies," I said as this rant went on. "On that note, I need a sip of water." I backed away and headed toward the standing bartender Marcy had positioned temporarily in the dining room.

"Sex?!" I heard someone say as I walked away. "Who's having sex with them? I leave that to someone else."

The day was beginning to wear me down and I was feeling ready to head upstairs to get some sleep. The baby felt heavy in my stomach. He'd gone to sleep and while the night was young, he was taking me down with him.

After chatting with a few of Jamison's friends, I found myself sipping on a glass of water in the corner of the room. With no one to talk to, I was thinking about Jamison and feeling sad again.

Piper appeared from out of nowhere. It was as if she sensed my tiredness and crept up beside me with ninja-like silence to catch me in a vulnerable state. If I ever forgot why I hated these women, Piper was always there to remind me.

"Drink too much water and your water will break," Piper said another one of her corny jokes.

"Funny," I pretended to laugh like most people.

"My mother used to say that to me."

"Well, mine had a different philosophy," I said, imagining what my mother would be sipping on at the moment.

"You know, I wished I was invited to your shower," she ambushed me. Piper was not one of my friends and there was no reason in the world for her to have been invited to the shower.

"Well, it was a small gathering," I responded.

"Yeah, but sometimes I just wish we were closer." She sighed and it was almost sincere. "Like if you'd pledged or something, we might be best friends. We have a lot more in common than you and Marcy. . . . Same family, same history. . . . We could have been close." She paused, expecting me to respond, I supposed.

"Sure," I said.

"Oh, it just makes me so sad that I couldn't be there for you right now . . . with Jamison," she finally said.

"Be there? Jamison?"

"Yeah, like through all of this . . . that I couldn't be your friend and comfort you."

"All of this?" I assumed she was talking about the baby, but the tone in her voice. . . Maybe it was the alcohol I smelled on her breath talking.

"Jamison . . . and why he's not here."

"Why he's not here? And why isn't he here?" My heart skipped a beat.

"I know about the other woman," Piper whispered, gritting her teeth.

"Really," I said to stop myself from saying a long list of other things. I didn't want to give Piper that satisfaction. She was no shoulder to lean on. She was just as fake as the filler she'd had pumped into her lips. I began to block Piper out and searched the room for the source of this drama beside me. Marcy was the only person who could have told her.

"No problem, Kerry," I heard Piper say. "You know I have your back. I always will . . ."

I felt the fire raging in my stomach. I held tight to my glass to stop my fist from meeting Piper's jaw.

"You're a troll," I heard myself say.

"Excuse me?" Piper placed her hand over her heart.

"You heard me," I said rather loud. The people standing closest to us turned around. "What gives you the right to come over here and say something like that to me? Who do you think you are?"

"Kerry!"

"No, not Kerry to you. And if you really want to know why I didn't join your sorority, it was because of simple women like you that I have no desire to associate myself with. In fact, that sorority would be better off without women like you. The world would be better off without you." I threw what was left in my glass in her face. "Now that's water under the bridge." I slammed the glass on a table. "My mother used to say that to me."

I walked away as the crowd around us grew. Piper stood there gasping as if I'd had a full gallon of water in that little glass.

"What did you do?" Marcy asked, pulling me into the kitchen.

"Don't you dare touch me," I said.

"What?"

"You told her? I can't believe you did that! I just can't believe you're up to your old stuff, Marcy."

"I didn't."

"Don't lie. Because I already know. There's no way out of this one." I was fuming.

"I didn't tell her."

"Why did you do it? Needed something to chat about on the phone?"

"I wouldn't do that. I just wanted to protect—"

"You know what? Don't say anything else." I cut her off. "I don't want to hear it. You did the same stuff in college and I've had enough. Just stay away from me." I turned and headed up the staircase in the kitchen. It was time for me to go.

"Kerry," she called after me, but it was too late. This was a deep cut and I was in no condition to pretend to patch it up.

After five minutes of fussing with the dress and realizing that it was going to take me much longer to get out of it than I needed to make a quick departure, I just grabbed my purse and headed for the staircase. I needed to get out of that house and away from Marcy before I broke down and cursed everyone out. How could she betray me like that? After all of these years and all of these promises she made never to share my business? She was supposed to be there for me. Especially at a time like this. Not out spreading my business.

Struggling down the hallway, I stopped at Milicent's door to say good night. I didn't want her to have to suffer for her mother's shortcomings. She was my godchild and I would always love her.

I swung my purse over my shoulder and opened her bedroom door. And there, sitting in front of a mirror, was a Millicent with about a pound of caked-on white foundation on her face. Iris was beside her, applying red lipstick. Milicent looked like she was in whiteface. "Now we look just alike," Iris said. Milicent saw me in the mirror and turned around quickly.

"Aunt Kerry, we're just playing," she said, clearly knowing she was doing something wrong.

"Take it off," I said with a sense of urgency in my voice that was familiar. Painful. "Now!" I snarled, causing both Milicent and Iris to jump.

"Kerry," I heard Damien say from the other side of the door. Milicent looked at me with a fear in her eyes that begged me not to say anything.

I hurried and stepped out of the room, closing the door behind me, just as Damien got close.

"Everything okay?" he said, looking at the door.

"Yeah, they're watching television. I just . . . wanted to say good night and . . ."

"Yeah, Marcy just told me what happened. I wanted to come and see if you were okay."

"Oh, don't worry about me," I managed.

"I'm really sorry about all of this. I spoke to Jamison and he feels real bad—"

"I don't want to hear that right now." I stepped away from the door.

"Come on, don't—"

"I'm angry. I'm real angry right now and I just want to be alone."

"Jamison's not going to leave you. He's not that kind of man. He's—"

"Like you?"

"You know what I mean, Kerry," he said.

"Did you know about her?" I asked.

"Let's not go there."

"You did?" I eyed him hard. "You knew about this?! You were in my house. With my family. And you lied to me?!"

"It's not about that . . ."

"If cheating isn't about lies then what is it about?" I said. I felt my heart break again. This time for my friendships. "Give me my keys so I can go home." I put out my hand.

"I don't think you should do that. Not in your condition. You're eight months—"

"Fuck my condition," I yelled. "Give me the God-damned keys."

Together Forever

Romance is the easiest thing to do when you're in love. Flowers. Chocolate. Poems. Candles. Dinner. These all seemed like silly tokens of affection to me—until I fell in love for the first time. Now I'd liked men before. There was this one boy, Christian Nelson, I had a huge crush on when I was eleven. He was one of my mother's friend's children, and whenever they came to visit, I was all googly-eyed over him. I'd sit for hours, looking into his eyes and saying stupid stuff, but that childhood crush in no way prepared me for what I'd feel inside once I truly fell in love with someone.

After that first night with Jamison, all I could think of was flowers and chocolate, poems, candles, and dinner. He was the air I breathed, the wind beneath my wings, and any other cliché ever concocted. What was so great about our love back then was that I could depend on Jamison. He was always there, always willing to hold me and show me that no matter what other people thought or said, our world was ours, and there, we had love.

For this reason, when I began planning a romantic dinner for his twenty-first birthday, I wanted everything to be perfect. My strong, handsome "Ken" had finally arrived and I wanted to show Jamison how much I appreciated and adored him. Plus, it was just a few weeks until graduation and a long list of questions lingered in the air about our relationship. We already knew that he was headed to school in New York; the question was where I was going to go and how were we going to handle the separation.

If it was to be the first and last birthday I spent with Jamison, my first love, I wanted it to be amazing. From the French dinner I'd ordered, to the Tiffany cuff links I bought to go with his first French-cuff shirt, I wanted to show him the world we'd find together. The success we'd both share as we grew. No more macaroni and cheese in the microwave or business shirts passed down from his mentors; Jamison was on his way to the top.

Of course, the matter of my lacking a real plan after graduation was haunting my subconscious, but I wanted so badly to put that on hold for my Jamison. I wanted to be happy and really feel the love in the moment.

Well, the moment just happened to include the last letter of rejection that came from the last med school I'd applied to arriving in the mail. Something told me not to check the box, but against my better judgment, I did, and the slender envelope told the story Yale wanted to tell before I even opened the letter. I'd sunk a million stories into sadness by the time I heard Jamison parking his car outside of my apartment. I'd managed to hold back tears—for fear it would ruin my makeup—but my spirit was shattered, and while I was in love, my heart was breaking fast.

When Jamison knocked on the door . . . the slow four-point knock he claimed was our little secret . . . I jumped up and reminded myself of the reason for the night. The candles were lit, the dinner was warm, and the reason for the evening was there. I didn't need to talk about my letter. I had to focus on my man. I'd have to suck it all up . . . for the moment.

"Ker Bear," Jamison said when I opened the door. He stepped inside and with eyes full of an innocent love that I'd later realize was priceless and temporary, he pulled me to his chest and nestled my head beneath his chin. We must have stood there in the foyer for ten minutes, just hugging each other in silence. I could feel his breathing beneath the thin polo shirt he was wearing. It was slow and calm, sweet and longing. He was all into me, around me, and holding me as if it was the first and last time ever. We'd done this before and would again many times after, but this time it was especially sweet. Standing there barefoot and defenseless in his arms, I felt as if anything was possible. I felt safe and loved and desired. And while he had no clue what I'd been going through mentally since I'd checked the mail that morning, it didn't matter. What he was showing me at that moment was that it didn't make a difference where I was going. He'd be there. He'd hold me. And that was enough to help me hold back any tears and put my fears to the side.

"What you got for big daddy?" he finally said, stepping back and kissing me on the forehead.

"You're so crazy," I said. "It's just dinner. For your birthday."

"It don't look like dinner! It looks like heaven." He walked into the living room that I'd decorated with roses and gardenia-scented, white pillar candles. After I forced Marcy to help me pick up twenty-one dozen golden roses and place them around the living room, I sent her to Damien's house for the evening. We were alone and there would be no interruptions. I wanted to play my favorite Enya CD, but Jamison said her howling sounded like a dying wolf, so I settled for his favorite, Sade. As I'd planned, when he walked in the door, "Your Love Is King" was playing.

"It is heaven," I replied sweetly. "Because you're here."

"Damn, girl. . . . You're about to propose to a brother tonight?" he joked. "I don't know . . . I mean, I'm not ready for all that. I have so much to see in the world and I—"

"Stop playing, Jamison." I was pouting, but I couldn't stop laughing. "I'm serious. This is supposed to be a romantic evening to celebrate your birthday." Since we'd started dating, I realized that Jamison wasn't exactly romantic. He was silly and playful and whenever I tried to make him be serious, he'd tell a joke and make me laugh. It made me upset because that just wasn't how I'd envisioned my romantic evenings—laughing until my gut hurt—but it also made me happy because it was why I was in love with Jamison in the first place. He could make me smile once more when my cheeks were already hurting, and on my worst days his playful nature made me forget that the word "sadness" even existed. His imitations of my mother even managed to make her seem funny.

"Okay, Ker Bear wants me to be serious?" Jamison blinked and pretended he was becoming some kind of character by wiping his hand over his face. "I am now Jamison the serious man," he said like a robot.

"See, you want me to laugh," I said . . . laughing, of course. "But I won't." I struggled to hold it in, but when he started doing the robot, it was too much to hold back.

Jamison was dancing in the middle of my romantic evening and Paris for his birthday was ruined. But I was laughing. In fact, I was laughing so hard I started coughing and had to bend over to catch my breath. Jamison began patting my back and when I stood up, he hugged me from behind.

"Tyrian purple," he whispered in my ear.

"What?" I asked, shaking off the last bit of my laughter.

"Tyrian purple," he said again. "That's what you are."

"Tyrian?" I turned to face him.

"When I was seven years old, my science teacher, who'd

been trying to teach us about the five senses, brought in this cloth his grandfather passed down to him. The day before, he claimed that the cloth was royal—that its color was one of the finest in the world, a scientific wonder that could confuse the senses and make you not only see but also feel color," Jamison said. "And I was so hard back then, so hardened by the street and stuff going on in my life that I could not care less about what he was talking about. Some old cloth some crotchety white man who probably hated little black boys like me passed down to my lame science teacher??? Who cared? I'd seen color. Nobody could feel color. It was stupid. I hardly made it to school that day. And, as usual, when I got to science, I sat in the last row, in the last seat. I was falling asleep when he finally got to the cloth, but I remember it like yesterday." Jamison's eyes glimmered as if in his mind he was going back to this moment in his memory. "And when he took it out and held it up, I swear, Kerry, it was the most beautiful thing I'd ever seen. I was still in the back seat in the last row, but my eyes, my mind were up front, you know? And while I'd seen murder and drugs and all this other stuff, the cloth, that color, made me so soft I might as well have been born again that day." Jamison's eyes went watery and he sank deeper into his memory. "'Tyrian purple,' my teacher said. 'This is Tyrian purple . . . the color of royalty. The rarest color of all.'" Jamison paused again and came back to the moment, looking in my eyes. "Ever since that day, I've been trying to find something else in the world that was Tyrian purple. I've seen shades of it. Sometimes paint that has come close, but nothing quite as special. But when I saw you at the Valentine's dance, when I first looked into your eyes—how happy and sad and excited and scared and nervous and bold you looked— the first thing I thought was, 'Tyrian purple.'"

I was about to say something, but Jamison placed a single finger over my lips.

"I didn't see the color, I felt it inside. I felt what my old teacher was talking about. I felt color and I wasn't even looking at it. Tyrian purple. The color that can make you feel. You're my Tyrian purple."

Jamison and I ended up eating our French meal in bed the next morning. The candles had all melted, the roses had began to droop, his gift was a day late, and nothing about my evening had gone as planned, but I was Tyrian purple and everything was all right by me.

TO: Jamison.Taylor@rakeitup.net
FROM: coreenissocute@yahoo.com
DATE: 4/25/07
TIME: 2:16 AM

I just walked in the house from our fifth time hanging out and I couldn't go to bed without writing you. I know I've been drinking a lot (I'm never doing shots with you again!) but I figure maybe that's a good thing because the alcohol will loosen me up and let me put everything I'm feeling on the page.

Jamison, the past month that I've been trying to get to know you has been amazing. You are the best man I've ever known and while I loved Duane with all my heart, he in no way compared to you. It's just the little things you do for me that I really love. . . . Getting me all those scholarship books for college and talking to your friend at Georgia Perimeter to see if I can sit in on one of his classes to see what it's like. Those are the signs of a good man that isn't afraid to help people. I love that spirit in you. That you don't look down on me because I don't have what you have and are willing to help lift me up. What a man!

Every time I see you, I just smile because I think of how lucky I am to know someone like you. Even though it's just a month, I feel like I've known you forever. And I look forward to the future. I know that sounds crazy, because we're friends, but it's how I feel. And some-times I know I'm not the only one.

I see how you look at me too and I can't lie and say it doesn't feel good. I haven't been to bed with another man since Duane and I'm about to burst! So, when you placed your hand on my shoulder when we walked into the movie tonight, I wanted so badly to turn around and just tongue you down right there in front of everyone. I didn't care. I wanted to feel your lips against mine. Feel your heat. Let you know how soft my tongue is and how it might feel against your body. Am I the only one thinking this? I know I'm not crazy!!!

I'm not trying to make you do anything, but I know how I feel and I'm old enough to know what I want. I also know what you need and what you're not getting at home. I don't see why two friends can't help each other out.

I can't even believe I just wrote that, but fuck it. It's how I feel. And I'm tired of hiding it and pretending it's not. Alcohol or no alcohol, it's what's inside and I'm going to hit send before I lose my nerve................

E-MAIL TRANSMISSION

TO: coreenissocute@yahoo.com
FROM: Jamison.Taylor@rakeitup.net
DATE: 4/27/07
TIME: 1:15 PM

First, I have to apologize for taking so long to write you back and not returning your calls over the last two days. I have read your e-mail many times and I wanted to wait a second before I responded.

You're not the only one feeling what you're feeling. I like you too and I'm attracted to you. You're a beautiful woman. Believe me I have been wrestling with both of these feelings and while I first thought the answer was to stop being around you, the truth is that I can't. You make feel good. I look forward to seeing you and how you look at me with those pretty eyes and something inside of me won't let me stop. I'm not sure what it is yet, but I'm man enough to admit that it's there. When you came into my life it was by chance and then it seems like everything I feel, think, and say is changing.

I've never questioned anything about my life before, but now I am and I realize that I've been holding a few things back. I used to just make decisions I thought were right and noble and then I stood by that. But right now, I am not sure what's right and noble. I just know what I'm feeling. But all that is beside the point. I guess the real question is, what are we going do?

The Morning After

*When it rains it pours. . . . And when it pours . . . you'd bet-
ter have buckets to keep from drowning.*

Sometimes you need to remind yourself of old sayings you'd
heard and ignored in the past in order to get out of bed in the
morning. And it was raining the morning after the worst day of
my life, so the saying just came to my mind. My entire body was
hurting when morning came to wake me. Before I even opened
my eyes, I knew it would take me minutes, maybe even an hour
to convince my overstretched body to rise. When I opened my
eyes and found that I wasn't sleeping in the bed I shared with
my husband, but rather the bed my mother put in the room that
was once my bedroom, I recalled the events of the night before
and how I reasoned that the only place I wanted to be, could be
with any emotional sanity, was home . . . the home I grew up in.
It wasn't a decision I'd come to lightly.

After I left Marcy's, I had been sitting in the driver's seat of
my car with my head spinning in a vat of drama. *Jamison. My
mother. Marcy. Milicent . . .* It seemed the whole world was off.
Crumbling. Falling apart. And I didn't know what to do. I
needed these people right now. I'd waited thirty-three years to
get pregnant. And I needed something to go right. Just someone to lean on. But now they all seemed out of place.

Was this me? My life? I was so confused that without think-ing, I drove straight to where my mind had been programmed to take me—my home. But when I pulled up in the driveway, I saw Jamison's truck and realized that I wasn't ready to talk to him yet. That truck outside, the man inside, had been some-where else just one night ago and that was still heavy on my heart. What was there to say between us? Ask about the thing?

After sitting there for a few minutes, I decided to drive to a hotel, but when I got there, I thought of how ridiculous I'd look—eight months pregnant, checking into a hotel with a local driver's license. . . . Even in my "unright" mind, this was a low I wasn't ready for.

So I kept driving. My foot to the pedal, just as firmly as it had been the night before, I kept driving and realized that the only place left was my mother's house. Then I got mad. Mad that she'd come up with some silly excuse not to come pick me up from the jail when both of us knew she wasn't going anywhere. This wasn't about scheduling. This was about pride and order and I was tired of both. If not one of the people in my life was there for me, even my own husband, my mother was supposed to be. I wasn't going to drive around like a homeless, motherless child when it wasn't true. She was about to have to do her God-given job, like it or not.

So, I woke up in the bed in the guest room that was once my bedroom. My back aflame, my ankles completely swollen, my baby shifting from side to side, begging for food, if I'd forgotten just how pregnant I was the day before, it was clear now. Everyone was right. I had no business being out like that. But you try telling that to a pregnant woman who'd just found her husband cheating.

"Mother," I called without moving a muscle a bit. She knew I was in the house. She was an old, Southern woman who dared not even snore in her sleep for fear of seeming crass. If one thing moved in that house, she knew it.

"Mother," I cried again.

I tried to pull myself up in the bed, but it was useless. My back had been hurting since the fifth month, and now it was next to unbearable.

"Mother," I hollered this time. The door opened slowly and my mother poked her head in as if unaffected by my screams. She was never a fan of loud voices and things. She always said the home was to be a place of serenity and calm. But then, she used to say a lot of things.

"You are in here hollering like my house is some saloon," she said. She was dressed in a blush night robe with a floral head scarf tied toward the back of her head.

"I just need you to help me get up," I said. "My back hurts."

"Of course it does. That's what happens when you're eight months pregnant and out in the street chasing some man."

"The man is my *husband*," I replied. "And I wasn't out chasing anyone. . . . Look, would you just give me a hand."

She frowned and after much reluctance came over to help.

"Oh, I see you're sleeping in your clothes now," she said. I was still wearing the dress from Marcy's. "Did you pick that up in jail?"

"Whatever," I said. I'd gotten used to my mother's quick and dry judgments. She wasn't the kind of person who could see a problem and just let it slide. She had to let the world know if one thing was out of place, one item wasn't meeting her standards. She'd always been that way even when I was a child, but like everything else, it only got worse when my dad left. Then she became the judge, and the rest of us . . . the defendants.

"Oh, and you're cursing at your mother now too?"

"Mother," I said, "Since when did *whatever* become a curse?"

She looked at me blankly. I was out of order.

"Look, could you just help me out of this dress, so I can put on something clean?"

"Hum . . ." she responded, but I could tell she was struggling not to say something else.

"Well, I had Edith put some clothes out for you in the bathroom," she said, unzipping me. "And there's a towel for you in there too."

"Clothes?"

"I sent her to the store this morning. I knew you didn't come with anything."

"Thanks, Mother," I said and I really meant it.

"And please comb your hair before you come down. I don't need you looking like a convict at the breakfast table. There's been enough going on around here," she said. "Your Aunt Luchie is coming over here for breakfast and I don't want her getting wind of what's happened."

"Aunt Luchie is coming," I said happily. My mother rolled her eyes. Her oldest sister, Aunt Luchie, was the most beloved of all of my mother's siblings. She was the free spirit of the family. She'd been a teacher, a chef, and preacher, and once a jazz singer. She always had a smile on her beautiful face, a new song to sing to you, and the ability to make everyone feel special and important. And for this, everyone, everywhere loved Aunt Luchie. And while my mother too shared in the energy of the communal crush, she couldn't help but to make it obvious that she was jealous of how everyone received, with open arms, her big sister, especially where I was concerned. When I was smaller, I'd scream and holler whenever Aunt Luchie tried to leave our house. My mother would look at me angrily and send me to my room. "Never beg anyone for anything," she'd say.

"She's coming over to try to get money for that old hospital downtown," my mother said emptily. While Aunt Luchie was the oldest, her rebelliousness led to my grandparents leaving my mother in charge of their estate when they passed. Now Mother held the old purse strings and all of her siblings, including Aunt Luchie, had to come to her for everything.

"Grady?" I asked. I'd heard about them closing the hospital on the news.

"Apparently."

After taking a long shower, I dressed and followed the direction of Aunt Luchie's laugh toward the kitchen. It was loud, cackling, and lacking any melodic qualities. I was sure my mother was sitting beside her cringing at the inconvenience.

"He called you, girl," Ms. Edith, who'd been my mother's maid for as long as I'd been out of the house, said when I turned into the hallway that led to the kitchen. Ms. Edith was a sweet, old woman who always seemed to have her wig on crooked. She loved taking care of my mother, watching *Wheel of Fortune* and having a secret to share. It seemed like every time I walked into the house, Ms. Edith would come over to me, trying to share a secret she'd been saving.

"Who called?" I played into her. I knew she was talking about Jamison, but Ms. Edith liked to reveal her secrets slowly. An old Southern woman cooking up the latest headline.

"Your husband," she stepped back and gave me the thin, questioning detective eye. "He's called every hour, on the hour, since we been up this morning. Now, your mama, she done told me not to tell you, but you know Ms. Edith got your back, right?" She snapped her finger and winked. "A woman needs to know if her husband is trying to reach her—no matter what he done," she tried to whisper in my ear. "Your mama thinks I don't know what went down yesterday with you in that jail all alone," she pulled all of me—and I do mean all of me—into her arms and squeezed me tight like I was about to be put away for life, "all alone . . . not my Kerry Ann! I wanted to come get you, but you know that mother of yours done come up with a million things for me to do in this house, so I couldn't get a foot out the door."

"Well, thank you," I said, kissing her on the cheek. Ms. Edith was about to go into her other favorite topic—how clean she keeps my mother's house.

"Now, you know there wasn't much for me to do around here," she went on. "I keep this place clean as a whistle. Even when she have those people come drunk around here, acting like they sixteen years old, I still keep it cleaner than a hospital."

"You sure do," I said.

"Is that my niece I hear?" Aunt Luchie called. "Come in here, gal, and give your aunt a big old hug . . . if you can." She started laughing at her joke before I even entered the kitchen.

"Very funny," I said, walking in to see that Ms. Edith had set up a formal breakfast table for us.

"Sugar, sugar, sugar," Aunt Luchie said, running to me. As usual, she was wearing a silky sweat suit that was made of every color in the coloring box and short heels—she was sporty, but her upbringing still hadn't allowed her to wear sneakers. Aunt Luchie had to be one of the most beautiful sixty-nine-year-olds I'd ever seen. Her smooth, coal-colored skin, thick eyelashes, and perfectly grayed hair (that she called platinum) made you fear getting that old a bit less. She'd aged with the grace of a dancer . . . which I think she'd been at one point.

"Look at you!" she kissed me on the cheek and looked me over as if she hadn't seen me less than a month ago at my baby shower.

"Yeah, he's growing," I said.

"Don't worry, baby. He'll be out in about four days. Five at the most," she said, rubbing my stomach.

"Oh, Luchie, stop all that old talk," my mother cut in. "She isn't due for at least two weeks."

Aunt Luchie had never had a child of her own, but she always seemed to know a lot about babies—when they were coming, what kind of person they'd grow up to be, what kind of illnesses they'd have. She called it her gift, but my grandparents told her it wasn't appropriate for someone like her to go around speaking in such a way. They were Christian and didn't believe in such things. But that never stopped even the most upstanding women of our church from stopping to ask for my Aunt Luchie to lay hands on their new baby.

"You mark my words," she said to me. "I was only a day off when you were coming—"

"Two days," Mother said.

"Twenty-seven hours," Aunt Luchie retorted. "Anyway, don't go listening to that old hen. I *know* . . ." She took my hand and led me to the table. "Now, what you doing staying at your mother's house?" She placed a scone on a saucer in front of me.

"*She*," my mother cut in again, "was just here helping me with some things."

Aunt Luchie frowned.

"What *things*?" Aunt Luchie asked suspiciously.

"What does it matter to you, old woman?" my mother said.

Suddenly, Ms. Edith appeared, plopping a second and unnecessary carafe of coffee on the table.

"Hum," she said loudly.

"I thought you were coming over here to talk about the hospital," my mother said. "Now, let's talk about that."

"Please, Thirjane. Now you want to talk about the hospital?" Aunt Luchie said. "Let the girl speak."

"It's nothing; I was just in a disagreement with Jamison," I said. My mother sank down in her seat.

"A disagreement?" Aunt Luchie asked.

"Yes," my mother said.

"Who is she?" Aunt Luchie asked knowingly.

I wanted so badly not to answer her, to keep the whole thing a secret, but I needed to talk about it.

"What makes you think it's that?" my mother asked.

"The girl is about to give birth any day . . . what else would make her leave her home and come . . . here?"

"Um . . . hum," Ms. Edith said. My mother shot her eyes at her and she turned to pretend she was cutting fruit on the counter top.

"It was just a small argument and they will be back—"

"Her name is Coreen," I said, cutting my mother off. With the mentioning of a name, even my mother fell silent.

"How long he been stepping out?" Aunt Luchie asked.

"I don't know, six, maybe seven months. That's all I know of."

"You knew all this time?"

"Some of it. But . . . I just didn't know what to do. He kept saying she was just a friend. And that I was being paranoid. But my gut kept telling me something was wrong."

"Well, why didn't you follow your gut?"

"I don't know, Aunt Luchie. He kept saying I was wrong and that I needed to trust him."

"Always trust yourself first," she said. "When you see something evil, you call it what it is. You ball up your fist and you fight the thing when you first see it. All this posing and prissing like you too good to fight to be treated right. That won't get you anywhere."

"And fighting has gotten you somewhere, Luchie?" my mother asked. "You don't even have a husband *to* cheat on you."

My mother was throwing big stones. Aunt Luchie had only one love of her entire life to speak of. A trumpet player named

Red who never married her. He'd left her at the altar twice and finally she found out he had a family in France.

"Well, I don't see a plethora of men walking around here," Aunt Luchie said. "Unless, you count the fully married judge who seems to stay late after all your parties."

Ms. Edith coughed loudly. My mother turned to her quickly and she went back to cutting her fruit.

"Will you two stop," I said. They frowned at each other like little girls arguing over a teddy bear.

"You're right, baby," Aunt Luchie said finally. "Now what happened that led you here?"

"I went and saw him with her. At her house . . . and I was so angry . . . I slapped him . . ." My mother set her coffee mug hard on the table.

"You slapped him?" Aunt Luchie's eyes widened as Ms. Edith picked up the fruit tray and came over to get a better listen.

"I know I shouldn't have. . . . But I was just so angry."

"You're right. You shouldn't have hit him. I would've cut him if I was there." We all laughed at Aunt Luchie, even my mother. Ms. Edith took the break to sit down at the table.

"Shoot, I'm proud of you," she went on. "You stood up for yourself. There's nothing to be ashamed of about that. Not in my book. Sometimes you have to scream in order for people to hear you . . . and sometimes if that doesn't work, you have to start swinging."

"Well, that would've been fine if the cops weren't there," I said.

"Cops?" Aunt Luchie's eyes grew even wider.

My mother sank farther into her seat.

"Yeah, the cops were there. It was a mess. They saw me slap him, and they arrested me."

"Arrested you?" Ms. Edith asked. My mother didn't even

bother to look at her. I guessed it was because she actually wanted to know how everything happened.

"Yeah, I went to jail."

"I've been there. We had this sit-in downtown back in '63 and I tell you, we all got locked up. Even my teacher."

"Luchie!" my mother said.

"How was it there?" Ms. Edith asked.

"It was just a bunch of women," I started and told them all about the odd friends I'd made in the big house.

"Well, what you gonna do now?" Aunt Luchie asked.

"Do?" I said. "I don't know. . . . I just needed to get away from him right now . . . and then I guess I'll need a divorce."

It was the first time I'd said and thought the word. Was that what I was doing? *Divorcing* Jamison? Was this how it happened? I was getting a divorce.

"The bastard," my mother said. "I knew it."

"You knew what, Thirjane?" Aunt Luchie asked.

"That he was no good for my baby." My mother looked over to me. "I always knew he was trash and that he'd cheat on you or steal or something like that. He's no good. Never was good enough to even be with you."

"Oh, Mother. I don't want to hear that right now."

"I didn't want to say I told you so, but there it is. I told you never to marry that man. He was just trying to marry up. And once he got you, he didn't know what to do. And that's why he was cheating with that woman. She's probably trash just like him."

"Everyone already knows what you think about him," Aunt Luchie said. "That's not what I want to know. I want to know what Kerry Ann thinks. What she's going to do. Because this isn't a simple matter to her. You may have thought whatever you wanted about that boy, but she loved him for the reasons she did and that's her business. Not yours."

I heard what Aunt Luchie was saying, but I was beginning to think that maybe my mother was right. Maybe Jamison was bad for me. Maybe I'd been fooled all these years and the real him was coming out now.

"How is it not my business?" my mother said. "She's my child."

"Yeah, and I'm my mother's child and she pushed away the only man I've ever loved," Aunt Luchie said with her eyes saddening. "No, I never married Red, but I loved him and I know he loved me. But you all pushed him away."

"Pushed him away?" my mother asked.

"Yes, with you judging him and judging me. What kind of man would want to be around that? A family judging him and his woman for everything they do, everything they are? Red asked me so many times to leave here, to go with him to France, but I just had to be here in *the South* like I didn't know any other place existed. Well, I lost him for it. For allowing other people to decide for me what I needed and now I have nothing."

"Is that true, Aunt Luchie?" I asked. "That he wanted you to go with him to France?"

"Yes, baby. He asked me years before he ever met that other woman," she said. "But I was too young, and still caught up in doing what my family said a woman like me was supposed to do. I turned him down. And then I had to watch him live my life with someone else. And that's what I don't want to happen to you."

"Please," my mother hissed.

"Look, Kerry, have you spoken to him?" Aunt Luchie asked.

"I don't know what I'll say."

"Not knowing what to say never stopped two people who love each other from speaking."

"Love?" my mother said.

"Yes, *love*," Aunt Luchie said with a look that sobered my

mother fast. Her "love" was hard and deliberate in a way that could only conjure, invisibly, the love my mother shared with my father. But she dared not say it. Not his name. Not in my mother's presence.

"You need to talk to him," Aunt Luchie said, her eyes back on me. "You need to stop running to all these other people with your problems and talk to your husband. Find out what's happening in your home."

"He called," Ms. Edith burst out. "Five times today. The boy was crying," she added.

"Edith, don't you have something do, somewhere in the house?" my mother asked. Ms. Edith got up from the table, taking with her the fruit that I supposed she'd cut for herself.

"Edith, can you hand an old lady the phone," Aunt Luchie said. "I need to call the pharmacy, so I can pick up my pills today."

"Yes," Ms. Edith said, picking up the phone from the receiver and handing it to Aunt Luchie.

"Pills for what?" my mother asked. "I haven't seen you sick a day in my life."

"I'm ten years older than you . . . it isn't any of your business what pills I have, Thirjane." Aunt Luchie held the phone far from her face so she could see the buttons. "Look, Edith, could you do me a favor and dial the pharmacy for me? I can't see a thing on this little phone." She handed the phone to Ms. Edith and the two exchanged slow glances.

"Okay," Ms Edith said.

"How does she know the number to your pharmacist?" my mother asked.

"Here you go, Ms. Luchie." Ms. Edith handed my aunt the phone.

"Hello?" Aunt Luchie said. "Who is this, baby? I can't hear you?" She scrunched up her face. "Look, hold on, I'm going to

hand the phone to my niece, so she can give you the order. Hold
on now." She slid the phone from her face and pushed it across
the table. "Talk to him," she said, making it clear who was on
the phone.

My mother and aunt were sitting on either side of me. I
turned to see Ms. Edith standing behind me. I couldn't do it. I
couldn't reach for the phone.

"See," my mother said, taking the phone, "she doesn't want
to talk to him."

"Hand me the phone," I said suddenly. "Give it to me."

Aunt Luchie nodded and snatched the phone from my
mother.

"Here," she said, handing it to me. "Talk to your husband."

"Kerry," I heard Jamison say before I put the phone to my
ear.

"Yes," I said.

"I. . . . Look, it's not what you think it is. She's . . ."

"She's what? Your friend? Let's not start this by lying. That's
not why I'm talking to you."

"Okay, you're right," Jamison said. "But I need you to know
that it's over between me and her. It's been over."

"It?" I asked. My throat tightened. "So you admit it?"

Everyone moved in closer around me. My mother placed her
hand on my arm.

"I—" he started.

"You cheated? Is that what you're about to say? Because I
don't want to hear anything else. I can't. I need to hear the
truth from you right now." I folded into the table and started
crying again.

"Is that what you want me to say?" he asked.

"Want? I want you to tell me it never happened. That you
didn't cheat on me. And ruin our family. I want you to tell me
that you loved me too much to cheat on me. That I'm too impor-

tant to you. That we're too important to you. That's what I want you to say."

"Kerry, you're making yourself upset," he said. "I didn't want this to happen this way." His voice cracked.

"Why didn't you just say something to me? To me? Why couldn't you just tell me about this and . . ."

"And what?" he asked. "And all of this could happen?"

"Do you love her?" I asked.

"I told you it was over," he said. "I broke it off the moment I found out you were pregnant."

"That's not what I asked you."

"Kerry, let's not do all of that."

"Do what?"

"You're just setting this up to be an argument. I don't love her. Of course not."

"Breathe," Aunt Luchie said, taking my hand. That's when I realized that all of the women had their hands on me. My mother was holding my arm. Ms. Edith was rubbing my back.

"I want to talk to you about this," he said, "in person."

"Jamison, I don't know about that."

"Breathe," Aunt Luchie said again. She looked into my eyes and nodded meaningfully.

"Kerry, baby, I just want you to come home. Can you do that? So I can talk to you? You don't even have to say anything. I just want you to hear me out. So I can tell you everything. Can you do that?"

Aunt Luchie nodded again.

"Breathe," she said.

Family Gathering

"I have to give a toast to my beautiful girlfriend, Kerry Ann," Jamison said, giving a toast at the graduation dinner his mother planned and reluctantly invited me to. I didn't care to ever see that woman again—she was pure evil unleashed, as far as I was concerned—yet, there I was sitting beside my mother (who I had begged to come, swearing I'd never speak to her again and get pregnant by some trucker I met a rest stop) at a dinner table in the very living room where Jamison's mother had dug into me like an alley cat in a street fight.

"Without Kerry," Jamison went on, "I don't think I could've made it."

His mother managed an unconvincing smile. Her eyes narrowed to tight slits, revealing suspicion, she moved not one inch to look in my direction, nodding only when Jamison looked at her. I supposed this was her noble self, her attempt to appear collected and temperate. Yet everyone around the table sat in a quiet nervousness, their eyes transfixed as they waited for her to start the show.

"You put up with me through finals and all of my stress," Jamison said. "And I just want to say thank you and that your support was needed and appreciated. Cheers!"

He raised one of the two-piece plastic champagne flutes his mother had placed around the table in her poor attempt to decorate (my mother didn't even bother to pick one up) and took a sip.

"And," he started, "I have another announcement."

My mother pinched my arm.

"I know this boy is not about to ask you to marry him!" she tried to whisper. "You brought me here for this? Around these people to embarrass me?"

The transfixed eyes moved from Jamison's mother to mine, the other sleeper cell awaiting activation.

"You had better say no," she demanded beneath her breath as she smiled at the onlookers.

"Mother, stop it," I said.

"This negro is trying to marry up," my mother said, "and I'm not having it. Not my daughter. I will not allow you to assign your life to this meagerness . . . this place." She looked around the room as if we were sitting in a zoo.

"I'm not going to med school," Jamison said finally, catching my eyes.

"What?" his mother said, her eyes widening, a deer about to be hit by a truck. Only I felt the same way. I'd had no wind of what Jamison was talking about. As far as I knew, Jamison was leaving for Cornell.

"I've decided to take advantage of my one-year wait, so I can stay here in Atlanta to take care of some things." He looked straight at me.

"Things? What things?" his mother asked, looking down toward me for the first time. "Hell, no," his mother jumped up. "You will not ruin everything I've worked for to be with that."

"That?" My mother jumped up too, her flute falling to the floor and splitting in two. "Who are you calling a THAT?"

"That thang on the other end of the table, that's who!"

"Mother." I tugged at her arm. "Sit down."

"Oh, I know how to handle women like this." My mother went to her purse.

"Gun!" someone screamed. And everyone hit the floor in unison, leaving me, Jamison, and our mothers standing. I kept my eyes locked on Jamison's. What was he doing? Was he giving up med school for me? It didn't make any sense.

My mother finally pulled a sizable gray cell phone from her purse

"Oh, it's a phone," someone else said.

"I'm calling the police," my mother said, bringing the room back to order.

"Mother." I snatched the phone. "Just stop."

"I know what you're going to say, but I already called Cornell. I told them I need a year to handle some personal stuff in my life," Jamison said. We were walking down his street alone after I put my mother in the car.

"What personal stuff?" I asked.

"I can't leave you." He tried to hug me, but I pulled away. Cornell was his big chance. It was what he'd been working toward all of his life.

"I'm reapplying. I'll be somewhere next year," I said. "That's our dream; that's our plan. Right?"

"But what if it doesn't happen? What if you're not accepted?"

"I will be. I know it," I pleaded. "I just need to focus on it and it'll happen. Weren't you the one who told me to keep the faith?

"I can't leave you here . . . not with that woman." He looked down toward my mother in the car. "If you go home . . . I mean, Kerry, I've seen what she does to you. How she makes you feel when she's around—like you can't do anything right."

I started crying. Everything Jamison was saying was right, but he didn't understand. I needed him to do this . . . to go to school.

"I can't let you stay," I said.

"It's already done," he said with his voice hardened. "They gave me one year and I'm going to help you with applications and in the meantime, I'll help my cousin start this lawn care business."

"Lawn care?"

"Yeah, he already has a truck. I just need to help him find the work. You know, match my brains with his muscle. There's a lot of money in it right now. We can branch out. Grow it."

"What are you talking about? Grow it? You're going to med school. That's what we talked about."

"Baby," he pulled me into his arms "I'm going back to school. I promise. Just one year. Trust me."

DATE: 5/03/07
TIME: 12:43 AM

Coreenissocute: Helloooooooo. Are you there?
JamminJamison: What do you want, Coreen?
Coreenissocute: Come on, don't be like that.
JamminJamison: I told you I don't think we need to communicate on-line like this.
Coreenissocute: Look, if I was going to be a bitch and send e-mails to your wife, don't you think I would've done that already? I'm not like that. You know that. I just can't ever get you on the phone and I wanted to talk about what happened this weekend.
JamminJamison: I told you I specifically don't want to talk about that.
Coreenissocute: Why not?
JamminJamison: Because I just don't.
Coreenissocute: Why? It was wonderful. You were wonderful.
JamminJamison: Thank you.
Coreenissocute: That's all you have to say is thank you?
JamminJamison: I just said I don't want to talk about it.
Coreenissocute: You didn't enjoy it?
JamminJamison: Yes, I did.
Coreenissocute: What did you enjoy about it?
JamminJamison: Are you serious? I just said I don't want to talk about it.
Coreenissocute: Look, Jamison, all I'm asking is that you tell me what you liked. That's it.
JamminJamison: You. What you did. It was better than I imagined.
Coreenissocute: I didn't think it was going to happen. I'm not exactly a fan of giving oral sex in a moving car, but you're just irresistible.
JamminJamison: Irresistible?

Coreenissocute: Hell, yes. And what's in your pants is even more irresistible. I can't wait to see both your heads again.

JamminJamison: Coreen, don't go there. I'm at home.

Coreenissocute: You're probably hard just thinking about it. MY lips wrapped around you. Just bring that thing over here to me. I'll handle it like a woman should. All of it.

JamminJamison: Damn, girl.

Coreenissocute: I'm serious. I'm a little too old to be having sex in the back of a pickup truck on the side of the highway, but anytime you need me to meet you, I'm there.

JamminJamison: Don't play because you're about to have me in my car in like ten minutes.

Coreenissocute: I'm not playing. Round two? At my place? Or do you prefer the backyard? I know you like grass.

JamminJamison: Shit.

Coreenissocute: I know I sound open, but that's how I am for you.

Coreenissocute: I'll do whatever you want me to and we don't have to tell your wife until you're ready.

Coreenissocute: I know you're a good man and I respect that. I wouldn't do anything to mess up your life.

JamminJamison: Really?

Coreenissocute: Really. I'm not going anywhere. I'm whipped!

Coreenissocute: So, tell me something now. Honestly, did you plan on doing this from the moment we met?

JamminJamison: I don't know.

JamminJamison: I guess in certain respects I did like in my head I imagined you naked and what it would be like to be with you.

Coreenissocute: What is it like?

JamminJamison: Wild.

Coreenissocute: LOL. Is that what you like? Wild sex?

JamminJamison: Yeah. Ain't nothing wrong with a little screaming and scratching.

Coreenissocute: I DID NOT SCRATCH YOU!

JamminJamison: I have scratches on both of my ass cheeks. I've been showering at the gym.

Coreenissocute: Sorry. How can I make it up to you?

JamminJamison: Don't ask me that.

Coreenissocute: Why?

JamminJamison: You know the answer.

Coreenissocute: Can you come out tomorrow?

JamminJamison: Kerry is sick. Food poisoning or something.

Coreenissocute: Well let me know as soon as you can.

JamminJamison: Will do.

Coreenissocute: And clean out that truck. I can't find my thong.

JamminJamison: Stop playing.

Coreenissocute: Kidding. Kidding. Kidding. Kidding.

JamminJamison: Have a good night.

Coreenissocute: You too.

TIME END: 2:03 AM

Face-to-Face

When this all began, I realized that Jamison's cheating was turning me into a paranoid mess. Before I even really knew about Coreen, I felt inside that something was wrong with Jamison, something was different in how he responded to me. This grew into a paranoia where my mind was busy with worry. The phone ringing, Jamison being late for dinner, unanswered questions . . . I tried to break into his e-mail. . . . I even found myself looking through the garbage to see if he'd thrown away any receipts from restaurants. I was looking for clues to confirm what I'd already known. I felt like a fool for doing it, but really, if there was something to be found, I'd feel like more of a fool for not knowing what was going on. Seeing Coreen was only making this worse.

When I walked into our house to meet Jamison as I'd promised over the phone, my thoughts led my eyes to spy every single inch of the house to see if anything had changed. If there was a sign, a clue, an item that would reveal that something was still amiss and that woman had been there.

As I waited for Jamison, I wasn't sure if I was paranoid or just plain perceptive, but I noticed that Isabella wouldn't look at me. Feeling like a visitor in my own house, I sat down at the kitchen table and watched her work. She'd wiped the counters, scrubbed the inside of the sink and started the dishwasher, all without taking a second to look at me. There was nothing but silence between us. After she said hello when I walked in the front door and explained that Jamison called to say he was on his way, she turned her back and got busy, cleaning around me and the chair I was sitting in.

While it was rather rude, it wasn't exactly a surprise. Isabella never liked me; she was probably happy when I didn't come home the night before. Hell, she was probably trying to put the moves on Jamison herself. That would be a quick step up.

While it was my idea to hire a maid when Jamison's business started to take off, I wasn't there for Isabella's initial interview. Apparently, the two hit it off. She was an immigrant from El Salvador, who'd managed to secure legal residence for herself and her three children and had been providing for all of them with the meager cleaning salary. Jamison said her strength reminded him of his own mother, how she raised him with her heart and hard work, and that he was sure Isabella was the perfect fit for us. When Isabella showed up at our house for the second interview and saw me when I opened the door, I could tell she was taken aback. While Jamison said she spoke perfect English, she was stuttering and kept trying to recall English words to match the Spanish ones in her mind. Jamison claimed I was reading into it, but I knew why she was having such a hard time—old Isabella was surprised to see that such a successful man had a black wife on his arm—one who needed a maid. A black woman not cleaning? Not cooking? If I was white, she would've smiled, called me senorita and fluffed my pillows. She would've expected that. And I have to suppose that if I was a little lighter, perhaps it would've been an easier pill for her to swallow. But, no, I was just little old me. The dark-skinned, rich black woman whose underwear she'd have to wash from now on.

When it came down to it, I wasn't on the "Let's Hire Isabella" campaign, but I let Jamison win that battle. From that day on, she was my maid, but Jamison's friend. They laughed together, took up for one another, and between the two of them, I always came out looking like wire hanger–hating Mommy Dearest.

"Excuse me, Ms. Kerry," she said, pushing past me with a broom in her hand.

"Sure," I said. But I really wanted to snatch the broom and snap it in two. "When will Jamison be back? Did he say?"

"Um . . . How you say???? He's back soon," she said, still with her eyes averted. Please, she'd been in Georgia for too long to play the "I barely speak English" card. I wondered what secret she was keeping for Jamison . . . if Coreen had been in my house. Had she been in my house, my bed, with my husband, and Isabella was just laughing at me? Sweeping and laughing . . .

"Did he say where he was going?" I asked.

"No say, he never say. He say he be right back," she said clearly struggling to inject nonchalance into her voice. But I knew she was aware of the matter in my home. If Ms. Edith knew, of course she did. Those maid hot lines were far-reaching, and they crossed color barriers too. If one household was dirty, or the kids were wild and crazy acting, the whole maid circuit knew. That was why my mother cleaned our house before the maid came when I was smaller.

I sat back in the seat and tried to relax, but it was impossible. The silence was tearing at my brain. Birthing my paranoia. I knew what I knew. All I kept thinking was that Isabella knew something else too. She had to know something. She had to have been covering up for Jamison. Maybe she was covering up

for him now. I was tired of thinking these things, tired of being
in the dark, of everyone knowing about my marriage but me.
Well, if Isabella wasn't going to tell me where my husband was
and why he was taking so long, I'd find out for myself. How
could Jamison do this to me? He'd begged me to come home to
talk and here he was abandoning me . . . again. Well I'd be his
fool once, but twice wasn't my style.

Angry, I got up from the chair and hobbled to the car to
squeeze back into the driver's seat. Isabella followed me, saying
Jamison was on his way, but my mind was seared with anger; I
just kept hearing that broom sweep against the floor, seeing her
eyes turn away from me. Something was going on. She couldn't
cover up for Jamison. I had to find him and if memory served me
correctly, the last time he was late, he was down Highway 85.

Driving to Coreen's, I was sweating from the inside as if I
had a fever. I turned the air conditioning in the car on high, but
I couldn't escape the heat inside my body. I was hot, my head
was pulsating, and I couldn't keep my thoughts straight. My
nerves were striking a heated tune as I charged down that
highway, in broad daylight this time. It was no secret. No darkness to hide what was coming. I just wanted to know everything. And have my say this time.

But when I got there, something was wrong. I was on the
right street. At the right house. But Jamison's truck wasn't in
the driveway. I turned off the ignition and wiped my brow. He
wasn't there. Suddenly, I felt ill. Like the heat had burrowed itself deep into my stomach and rotted into shame, anger, loneliness. What was I doing here? I looked at the door, at the little
lace square covering the window. My marriage was falling apart
because of the woman inside. I was falling apart because of the
woman inside. Driving around the city, eight-and-a-half months
pregnant. Endangering my child's life.

I wondered what made Coreen think she could have my husband; just come in and take him from me. What had Jamison told her about me? What did she know about me? About my marriage?

Then the door opened. Coreen stepped outside. She was walking toward the car, toward me. Charging with her fists balled tight. This woman who'd tried to tear my family apart wanted a confrontation, and she was going to get one.

I wiggled out of the car and walked toward her, pushing my feet hard into the dirt on her yard, trying to keep my balance.

With each step, as we came closer to one another, my mind cluttered with insults, angry words and thoughts of what I wanted to do to her.

The air was thick with hate when we came toe to toe in the grass. Her hands were by her side, mine were on my hips. Something was about to happen.

"You," I said with my face only a spoon away from hers. I felt the baby twist and turn quickly in my stomach.

"You," she said, coming in even closer.

"Where's my husband?"

"You don't know?"

"Don't you dare try that with me," I said, and then something inside of me just dropped. It was like an anvil that had been dangling from my throat had fallen and landed in my stomach. The pressure where it sat tightened and then released.

"Kerry," Coreen said, stepping back and pointing toward the ground.

"What?" I looked down to see water streaming in crisscrossing lines down my legs. Water was pouring from my middle, and the front of my dress was soiled.

"Your water broke," Coreen said.

"Oh, no," I said. "No, not now!" But the water kept flowing down my legs and into the grass beneath me.

"The baby . . . It's coming," she said.

"I have to go." I gathered my dress and tried to walk back to the car. I had to get to the hospital.

"Kerry," Coreen cried after me. "You can't go alone." She was following behind me, hesitating with each word.

I tried to open the car door, but she grabbed my arm.

"You can't drive like this," she said. "I have to take you. It's not safe."

"Please, let me go," I said, feeling my stomach tighten into little cramps. I pushed her away and opened the door. "I don't want to be here."

"Kerry, don't be stupid. You can't drive."

"I don't need you," I said. I slid into the driver's seat and a bigger cramp came striking up my spine. I buckled forward and took a deep breath.

"You okay?"

"I'll be fine," I said. The pain came again and instead of pushing the key into the ignition, I dropped it on the floor. Coreen grabbed it.

"Give me the keys," I said, struggling to keep my breath. The contractions were coming faster and hitting me harder.

"I know you hate me, but I can't let you do this," she said.

"You slept with my husband and now you want to care about me and my baby?" Another contraction came, pulling me forward as I bent over to escape the pain.

"Breathe," Coreen said, pulling me out of the car. "Just breathe slowly and try to think about something else," she said as we walked to the passenger's side.

After helping me into the car, Coreen got into the driver's seat and turned the engine on. I couldn't believe what was happening. Where I was and who I was with.

My phone began ringing in my purse. I knew it had to be Jamison.

"Get my phone," I said, between breaths.

She pulled it from my purse and looked over at me.

"It's Jamison."

"Tell him to meet me there . . . at the hospital."

Coreen looked at me cross, but I didn't care anymore about fighting with her. I just wanted to get to the hospital and I needed my husband.

"I'm taking Kerry to the hospital," she said, opening the phone. "It's me . . . Coreen." She paused. I imagined Jamison was wondering how we'd ended up together.

"Just tell him I'm having the baby," I cried.

"He wants to speak to you," she said, handing me the phone.

"Kerry, are you okay?" Jamison asked with deep worry in voice.

"No," I said. "I'm having the baby. Meet me at the hospital."

"How did you end up with Coreen?" he asked. "Did she come to the house?"

"No," I said. "Just meet me at the hospital."

"It's over between us," Coreen said breaking the silence shortly after I hung up the phone. We turned onto the main road where the hospital was. "It's been over."

I really wanted to hear what she was saying, but inside I was still hurt to know that there was something.

"I'm sorry for what I've done to you . . . to your family." She started crying.

"Please," I said. "You're just sorry you got caught."

"It wasn't like that," she said. "It wasn't even my idea to meet him. . . . The whole thing was just . . ." She turned into the emergency room driveway. "Look, I can't tell you all of it. I swore . . . I swore I'd just—"

"Uggggggghhhh," I screamed as what felt like a jab thrust into my stomach.

"I've got to get you inside," Coreen said. She got out of the car and ran into the hospital. She came out with a nurse and a wheelchair.

"She's going to take care of you," Coreen said.

"How far apart are your contractions?" the nurse asked as I slid into the chair.

"I don't know. They're coming now though."

"Are you going in with her?" she said to Coreen.

"No," we both said.

"Well, you'll have to wait outside," she said, stopping in front of the emergency room doors.

"Okay," Coreen said. "Kerry, I'll just leave the car here for Jamison and I'll take a cab home."

I didn't say anything. That part of my journey was over. I wasn't thankful. I wasn't sorry. I just wanted her to go.

Rose Petals

I was mad. I know they say "only dogs get mad," but that day, there was no other way to describe my feelings than mad. One of Jamison's mentors invited us to the annual mayor's ball and I couldn't have been more excited. I'd been before, so it wasn't a huge deal, but after taking the MCAT for the second time and being completely stressed with the next batch of med school applications, I was happy to get out for a night and mix with good company. I'd spent the day at the spa with my mother and picked out the most beautiful Cavalli buttercup cocktail dress I'd ever seen. I certainly couldn't afford it on my budget, but I needed that dress. I wanted to show everyone that I was okay, that Jamison and I were doing fine. There was so much discussion going on. People wondered why neither of us had left Atlanta after graduation. And as they always did when there was no news, they simply made things up. According to Marcy, some gossips said Jamison had gotten me pregnant and moved into my mother's house. He was spending all of our money and forbade me from going to med school. It was ridiculous and I had to show them that it couldn't have been farther from the truth. Everyone who mattered would be at the ball. They'd see me in my Cavalli and with Jamison at my side and know that we were happy and clearly on our way up.

I was supposed to meet Jamison at his apartment at 7:00 PM, but when I got there, he was nowhere to be found. I could hear music playing inside, but his car wasn't outside and he wasn't answering the door. Now, it was 1996 and neither of us had cell phones, so all I could do was sit in my car and wait for him to show up or go home. I grew more and more angry with each minute that passed. Jamison hated these kinds of events, the kinds of people who would be there. I knew that. He didn't want to go and he was probably somewhere just sitting around eating a hot dog with his mother or something. I didn't understand why he couldn't just sacrifice his feelings for me for three hours. Yes, he hated these people, but these were my people and I needed to be there, we needed to be there together. If he was ever going to be successful he'd have to make partners with the people I knew.

By the time the mayor's ball was supposed to start, I was completely mad. Dog mad. Burn-down-a-house mad. Get-arrested mad.

Furious, I was about to leave, but then I decided to go and knock on his door one more time. Maybe he'd fallen down. Maybe he'd hit his head. Either way, when I got to him, I'd kill him. I got out of the car and walked to his door and knocked and knocked, but still, I could hear music, but there was no answer. This only made me more mad, and when I decided to walk back to the car I was so mad that I'd decided to break up with Jamison. If he couldn't understand, sacrifice for me, we couldn't be together. I'd sacrificed so much for him, and he couldn't even come to a party? He couldn't even tell me? He just stood me up? This was a first, and I was sure it was going to be a last.

When I walked out of the gate, I turned to my car and saw that it was covered with some little round things. As I got closer, I realized that they were purple flower petals. Rose petals. They were everywhere—on the roof, the windows, the hood.

I looked inside the car and there was a bouquet of purple roses in the passenger seat.

I was smiling. I remember that. I was smiling and opening the door.

I picked up a little gold card that was on top of the car and read it.

Do you feel this yet? it read.

I felt a tap on my shoulder. I turned to find Damien standing behind me, wearing a black suit with a gold tie and white gloves. He had a stern look on his face.

"Damien? What are you doing here? What are you wearing? Are you going to the ball too?"

"I'm here to escort you to your destination," he replied, extending his arm.

"To the ball?" I was intrigued, yet confused. "Where's Jamison?"

He simply winked suggestively and signaled for me to take his arm. He turned and walked away from Jamison's apartment, toward a small cabana area in the apartment complex where they had a pool.

"Where's Jamison?" I asked but Damien was silent. As we neared the pool area, entering a small garden of trees and bushes that were intricately set up around it, I could hear what sounded like humming.

When we turned toward the walkway that led toward the pool, two lines of Jamison's fraternity brothers stood facing each other, dressed in the same suits as Damien. They were holding candles and now I could make out that they were humming my favorite Stevie Wonder song, "Isn't She Lovely?"

"What's going on?" I asked to no one in particular. My eyes widened as I saw that the trees had been decorated with white lights and I saw that dozens of pictures of Jamison and me were hanging from gold ribbons.

"You will have to walk the rest of the way alone," Damien said, turning to me. "But before you decide to go any farther, please read this note." He handed me a piece of parchment paper that was rolled up like a scroll and walked away.

I was already crying before I opened the letter. The mayor's ball was far from my memory, and my mysterious surprise was taking my breath away.

Kerry Ann:
Sometimes, when I'm alone, I think of you. I become lonely and sad, yearning for the next time we'll be to-gether. But then, like a magician, I create you in my mind. I build you up—from your tiny round toes to the soft brown hair that grows around your navel. From the sweet scent of the insides of your palms to the back of your neck. From the calming sound of your voice when you say hello to the passion I feel when I kiss you. The point is that I have memorized every inch of you in my mind, from top to bottom. I do believe, Kerry Ann, from the depths of my soul, that you were made for me. I love you with every-thing that I am, was, and ever will be. You make me want to be the best man I can, and while the memory of you is good, I have decided that I don't want to spend another minute having to be a magician and recall you in my mind. I want you here always by my side forever.

Jamison

I could hardly read the last two lines. The tears had clouded my eyes and my heart was beating so fast. I looked up from the paper and the guys raised their candles high so I could walk down the path toward the pool.

As they continued to hum the song, one sang the words a

little slower, as my father used to do when I was young. It was like a dream.

At the end of the path, I saw the pool shining with lights and color. It was beautiful. Purple rose petals drifted in the water, around floating tea lights. A small wooden walkway that I'd never seen before had been built on top of the water, down the center of the pool, and right in the middle of the bridge was Jamison, standing dressed in white.

The men stopped humming and the soloist sang the chorus alone as I walked down the plank toward Jamison. I couldn't believe he'd done all of this for me. I knew the man who wrote those words in the letter. I knew him well, and I loved him so much. I wanted to wrap my arms around him and show him that I was worth that kind of love, that I could receive it and I could give it.

"Baby," I said, finally standing before him. The men had separated and now they were encircling the pool, their candles making the water shimmer even more beneath the dark sky. It was the kind of romantic moment women dreamed of. But I was living it, and feeling like the luckiest woman in the world.

"I don't ever want to be without you, Kerry," Jamison said. "I told you before that when I first saw you, for the first time, I felt something in my heart." He placed his hand over his heart. "And I know now that I never want to be without that feeling again."

Every hair on my body raised. What was he saying? Was Jamison about to ask me to marry him? Did he want me to be his wife? And . . . did I want him to be my husband? We hadn't talked about it. Not this. I loved him. I really did, but we were so different. From different worlds. Could our worlds ever come together? Would he love me forever? Could he? All of these thoughts raced through my mind in seconds. I was happy but nervous; overjoyed but scared as a baby. This man was in love with me. Not in love like I thought . . . he was innnnn lovvveeee. I knew I loved him, but I didn't want to let him down.

Jamison got down on one knee, reached into his pocket and pulled out a tiny, red ring box.

"No," I cried.

He looked up at me with terror on his face.

"I mean . . . not no, but no . . ."

"Kerry, I . . ." he tried.

"I mean, I know I want to marry you," I said. Everyone was silent. "I do, but . . ." I bent down by his side. "This is a big deal," I said. "I love you and I know I want to be with you, Jamison, but I just . . . I'm messed up."

"What are you saying?"

I was crying again, this time in sadness.

"I just have a lot in my past with my mother . . . and with your mother and with our difference, who knows . . . I mean, who knows—"

"Who knows what?" he asked.

"If you'll love me . . ." I said. I felt weak. "If you'll always love me. That's what I want to know, Jamison. If you'll always love me. Good or bad, me. Selfish me. All of me. Can you always love me? Will you? Can you do that and promise me you won't leave?" A crack came stinging through my heart. I saw my father's face in my mind. I felt his hand on my back as he hugged me, and realized right then how much I'd missed my father, and that I was hurt, hurting since he'd left. And I knew it didn't make any sense at all, but I couldn't bear to lose someone else the same way. Anyone else that I loved, through death or deception, I couldn't do it.

"You are the most perfect person I know," Jamison said. He was crying now too. "And do you know why?"

I shook my head no.

"It's because even in your flaws, you're still being you. And that's part of what I love about you," he said. "Some people's cracks are a little less visible, but you wear yours. And right or wrong, you are what you are. So, if the question is if I can deal with all of that, the answer is, I already am dealing with it. And I always will. Because if that's what it's going to take to have you, point blank, baby, I'm down. So, our mothers will have to change. And in some ways, we'll have to change, but we'll do it together."

I smiled.

"So . . . Kerry Ann . . . perfect Kerry Ann, would you please rise?" He wiped my tears and straightened his back.

"Huh?" I asked.

"So, I can . . ." He held up the ring.

"Oh," I giggled and stood up. I looked at Jamison and wiped a single tear that was still left on his cheek with my hand.

"Kerry," he said, taking my hand into his. He held up the ring to my ring finger and looked back up at me. "I would be blessed if you would do me the honor of being my wife. Will you marry me?"

"Yes," I cried with joy. "I will. I do. I will and I do."

Jamison slid the ring on and everyone started cheering. He stood up and we hugged each other tightly.

"I love you, baby, and I always will be there for you," he whispered in my ear.

I could see Marcy standing on the other side of the pool with Damien. She smiled and waved at me.

"I love you too, Jamison," I said.

TO: Jamison.Taylor@rakeitup.net
FROM: coreenissocute@yahoo.com
DATE: 5/09/07
TIME: 5:20 PM

This is ridiculous. You won't answer any of my calls, return my e-mails, or sign on to chat. What the hell is going on? I'm getting tired of you disappearing like this on me. And then it's like I can't even say anything. I know I sound angry, but damn it's been three days since I last saw you and you seem like you just want to come and go out of my life as you please. It's not fair. I'm not angry. I just miss you and want to know what's going on. Did I do something wrong?

TO: coreenissocute@yahoo.com
FROM: Jamison.Taylor@rakeitup.net
DATE: 5/10/07
TIME: 1:26 AM

Coreen:

I don't know how to say this and I don't know if there's a right way to do it, so I'm just going to come out and tell you that I can't see you anymore. Remember, I told you my wife was sick? Well, we just found out that she's about two months pregnant. We didn't plan it, but it's what's happening.

I have to ask that you not try to contact me anymore. I have to be there for my family and make some right decisions for my wife and child. I'm not trying to be mean, Coreen, and I know e-mail is not the best way to do this, but I don't have the nerve to do it any other way. It's not that I don't respect you, but I'm married and I can't make this just go away. I hope you understand.

Jamison

E-MAIL TRANSMISSION

TO: coreenissocute@yahoo.com
FROM: Jamison.Taylor@rakeitup.net
DATE: 5/10/07
TIME: 3:15 AM

I can't stop crying. I can't even believe what I just read. How could this happen? I guess I should've expected it. But I didn't expect you to lie to me. You said you haven't been having sex with Kerry, so how did she get pregnant? Sounds like someone's caught in a lie.

But that's OK. I guess I got what I asked for dealing with a married man. I just thought you were different. That maybe we had something.

E-MAIL TRANSMISSION

TO: coreenissocute@yahoo.com
FROM: Jamison.Taylor@rakeitup.net
DATE: 5/10/07
TIME: 5:33 AM

I'm sorry you feel that way. I never meant to hurt you. It wasn't like that at all. This just happened and I have to be a man and deal with it. I have to do what we both know is right, no matter how I feel. So, again, I have to ask that you not contact me anymore. I'm sorry. You have to know this hurts me too. But this is my family. I love my wife. I always have. And I just can't continue to do this to her.

Tyrian Purple

After everything I'd been through, I was still relieved when one of the nurses came in and said Jamison was on his way into delivery. The weirdest thing about being angry with someone you love is that when you really need them, you tend to feel less of the anger riding your heart. And lying in the hospital bed alone with my legs cocked up and nurses and my doctor walking in and out of the room on a rotating basis, I needed and wanted no one else there but my husband. Cheat or no cheat, this was our baby coming out of me and I didn't want to go it alone. That wasn't how it was supposed to be. Not how I imagined it. I didn't want to someday tell my child that his father was not there the day he was born. I wanted to feel the love I felt when my child was conceived, see the man I loved, and share, even if it was for the last time, a part of the family we'd created. So, when Jamison came into the room, while I was silent and wondering what I'd say, I'd be lying if I said my heart didn't soften.

"Baby, I'm here," he said, rushing over to my bedside.

I didn't say anything. After an hour or so of trying to breathe between the thumps in my gut, all I could do was cry. Seeing my husband, the moment finally hit me. So much had happened, but here I was now, Kerry, giving birth to my first child. And now my husband was by my side. It was happening. We were giving birth.

"I came as soon as I got the ca— Are you all right? You need anything? You need me to . . ." He was nervous. Jamison tended to ask a lot of questions when he was nervous. "Get you something? Something to eat?"

"Sir, she can't eat right now," the only nurse left in the room said, laughing.

We both looked at her blankly.

"I guess I'll let you two be alone for a second," she said.

"Baby, I—" Jamison started.

"Don't say anything," I said with my voice cracking. "I'm just glad you're here. I just want you here right now."

"And I want to be here too. I can't believe he's coming. Can you, baby? Our son?"

"No," I said.

"I love you."

"I—" A contraction came that was so powerful, I felt as if I was going to fall off of the bed. "Ahhh," I hollered, and I don't believe I even recognized the voice. It felt as if I was suddenly hit with the worst menstrual cramp I'd ever felt, a swift kick in the belly. I sucked in deeply and then released, this seemed to make the other contractions stop, but it just came back and this time it was harder.

"Jamison," I hollered after what seemed like ten minutes but must've been a second because Jamison still hadn't said a word.

"I know, and I'm sorry, but I—" he tried.

"No, get the nurse," I managed.

"Oh," Jamison said. He hustled out the door and the next thing I knew the nurses had wheeled me into delivery and I was giving birth. I always thought birth would be the most painful part, but the birth had nothing on those last, awful contractions. I felt as if everything inside of me was trying to get out and tear me wide open, so by the time the doctor announced that I was crowning, I felt at peace and ready for the whole thing to be done. I was so hot and sweating, and every five seconds it seemed like my doctor was telling me to push harder and again and then harder and two more times. I wanted the pressure to stop and when the last push came, I grabbed Jamison's hand so tight. He looked into my eyes and for that second, time stood still. I saw fear and happiness, confusion and clarity. We were beginning something. Someone was joining us. A part of both of us. It was arresting, baptismal, and I was so happy to share that moment with him.

"This is it," my doctor said. "One more push and he's here."

Jamison nodded his head and I pushed and our son came into the world.

I'd imagined having so many beautiful things to say about my son when the nurse placed him in my arms for the first time, but nothing came out. I just kept crying and laughing. I was so happy to see his little wrinkly face, his questioning eyes that seemed to ask the inevitable, "Where am I and who are you?"

"He's ours," I said to Jamison, who was standing beside me and crying.

He bent over and kissed him on the forehead.

"Tyrian," he said and then kissed me on the forehead too.

"Tyrian," I said too.

PART TWO

Life

*"I know our love will never be the same
But I can't stand the growing pains"*

—Erykah Badu,
"Green Eyes"

Jamison's Wedding Day

Like most men I know, I have to admit that I hate weddings. But unlike like most men I know, this isn't because of the frills and forced intimacy in front of hundreds of sappy spectators—most of whom you don't know. When I fell in love with Tanya Tolliver in fifth grade and spent every red cent in my piggy bank to buy her a dozen pink roses (she was always wearing this pink sweater and I knew she would like them), I accepted that I was a hopeless romantic when it came to the woman who had my eye, so romance never bothered me, much less public displays of it. What bothered me about weddings was the crying. Rows and rows of wet eyes and cheeks, falling back like dominoes from the person who likely started the whole thing—the groom. I noticed at every wedding I went to that the tears in the church always seemed to start with stormy tears gushing from some brother's eyes. Now, this too, in light of the situation (seeing the woman that was supposed to be the love of his life giving her life to him) wasn't completely deplorable. But even with my sensitive side, I'm still a boy from southwest Atlanta, and seeing some otherwise strong brother standing in front of a room full of people crying just wasn't my idea of a good time. Was he happy? Was he sad? Was he a damn punk? Come on, brother! Love was deep for me; the love I had for Kerry was the deepest thing I'd ever experienced. But on our wedding day, I was determined that I wasn't going to be that dude crying.

That morning, during Damien's "Bros Only Pre-Wedding Chat," he broke it down for me and gave me some "dry eye," man-up advice.

"No way out of this crying thing?" I asked.

"Nah, dog," he said frankly. "The whole damn thing really is set up to make you cry. See, when Kerry comes walking down that aisle, she's gonna be wearing this white dress. Now, I know you're thinking you've seen her in white, so who cares? But you haven't seen her in *that* white dress. And *that* white dress is *real* white. It's gonna look big, huge, flowing and glowing and shit in the church like you're hallucinating and seeing an angel. So already then, you're gonna think you're having a dream like in some alternate reality where brothers are supposed to cry. But it doesn't stop there. That's not what takes you out the game."

"No?"

"No, because then she's gonna start floating and gliding straight to you like you're rolling down the street in a Spike Lee movie, and everybody's eyes are going to be moving from her to you to see your reaction. Now, you're gonna try to control your reaction because of the eyes on you, but then you're all proud and shit, because that's your woman. So you might smile a little. Let folks know you're impressed and happy. Cool. Nobody likes a scared groom. And you got that. No tears yet. You're smiling. Proud. You got it. Right?"

"Hell, yeah," I agreed. I got it.

"Hell, nah! Because then, man, they're gonna move that veil from Kerry's face. And while you're trying to be strong, when you see her face, man, how nervous and innocent and happy she looks, that's it. She's gonna take your breath away from you . . . then you're ass is gonna cry."

"Damn," I said. "Take my breath away?"

"Like a fucking cat," he said. "That's what they do."

"And there's no way out?"

"Well," Damien started, "I did get some advice on my wedding day."

"What?"

"My uncle told me to hold my breath when they raise the veil, and my father told me not to look at her face at all. Not into her eyes. He said to look at her ears, so everybody thinks you're looking at her eyes. But you can't look at her eyes because then you're definitely going to break down."

"Any of that work for you?" I asked.

"Hell, nah, J." he said. "You were at my wedding. You saw how I showed out when Marcy came down the aisle. Shit, I was already crying when I remembered what they told me. Good luck."

When Kerry walked into the church and the organ started playing the wedding march, I kept reminding myself to hold my breath and look at her ears.

"Breath. Ears! Breath. Ears!"

Shit, I said that to myself so much that aside from saying it, I totally forgot to do it. First Kerry entered the church. Then, just like Damien said, she was an angel floating toward me in *that* white dress. Then her uncle was raising her veil. Then everybody was looking at me. Then I was looking at Kerry. Her eyes soft. Her lips quivering. A smile suddenly on her face, just to me, just for me. My breath was gone. Like someone had punched me right in the gut. Then I was crying. And still saying to myself, "Breath. Ears!"

I was the punk I never wanted to be. But I really didn't care. Kerry was more than I could've asked for. More than I even dared hope for until I asked her out on our first date and she said yes. I loved that girl through and through. Even with her ways. It was no secret that Kerry was a bit of a perfectionist. I knew this when we started dating; it was what turned me on to her—that she cared about the fine points. That she was passionate. Confused as hell, courtesy of her confused-ass mother, but still passionate about the little things. Feeling. The girl arranged her underwear drawer by putting matching sets into little plastic bags. She lined my shoes up in the closet in order first of activity, second usage, and third color. To most people this was a sign that she was a little over the edge, but to me it was like a light to let me know just how sensitive she was. While Kerry tried to play Ms. Hard-as-Nails-in-Complete-Control, she really needed the world to comply with her. She really needed me to comply with her. Because if one of those things was out of place, if I wasn't there when she needed me to be there, she'd protest. So even with the pretending and crazy mother, my baby felt things deeper than most people, more than any other woman I'd ever known. And to me, that was what made her heart beat the loudest in any crowd. I couldn't ignore that beat.

Now, Kerry had spent every waking moment since the engagement planning the wedding with her mother. While I didn't exactly agree with the 600-deep guest list, filled with only about 90 or so people I knew and 450 Kerry thought she knew (the rest were her mother's "associates" and people that "had to see us get married"), it was her dream day and I wanted her to have whatever she needed. But at some point she turned from my little passionate perfectionist to a member of the Third Wedding Reich—with the wicked führer being her mother—Lady Hitler herself. I sat back and let them do their crazy wedding thing, sure it would pass . . . kinda wondering when it would pass. Usually when Kerry got trapped in her mother's control, after a certain point they'd end up fighting and Kerry would come out of it and run back to me. This hadn't happened yet, and I was waiting for it.

Standing at the altar, a part of me was wondering if the spell would ever break this time. But then it happened. When Kerry was supposed to say the vows she'd typed and spent the last month memorizing in the shower, she opened her mouth and nothing came out. Nervous, I started mouthing the words to her (I'd memorized them too by default), hoping she needed a refresher, but she was frozen. Just looking at me, her eyes wide and still.

"Jamison," she finally said. But it wasn't like she was supposed to say it—like the salutations before a speech. It was more like she was unsure I'd answer. Like she was looking for me in a crowded room. "I love you. And I know I love you because I . . ." She paused and looked deeper into my eyes. "I feel it deep inside of me. Like when I'm with you I'm just where I'm supposed to be. I never told you this before, I never told anyone, but I used to feel like I was alone a lot before you came into my life. I felt like I was alone and that no one really understood me. Not who I really was. They all looked at me, but no one could see me. Not the real me. But you always did."

Tears streamed down her cheeks. It was the most vulnerable I'd ever seen Kerry. I reached over and took her hand.

"You always cared to really see me, Jamison. To really hear me. . . . And you accepted me. And that meant everything to me. Even though we're different and sometimes don't agree, you always take the time to see and hear me." Her voice cracked and I squeezed her hand tighter. "And I want to say today that I want to give that back to you. I want to spend the rest of our days together hearing and seeing each other for who and what we are. That's what I want to do . . . that's what I want to do with you for the rest of our lives together."

"Okay," I said, nodding and trying to see her through the tears in my eyes.

If Kerry floated down the aisle toward me to start the wedding, after the preacher announced that we were man and wife, we must've sprinted out. I felt weightless, on cloud 99.9. I was ready to start the rest of my life with my wife, but it seemed like the rest of my life wasn't coming toward me fast enough.

But like most track stars, after sprinting out of that church, I learned that course-changing injuries came quick, and when least expected. Torn ACLs, pulled muscles . . . My injury came in the form of a permed-out Hitler that I was forced to dance with at the wedding reception.

There I was doing my best to enjoy my wedding, waiting for it to be over with so Kerry and I could get back to the hotel to . . . seal the deal, when Kerry whispered that I had to dance with her mother. Now we both knew this "Mother-in-Law/Groom Dance" was a bad idea. I hated Kerry's mother; she hated mine. We'd accepted that and decided to rise above it. Kerry didn't have to dance with my mother. I was doing a pretty good job of keeping the two of the them apart, so why in the hell did I have to dance with her mother? I'd never seen it done before, but Kerry said it was symbolic of bringing the families together and that it was her dream. I damn sure didn't want to do it, but when the dance was announced, Kerry pinched me under the table and I put a quick smile on my face to join the crone on the dance floor. Dread wasn't word enough to describe the moment. It was more like disgust . . . abhorrence. And it wasn't because of the normal reasons other men didn't get along with their mothers-in-law. Kerry's mother had them all beat. She took pushy and nosy to the next level when it came to my relationship with Kerry. If she wasn't talking about what we weren't doing correctly, she was talking about what we needed to do. If she wasn't telling me how she thought I should behave, feel, think, see, and breathe, she was complaining about the way I did all of those things—but never to my face. Of course it was never to my face. No, she'd get Kerry on the phone and get her all riled up and send her to me with the message. So I'd get home and find Kerry pacing the floor. I'd ask what was wrong and she'd say that "I" needed to get a home phone because it didn't look right for people not to have a home phone, or "we" needed to attend church every week together at her mother's church before we announced the wedding. Kerry would try to stand firm on this opinion, pretending it was her own, but after we'd discuss it for a little while, or sometimes argue, it would almost always come out that the whole idea came from conversation she'd had with her mother. One day I actually overheard them. "That boy needs to stop letting people call him J," I heard her mother say. "His name is Jamison and that's much more acceptable. J is some kind of street name." I was furious. But I didn't say anything to Kerry. I just went into the bathroom and shut the door. I guessed Kerry knew not to bring that garbage to me though, because she never brought it up. But even with all of her mother's drama, she really didn't bother me that much. Not to call a woman a bitch (my mother raised me better than that), but I'd known many females that could be classified as dogs in my life and they didn't scare me. I can bark and bite too, so I was cool. What really bothered me about Lady Cujo though was how she got to Kerry. Her nagging and constant critiques had led to Kerry being much too self-conscious about the world and what other people thought of her. Whenever Kerry was happy or had done some great thing, her mother came talking about how so-and-so could have been better. Kerry would be crushed and start second-guessing herself. It seemed like since Kerry's father got ill, the two of them were cells floating around, bumping into each other to see who hurt the most.

That was partially why I didn't go to medical school. I didn't want to leave Kerry alone, floating with her mother as they both starved for love from Kerry's dad. They needed a buffer. I didn't want to leave Kerry alone in Atlanta to crash and burn. I loved her and if protecting her meant that I had to put some of my dreams on hold, I was willing to be a man and do that. I'd lose one dream, but gain another in a woman who I knew I would make my wife.

My dream did not include dancing with Kerry's mother at the wedding. But there I was, trying hard not to vomit and thinking it was so typical of that woman to be all smiling and cheesing for the cameras. She actually looked like she liked me. Like she was proud I was her son-in-law—the steet boy on the come-up who at the time was actually driving a lawn care truck and cutting lawns himself to get his business off the ground. That wasn't what she'd wanted for Kerry. I needed a more recognizable name and a bus-load more of dollars in the bank. Shoot, according to her, I wasn't even going to the right church. She hated me. Period. I was also quite surprised when she started talking to me during the dance. "You were a lovely groom," she'd said, smiling. "And this was a wonderful day for my daughter." I just smiled, waiting for the punch line. There was always a punch line in situations like that. But she just smiled. Then I thought maybe, just maybe, she'd changed. Maybe she'd accepted me into the family. Maybe she wasn't as bad as I thought she was. She was turning over a new leaf. Old dogs could learn new tricks. I looked at Kerry and smiled. This was the family I'd imagined. If only we could get my mother to say two words to Kerry without accusing her of ruining my life, we'd be perfect then. "You looked lovely tonight," I said, trying to return her nice words. I looked to Kerry again. She

winked at me, nudging me on. Her mother looked at me with
honesty in her eyes and nodded her head. As the song came to
a close, the crowd began to clap and she opened her arms wide
for a hug, which made them clap even louder, as if they knew
the magnitude of the moment. I played along and hugged her
tightly, and when I tried to let her go, she pressed her lips
against my lips for a kiss. Then she whispered in my ear, "Good
luck." She stepped back and smiled again, only the look on her
face had shifted from fake jubilation to pure evil. "You're her
first husband," she added just before we parted.

It took me a minute to understand what she was saying. It
sounded really positive at first. Her first? Like I was *the man*
or something. But on the way back to my seat, I realized that
this wasn't a friendly communication by any means. It was
Kerry's mother in her real form. I decided I really hated that
woman at that moment. I hated everything about her. And,
Lord, I hated her for saying what she'd said. I wanted so much
to forget it. But like she'd hoped, I never did.

Baby Week II

November 2007

I always thought it sounded cliché when I'd see a friend who'd just given birth and I'd ask how old the baby was and she'd give me a long, drawn-out answer like, "Two years, four months, two weeks, and a day!"

But my first two weeks with Tyrian were nothing short of cliché. He was the "apple of my eye," "the beat of my heart," and, clearly, "the most beautiful baby in the world." So, whenever Jamison and I would run into folks at the doctor's office, and they'd ask how old he was, I'd count each second of his life and offer it up with pride. I'd explain that my beautiful baby boy was two weeks, one day, and eighteen hours old. I'd add that since he'd met the world, Tyrian had managed to figure out how to scream to indicate that he was very hungry (which was quite different than his "I'm awake, so I can eat now" hungry cry), blink his eyes without falling back to sleep, and keep his hand open. Then I'd pull out my digital camera to prove that he'd indeed achieved all of these things. The poor innocent bystander would then smile graciously, and inside I'd know that they thought I was crazy (like I once thought of the other mothers I knew), but I didn't care. I was in baby bliss land and no lack of outside participation could stop me.

Tyrian really was the most beautiful baby I'd ever seen. Really. His color was the perfect mix of mine and Jamison's, a soft oatmeal with undertones of caramel and copper. When we first brought him home, he looked like a little scoop of toasted almond ice cream, but even in the cold winter months, he'd managed to find his rich color. His eyes, though, were a complete surprise to everyone. Jamison had been born with dark green eyes, the color of emeralds, so we expected Tyrian's to be the same, but instead his were an intense brown. So brown, in fact, that they looked black. Little marbles that pierced so deep, even in his two weeks of life when he could hardly focus long on one thing without falling asleep, people would comment about how serious and intense his eyes were. It was as if he could look into you, know that you were hiding something.

Now, my sweet boy, who wanted nothing of the world but to be fed and kissed on his hands (that calmed him), was on to something with these piercing eyes. We were hiding something, Jamison and I. We were hiding something from the world and even ourselves. In fact, we'd taken a few steps past hiding and were establishing permanent residence in the land of denial. That was because with all of the cute stuff we'd had to do with Tyrian, dedicating all of our positive energy to him from the moment he was born, we'd both nonverbally agreed to live separate emotional lives.

We'd smile at the baby, but never at each other. We'd talk to the baby, whoever was visiting the baby, even Isabella, but we never really spoke to one another. Yeah, we'd get through the day-to-day, negotiating compound and complex sentences within each other's presence, but these were all empty, demandless developments. Jamison would tell me that my cell phone was ringing in the den or ask me if I needed anything extra when he was going to the store, but other than that, the only smiles or laughter we shared was when our heads were pointed at the baby. If he'd seem to crack a smile or belch so hard his little body would shake, we'd laugh and look at the beautiful thing we'd made together with great pride and love. But that was it. The "talk" Jamison wanted to have never happened. When the baby came, it seemed impossible. It wasn't that I wanted to be the perfect family and pretend Coreen never existed. Instead, I was afraid of what I might do next.

The thought of the whole thing, of everything that was going on in my life outside of Tyrian made me feel like I was going to start screaming again and I did not know if I'd have the ability to stop. I was sure I'd lose control of myself again and the thought of that happening in front my child frightened me.

But that didn't stop me from feeling what I was feeling. When Jamison would walk into the house, my head would be full of questions. Not necessarily about whether he'd seen Coreen, but about how many times he'd walked into the house in the past after having been with her and wrapped his arms around me, and slept in my bed with her still on him. The thoughts stung me and, to be honest, I was simply afraid to really open that can of worms. So instead I'd roll my eyes when he walked into the room. Turn my back when he was getting ready for bed (he'd had sense enough to take up residence in one of the guest bedrooms). And mostly pretend he wasn't around.

But little, helpless babies who can do nothing when they are first born grow every day, and with each day, Tyrian seemed to want and demand more from us. He needed us on the spot, together. Or he'd cry and cry. Isabella couldn't calm him, Aunt Luchie couldn't calm him, and he hated my mother; but whenever Jamison and I would sit together and play kissing games with his hands, our son with the piercing eyes would sit quietly and soon drift off to sleep. It seemed Tyrian had another plan for his parents, and while we were trying hard to live with each other by living apart, Tyrian wasn't having it. "He's been here before," Aunt Luchie said once as Jamison and I were forced to sit on the couch in Tyrian's view. "He's got an old soul. You can see it in those brown eyes."

Tyrian just laid back in his carrier, his eyes half-focused on the two of us and if one even seemed to shift to move, he'd break out into his little pleading cry—even if he was asleep.

Our son was making our six-bedroom house quite small, and avoiding one another was becoming difficult.

When Jamison came in from a meeting he'd had with a new landscaper, I was sitting on the couch in the den, watching Tyrian nurse as I enjoyed doing seemingly every minute of my life. While my mother was strongly against breast-feeding, claiming it was completely crass to do in public, everyone at the hospital kept saying it was "best for the baby," so I decided to give it a shot, for the first month or so anyway. Plus, one of the nurses let me in on a little secret, that the baby weight went faster when you breast-fed. This news came just as I was on the fence about the whole thing. But while I couldn't decide, I was desperate to lose weight, so breast-feeding it was. This was no easy task, especially at four in the morning when both Tyrian and I wanted to sleep, but Aunt Luchie, who'd been staying with us to help out, insisted that I feed him on the clock, sleep or not.

"You two okay?" Jamison asked, poking his head into the den to ask his usual stupid question for the day. It was amazing how nearly everything that came out of his mouth sounded asinine to me now. Of course we were okay. We were sitting in the den, quietly. What did he think was going on?

"We're fine," I responded flatly and smiled at Tyrian, who stopped sucking when he heard his father's voice. "Your mother called about an hour ago. Right after you left." Isabella told me that the witch had called. I wasn't answering the house phone.

"I know; she called my cell phone. I went over there to see her."

I just shook my head. This was extra information I hadn't wanted nor asked for. He knew we weren't communicating like that. I didn't care about his comings and goings. He didn't seem to want to tell me where he was going when he was on his way to see Coreen, so why should I care now?

"She wanted to talk about Thanksgiving, next week," Jamison added, introducing a conversation without my participation. In fact, he walked past me and sat on the other side of the couch.

"Okay," I said, moving Tyrian from my breast and to my shoulder to pat his back.

"She thinks we should have it here . . . the dinner."

This simple announcement would've been accepted in any other household, but at this time and in this place it sounded like the announcement of an execution, a machine gun firing into a crowd. Tyrian punctuated his father's words with a resounding belch. I felt his little body shake on my chest, and while I wanted to strike out at Jamison, I knew I couldn't. I simply closed my eyes and prayed for patience. Jamison knew damn well that I hated having Thanksgiving with his mother. Those kinds of relationships just weren't suited for holidays. Jamison and I had spent six of the first ten years of our marriage at my uncle's house in Augusta with my mother and the other four times we were apart, as he'd gone to be with his family. This was also how we did Christmas, Easter, and any other holiday when black people felt a need to gather around the table. I couldn't stand his mother and I wasn't about to start pretending now. Not in my own house. I married the man, not the mother, and I was in no mood to put on a show. Not even with my son in the room.

"Here?" I said finally, my eyes still closed, my mind still in prayer. "We've never had any holidays here."

"Why not? We have the space. A formal and informal living room, two dens, a media room, kitchen, six bedrooms, it's the perfect place to have a big family Thanksgiving like I used to have when I was young," he said. "We can invite people from both sides of the family. So everyone can come see Tyrian. A lot of people haven't seen him yet."

"He's only two weeks old."

"He'll be three weeks then, past the time when the doctor said we can start letting people come over."

"Tyrian, where are you?" I heard Aunt Luchie calling from the kitchen. She'd taken to calling his name throughout the house whenever she was on her way to him. "Don't hide from your Aunt Luchie."

Jamison and I sat frozen, our eyes averted as if we didn't want anyone to know we'd been speaking.

Aunt Luchie appeared in the living room, fully dressed in an overcoat.

"There you are," she said to Tyrian's back. "Hiding in here with Mommy and Daddy."

She came over to me and gently took him from my arms.

"Off for our first official walk," she said, obviously trying her best to ignore the tension in the air.

"Oh, no, he's not ready yet. He could catch a cold," I said, getting up from the couch.

"Child, sit down," Aunt Luchie said so forcefully I had to sit down. "It's a beautiful day outside and this child has four snow-suits. He's no more likely to catch a cold than any of us if I wrap him up right. Plus, it's time he got some real air. And that you two had some quiet time."

"But I was just about to—"

"To do what?" she cut me off. I dared not say anything. Aunt Luchie was usually smiles and hugs, but when she put her foot down, that was it. I was angry, but not crazy. The last thing I wanted in my house was an angry old black woman. Her eyes went from me to Jamison, just begging us to say something.

"It's settled then," she said. "We'll be back in fifteen minutes or so. After that, I'm sure he'll be exhausted; I'll take him right upstairs for a nap."

When she left the room, I got up and went into the kitchen to fix myself a sandwich.

Pulling the ingredients from the refrigerator, I saw that Jamison had moved himself from the den to the kitchen too. He was sitting at the kitchen table looking just as stupid as he had in the den.

"We need to talk," he said.

"Talk?" There was a mix of sarcasm and comedy in my voice. I didn't know why though. It just was. I didn't want to talk to Jamison, but really inside I did. I hated him, but I still loved him. I wanted him to stop talking to me, but really I missed talking to him. I missed him. How could I feel all those things at once? But that didn't stop me from having an attitude. I was still mad, and wanting to talk or not, the attitude was staying.

"We can't go on like this, not speaking," he said. "It's driving me crazy."

"Look, I don't want to have Thanksgivings here. And that's it." I spread the mayonnaise on the bread in quick jerking strokes, nearly slicing it in two.

"Not that, about everything. We never spoke about it. About what happened."

"Hum," I said, putting two extra slices of cheese on the bread.

"Look, just come over here and sit down," he raised his voice. "I need to get this out."

"Oh, now you want me to sit down so you can get stuff out?" I slammed the sandwich down on the counter. "Okay then, if that's what this is about. You want me to sit and listen?" I walked over to the table and sat next to him. "What do you have to say?"

"Kerry, come on, can't we just be adults about this?"

"Adults? I'm sorry, I'm just remembering the other time I was supposed to meet you at this table to talk and you weren't even here," I said. "Do you remember that?" I paused. "No, don't answer, maybe you can recall all the other times I tried to sit down to talk to you about what was going on and all you could say was that it was nothing and that I should stop being paranoid. Do you remember that?" I paused again. "No—don't answer that either. Because maybe you can recall when I asked you to talk to me right in front of that bitch's house and you couldn't . . ." My voice cracked and just like that I was crying. "No, you wouldn't talk to me then. Do you remember that?"

"Stop it," Jamison said, reaching over to grab my hand. "Just stop." We sat in silence as I cried and tears gathered in the corners of his eyes.

"I didn't mean for none of this shit to happen," he continued. "It just did."

"How, Jamison? How could something like that *just* happen?"

"I don't know."

"We were married. And happy. I mean, what would make you do that?"

Jamison looked away.

"We were happy, right?" I said.

"I wasn't unhappy," he said. "But I wasn't happy. I'm not going to say that's what it was, because I'm a man and if I wasn't happy with you, I know how to open my mouth and say it."

"Then what was it?" I wiped my tears and sat up in the seat.

"Kerry, you're my wife and I swear to God I don't want another wife, but—" he said, "we just don't seem to connect on a lot of things, and it bothers me so much that sometimes I don't even want to talk to you."

"We don't connect? On what?" I asked.

"Come on, it's not necessary to give an example," he said.

"Yes, it is. If you say we don't connect, then tell me why."

"See you're making everything I say an absolute and it's not like that. We do connect. If we didn't, we wouldn't be married. If we didn't, I wouldn't be in love with you," he said. "But sometimes we don't connect and our differences come up and it makes me feel like I'm alone. Like I'm married to someone who could not care less about how I feel."

"How you feel about what?"

"The business—"

"Oh, the business," I said, cutting him off. "Here we go with that again."

"See, that's exactly what I mean," he said. "That brushing me off when you know how much I care about my business."

"Fine then, go ahead."

His elbow on the table, Jamison rested his forehead in the palm of his hand.

"Look," he started slowly, "I just know how you feel about it. That you don't like it. What I do for a living."

"Jamison, please, I got over that years ago. You know that," I said. We'd had that argument about ten million times after we'd gotten married and he made if obvious that Rake It Up was here to stay. Yes, I was mad that he never went to medical school, but this business was pulling in good money, and in the last five years he was making more money than he would've if he'd become a doctor.

The front door opened and we heard Aunt Luchie come in

with the baby. She was humming a song to him and we listened in silence as the hum faded as she carried Tyrian up to his bedroom.

"You're no more over the fact that I never went to medical school than my mother," Jamison said. "You say you don't care, but I can see it in your eyes. At least she says it."

"How can you tell me what I feel?" I raised my voice, but then lowered it again. "You don't know that."

"No, I don't know that, but I do know you. And I know in my heart that you wanted to be married to Jamison the doctor, not Jamison the man that owns a landscaping company. You can't lie and say it's not true. You didn't even want to take my last name. Now, I was too young and excited about my company when we first got married to see how unhappy you were about Rake It Up, but your feelings have been growing more obvious over the years and it eats me up."

Of course I wanted Jamison to be a doctor. Everyone did. Jamison was the only one who was ever down with the Rake It Up plan. He knew that. He knew what I had riding on his going to med school. It was no secret.

"'A *little* company.'"

"What?" I asked.

"That's what you said when the woman from *Black Enterprise* came over to interview me," he said with tears rising in the corners of his eyes again. "She asked how you felt about all the attention the company was getting, and you said you were surprised that people cared so much about such 'a little company.'" He paused and looked down at this feet. A tear fell to the floor. "That made me feel like shit. In my own house. In my own house I felt like shit. Like the money I'd made to pay for everything in here was nothing but some dirty money and it didn't matter to you just because of how I made it. Because there was no M.D. after my name, it wasn't worth as much as Damien's money. It's more, but it's not the same, right? Because I don't have the family name or the fucking title to validate me."

"That's not it," I said.

"Yes, it is, and you know it. My own wife," he said, "said my biggest dream was *little*." His voice fell to a whisper. "But," he paused and cleared his throat, "I told myself that it was just my Kerry being Kerry. The woman I loved was born with a silver spoon in her mouth, and I married her, so I'd have to deal with it. And it was easy to take like that. It was my cross to bear. But every time something like that would happen—you'd say you never wanted to come be with my family for the holidays, you acted like you didn't want any of my family in the house I've already paid off, and telling me who I should know and how I should speak to them and make sure to mention who your wife is and what family she's from like I'm some fucking nobody—and I just felt myself getting smaller and smaller and pulling away from you."

"Well, why didn't you say anything to me about it?" I pleaded.

"How am I supposed to say that to you? To say you make me feel like less of a man?"

"Less?"

"Kerry, if you don't believe in me, in my dream, then how can I feel like a man for you? The only thing I can feel like is less," he said. "And I didn't even know that was how I was feeling. Not until . . ."

"Until what?"

"Until I met Coreen."

"So, she makes you feel like more of a man? That's why you cheated on your wife? Because some tramp makes you feel like a man?" I heard myself screaming.

"Again, it's not that simple. You know me better than that," Jamison said.

"I thought I did."

"And I thought I knew you too, Kerry."

"What is that supposed to mean?"

"You've changed a lot over the years too," he said. I stood up. I couldn't take it anymore. He was just moving from one thing he hated about me to another. How was it that he was the one having an affair but this conversation was all about me? What about how he'd made me feel like less? How he'd changed?

"I don't want to hear this," I said, walking past the sandwich on the counter. I'd lost my appetite.

"Why not?" he asked, following behind me.

"Because it's not about me. This is about you, Jamison, not me."

"What happened to you going to med school?" he asked. I stopped. Right in the hallway between the front door and the kitchen, I stopped moving because I couldn't believe what I was hearing.

"Excuse me?" I asked turning to him.

"I'm not the only one who didn't go to med school in this house," he said.

"I changed because I didn't go back to school?" This was news to me. Jamison never once brought up anything about me going to school. I'd been there when he started his business, and after I didn't get into any schools the second time around I decided to help him with the business. Once it got off the ground and it was clear he didn't need me, we bought the house and I put all of my energy into the house, into making sure my husband had a lovely home to come back to.

"When we met, all you could do was talk about when you went to med school and how you were going to save the world," he said. "That was never my dream. That was yours. I loved science and it paid for me to got to college, so being a doctor was a great option for me. It was what made me sound legit when I was trying to pledge and make friends on campus and date you, but that was never my dream."

I had thought of going to back to school a few times, but my feelings had been so hurt after the second round of rejections that I gave up on it. Jamison knew that.

"Why did you give up on it, Kerry? Just because some people told you no? You know how many people told me no when I started my company? My own wife told me no. My own mother. But I kept fighting for my dream," he said. His words hurt me. It was like I was being rejected all over again. "You ever think that maybe the reason you kept trying to tear down my dream was because you didn't have your own anymore?" he said harshly.

"I can't do this," I said, turning from him. "I just can't talk about this anymore," I blurted out and ran up the steps to my bedroom. I just wanted to be alone.

DATE: 6/01/07
TIME: 11:27 AM

Coreenissocute: There?

Dablackannanicole: Yeah, I'm still here. I just had to put something in the fax machine. You OK?

Coreenissocute: Hell no. This shit is crazy!!!!!!

Dablackannanicole: I'm sorry to hear that. I know it has to hurt. We've all been down that road before. You know I'm here for you.

Coreenissocute: I just don't understand how he could do something like this. Just lie to me.

Dablackannanicole: Lie?

Coreenissocute: He said he wasn't sleeping with her . . . so how did she get pregnant?

Dablackannanicole: You know these dudes lie. I mean, the ass is in the house with him every night. He's gonna take it.

Coreenissocute: I know that, but still that doesn't make it any easier. I really loved him.

Dablackannanicole: I know you did.

Coreenissocute: I just feel like a damn fool. Like did I really think he was going to leave her for someone like me?

Dablackannanicole: Girl, who and what that girl is doesn't have anything to do with you. What he saw in you was different. And just because he decided to be with her doesn't mean he doesn't love you. Shit, he probably doesn't even love her. He's just there out of obligation like he said in the e-mail.

Coreenissocute: You think so?

Dablackannanicole: Hell yes! And, come on, DO YOU REALLY THINK he's never going to call you again? We're both old enough to know he will. He's just trying to play the good husband right now because he realized that he's about to be a father. But that will wear off and he'll come running right back around to you.

Coreenissocute: LIKE THEY ALL DO.

Dablackannanicole: Shit, she probably only got pregnant to keep him anyway. Don't you think she knows he's cheating and that he doesn't want to be with her anymore? Please, that whole having-a-baby-to-keep-your-man thing is sooooo played.

Coreenissocute: I know, but that doesn't change the fact that she has my man and now I have nothing. I'm just so tired of being alone. I'm 33 and I have nothing to show for it.

Dablackannanicole: Yes you do.

Coreenissocute: I have no husband. No children. I want that. I want my big house, my nice car, my maid, and my man that is busting his ass to give it to me.

Dablackannanicole: Well you just have to be patient. He'll come back.

Coreenissocute: I can't eat, girl. Can't sleep. My shit is just all messed up right now. I don't know what I'm going to do without him. I know we belong together. I'm crying right now. Damn.

Dablackannanicole: Girl, come on . . . don't be crying at work!

Coreenissocute: I know, I know, but this shit is that real to me. I LOVE JAMISON. I can't be without him.

Dablackannanicole: Maybe you should tell him that, Coreen. Like e-mail him or call him. Let him know how you really feel.

Coreenissocute: He said not to contact him. His wife is pregnant.

Dablackannanicole: Hum . . . well give him some time and then contact him. I mean, really, I know he'll contact you, but you have to be patient for that. But in the meantime, you have to get yourself together. I hate seeing you like this.

Coreenissocute: I know, it's just soooooo hard. I just know we're meant for each other. We're just alike. Even his mother said so.

Dablackannanicole: Girl, he introduced you to his mother?

Coreenissocute: Damn. No

Dablackannanicole: ????How do you know that?????

Coreenissocute: Never mind.

Dablackannanicole: Hell no! You can't be typing shit like that and expect me to take "never mind" for an answer. Don't make me come to your cubicle!

Coreenissocute: But it slipped. I swore I wouldn't say anything.

Dablackannanicole: About?????

Coreenissocute: I promised to keep my mouth shut.

Dablackannanicole: Girl, if you don't stop this!!!!

Coreenissocute: OK, look, I met Jamison through his mother.

Dablackannanicole: What?

Coreenissocute: She goes to my church. We're in the same Bible study group. She was helping me out when I moved here after Duane died, so we really got to know each other . . . and she said she wanted me to meet her son.

Dablackannanicole: Girl, you are fucking kidding me! That's some *Dynasty* shit.

Coreenissocute: I didn't want to at first. He's married. But she just kept telling me about him and how he's so unhappy and married to a woman that uses him and he doesn't even love the girl. He actually didn't go to medical school to be with her.

Dablackannanicole: What?????

Coreenissocute: Yeah, she said she always wanted more for her son, that she wanted someone like me for him, and that was the only way he was going to leave Kerry. To meet someone new. At first I wasn't down. I was getting over Duane, but then I was like, this is his mother. She knows what she's talking about . . . just meet him. I guess I was a little bored. Lonely. Definitely horny.

Dablackannanicole: LOL. ROTF.

Coreenissocute: So I agreed.

Dablackannanicole: How did she hook it up?

Coreenissocute: She stole his PalmPilot and gave it to me. She said I should e-mail him and claim I'd found it on the street.

Dablackannanicole: Damn, she's good.

Coreenissocute: So I did it. And then he showed up at my house.

Dablackannanicole: If only you would've met him first.

Coreenissocute: Right.

Dablackannanicole: I can't believe all of that. Did you tell him about his mother?

Coreenissocute: No. I promised I wouldn't.

Dablackannanicole: Damn. Well make sure you keep that on the down low.

Coreenissocute: I know.

Dablackannanicole: Oh yeah, and don't e-mail me at my work address anymore. I think Piper's been reading my e-mails. You'd think she had something better to do.

TIME END: 1:08 PM

In Bed

Thinking about everything Jamison had said to me in the kitchen, I cried most of the afternoon and into the evening. The weight was too much to carry. I wanted to know about Coreen, how it all happened, but when I heard it, that he thought I had something to do with it, I really wished he hadn't said anything at all. It stung me. My hurt went to aching and I needed so much to know that this wasn't how things would always be. I hated Jamison for what he'd done, but the thought of him feeling the way he said he'd felt about us terrified me. Was my husband falling out of love with me? Was our marriage really over?

Exhausted, at bedtime I was lying in bed, half asleep with the baby resting on a blanket beside me when the bedroom door opened. It was Jamison. I thought he was coming into the room to get a sleeping shirt or something so he could go back to the guestroom—he usually did this when I was out of the room, but Tyrian and I had been in the room for most of the night. But, while I heard the dresser drawer open and close, he didn't leave this time. My back to him, I listened as he stopped. I could feel his eyes on me. Then he started moving again, but his footsteps were coming closer and then the bed moved as he sat down. I didn't turn around. I just lay there and felt tears well up inside of me again. One dropped from my face onto the pillow and grew into a soft spot. I wanted to tell him to leave, but another side of me really wanted him to stay. I opened my eyes and looked at Tyrian as I felt Jamison lay down beside me.

"I'm sorry," Jamison whispered softly into my hair. "I love you and I'm not going anywhere. Not even if you tell me to. I'm not letting anything happen to our family. I promise you that."

I felt Tyrian shudder and readjust his body in his sleep. He whimpered a bit and then shifted his head from one side to the next, threatening to wake up. But then his chest moved up and down, and through my tears I watched as he found his way back to a restful sleep.

Jamison slid his arm over my waist as he'd done a million times before. Only this time, he did not wrap his arm around my waist and cradle my stomach. Instead he reached over and rested his hand on Tyrian's back, rocking him softly. He kissed me on the back of my neck and before he rested his head against pillow, a tear fell from his face to my cheek.

Marital Bliss

Kerry made everything just right. I'd come home from a day I thought was the worst I'd ever had, and there she was pretending we were in Mexico, throwing a fiesta in the middle of the living room. And everything would be in order—from the enchiladas she'd order from my favorite restaurant to the little sombrero she'd be wearing when I'd open the door. She'd be determined to make me feel better. Make me laugh and smile. I wanted to be mad and just wallow in my misery, but she wouldn't let me and I'd break sooner or later. That only made me love her more. She kept our house clean, herself looking pretty, and while she still wasn't cooking, she'd figured out how to make the only meal that mattered to me—Hamburger Helper. I always told her I didn't need to be taken care of. My mother raised me to clean up after myself and Moms made sure I could cook before I left her house. But Kerry wouldn't hear any of that. She had it set in her mind that things were supposed to be a certain way . . . the traditional way. I was sure this tradition didn't include a file of restaurant menus she kept in the kitchen cabinet where there should have been food, but I went along with it. Kerry was trying to make me happy and that's all I wanted. The gift was that I got to come home to her.

To lie with someone I knew really needed me and loved me more than she even knew.

And that couldn't have been an easy task. I wasn't the cash cow tradition said I should be. My Rake It Up venture wasn't exactly raking in the dough during its first years. I couldn't even really afford to contribute to the wedding. Her mother paid for most of it out of some wedding fund she started when Kerry was born.

In the first three years, I mostly drove my own truck and cut lawns myself with a few people I hired here and there. We lived off my limited funds and the money Kerry was making at a job she had at a doctor's office. Living check to check was an understatement. We were broke and both my mother and her mother had to pay a few bills. This made me feel bad. I didn't want to be broke. I wanted to be just as successful as Kerry wanted me to be. Shit, I even wanted to make my mother happy . . . and it would've been the icing on the cake to shut Kerry's mother up. But somewhere along the way Rake It Up shifted from a side thing I was doing until I went to med school to a dream I really believed in. I always liked working with my hands. Because I was good in science, I assumed this meant I was destined to be a surgeon. But once I got those yard cutters in my hands, it just seemed right. There was something so peaceful and calming to be out there cutting grass and shutting out the rest of the world. No one bothered you. And when you were done, you got to step back and see what your work went into. You'd made the world prettier or nicer for other people to enjoy, even if they didn't notice it. And the scientific mind everyone always said I had helped me do that. For me, cutting grass was a science. It took planning and balance, a vision of how you wanted things to look and feel to the senses.

I couldn't back away from that. That grass seemed to grow

into my being. It became my patient. I had to give myself to my company. Now, I was no fool. I knew two things: I liked money, and I didn't want to be cutting grass for the rest of my life. So, because I wasn't going back to med school, I knew I'd have to grow Rake It Up into something big. Something where I could give everything to Kerry she'd ever wanted. Not to shut her up. Not to shut her mother up. But because my wife deserved it.

"You need a secretary," Kerry said one day when I walked into the house from working. I was sweating like hell from being in the sun all day and my body smelled like everything dead. I just wanted to run to the shower, but it was clear Kerry wanted to talk, so I stood there. Plus, I wanted to hear what she was about to say, because I noticed that she'd just hung up the phone when I walked in the door. I didn't have to ask who was on the other end of the line.

"A secretary? For what?"

"For your jobs and stuff. So many people call you now to do jobs," she said. "A secretary would make the business more efficient and help you get more clients."

"Hum . . ." I said. I'd thought of that before, but the business wasn't there yet. I couldn't afford it.

"I know you're thinking you can't afford it," Kerry said, reading my mind. "But I have a proposal . . ." She came over to me and began unbuttoning my shirt right in the living room. She never touched me when I came in from work.

"My job isn't really bringing money home . . . and now that the company is growing, you could use me with you."

"But we can't afford it. We're already struggling."

"But with my help, we could really take the business to the next level."

"How?" I asked.

"Well," she pulled my shirt off, "I could do marketing and hook you up with some of my mother's friends. They all have businesses. They could hire you."

"No . . ." I protested. Kerry pulled me to her chest.

"Don't say no so quickly," she said. "Think about it."

"I'm thinking about." I pulled away. "And I'm thinking it's a bad idea. You know how it goes with me and your mother."

"But you won't be dealing with my mother. See, now you'll have a secretary. So I'll deal with her."

"But Kerry, what about your job? Didn't you say you wanted to stay there until you took the MCAT again?"

After Kerry didn't get accepted to the medical schools of her choice the second time around, she decided that instead of applying to different schools, she'd pull up her MCAT scores to prove herself. She signed up for the next test, but I didn't see her crack one of the study guides I'd gotten her when we got back from our honeymoon. Then Kerry said she'd been too busy planning the wedding and working to study, so the date came and went. She decided not to take the test that year. She'd wait and study for the next one.

"I'm studying. It'll be fine. I can work for you and study when I'm free," she said. I could tell it would be a bad idea to push the issue about the test. I realized before we even got married that it was a sore spot for Kerry. Between her mother constantly implying that Kerry had done something wrong and the stack of rejection letters Kerry still hadn't thrown out, she seemed to have enough anxiety about the whole thing.

I didn't say anything. I stepped away from Kerry and walked into the bedroom. I didn't want to fight with her.

"What, Jamison? What?" She was following behind me.

"Nothing," I said.

"Well, what do you think?"

"I think I'll have to keep thinking about it."

I walked into the bathroom and turned on the shower. When I went back into the bedroom, Kerry was sitting on the bed. I could tell she was crying.

I walked over to the closet and threw my pants into the laundry basket, trying to figure out how to avoid the drama. This was how Kerry got me to react. She knew that. She knew I couldn't just sit there and let her cry. What kind of man would do that? Not one who wanted to live in peace.

Wrapped in a towel, I sat down beside her on the bed.

I exhaled and looked at the wall next to the bed. There was a vase Kerry had filled with some of the rose petals that were on the ground when I proposed to her.

"I guess it won't be too bad," I said finally.

She sniffled.

"We can try it for a little while, but if it doesn't work out, we have to stop."

She sat up and wiped her tears.

"Okay?" I asked. I just wanted her to stop crying.

"Jamison, I want us to be a team. Is that so bad?"

"We are a team," I said. "I just never imagined you working with me. I thought you hated the company."

"But this is what's best for us," she said. "I want to do what will be good for us in the future."

"What about what's best for you?" I asked. "Your dreams."

"Well, I can put that on hold for a while, so this can work. So we can make sure it works. Then, with the money we can focus on med school," she said.

"Doesn't sound bad, I guess," I said, getting up and heading toward the shower. "But only until we get things together. Then we can focus on getting you back in school."

"Exactly." She got up too and came behind me. She started taking off her shirt.

"Woman, what are you doing?"

"Well," she said, smiling as if not one tear had fallen from her eyes, "if we're going to work together, we may as well shower together."

She slid off her pants and I watched as she walked naked into the bathroom. And, Lord, just like that old saying goes, "I hated to see her leave, but I sure liked watching her walk away."

"You coming in?" she called from the shower.

God permitting!

In two years, I'd learned two things about being married:

1. The worst part is fighting.
2. The best part is making up.

E-MAIL TRANSMISSION

TO: Jamison.Taylor@rakeitup.net
FROM: coreenissocute@yahoo.com
DATE: 9/11/07
TIME: 12:42 PM

Hello. I just wanted to say hi. Today is 9/11. The day Duane died. It's a very sad day for me. I wish you were here.

E-MAIL TRANSMISSION

TO: Jamison.Taylor@rakeitup.net
FROM: coreenissocute@yahoo.com
DATE: 10/19/07
TIME: 4:51 AM

It's my birthday. I don't know if you remembered that or if you even care, but I wanted to let you know that I have been thinking about you and I do miss you. Whether you miss me or not, that doesn't change how I feel.

Tonight I went out with one of my friends from work and when we were sitting at dinner I kept seeing all these couples walking around together and it made me so sad. I wanted that to be us and be-cause of the lies you fed me, I thought that would be us. I really did love you and every day I spend without you makes me sick. I can't eat. I've lost twenty pounds and while I tried to go to the classes you got me into at Perimeter, I'm too sad to be focusing on stuff like that.

I know you really don't want to hear all of this, but I'm tired of keep-ing it to myself. I think we're meant to be together. I know you know it too. You're just being a husband out of obligation and I understand that. But I want you to know that I'll always be here waiting for you. I feel crazy even saying that, but it really is how I feel. I need to be honest with myself right now. There's no other man for me.

I have been alone and lonely for a long time. Even when I was married, I felt alone. I always thought there had to be someone else out there for me. Something else. When I met you, I figured I'd found it. Not just because of who you are, but what you make me want to be. How you make me feel like being more than what I am. Now that you're gone, refusing to even return my e-mails, I feel alone again and I really don't know how I'm going to find my way out. I'm afraid to think of what I might do. But I'm a woman who has nothing. I can't even say that to anyone else. And it hurts me to even write it. And here I am crying again over a man that doesn't even want to be with me . . .

Turkey

The morning after Jamison found his way back to our bed, we woke up to a full Southern breakfast, courtesy of Aunt Luchie. Homemade biscuits, gravy, eggs, bacon, grits . . . There was so much food on the table, I thought it was already Thanksgiving. Aunt Luchie, Jamison, and I sat at the table as Tyrian rocked in a swing Isabella had set up in the kitchen. It was the first time we were eating as a family, and while we were just making small talk, it felt so good to be in that space. Like we were whole for the first time in a long time.

When we finished eating, Jamison got up from the table and kissed Tyrian and me on the cheek before heading to work. He did it methodically, so practiced, as if it was something he'd been doing or thinking of doing every morning for his entire life.

"Bye babies," he said, exiting with a hopeful smile on his face. I didn't respond. I just smiled back and nodded.

"Wow, that was great," I said to Aunt Luchie. I got up from the table and began helping her put the dishes away.

"Thank you, baby. I thought we could all use a little something extra on our stomachs this morning," she said. "I think Georgia saw its first real winter night last night. It was so cold."

Unlike my mother, Aunt Luchie didn't see it as being necessary to be completely dressed before you sat down at the breakfast table. She was wearing a brown silk bathrobe and had a colorful scarf on her head. She looked lovely, even that early in the morning, but I don't think I ever saw my mother at the breakfast table with something covering her head. She hated head scarves. Said they only had a place in the bedroom and made us look like Aunt Jemimas. If it wasn't for the pictures, I'd swear my mother and Aunt Luchie were raised by different people.

"Yeah, it sure was cold," I said.

"I had to get an extra blanket out of the closet."

"Oh, you could've turned up the central air," I said.

"No sense wasting money now. You and Jamison have enough to worry about." Aunt Luchie poured herself a cup of coffee and went back to the table. I set the dishes in the sink so Isabella could load the dishwasher later.

"So how did your talk go last night?" she went on. "I saw that Jamison wasn't in the guestroom this morning."

"Well, we talked a bit more before we went to sleep," I said. "We just agreed to start talking more and we both need to make some major changes." I got my cup of coffee and as I sat down across the table from Aunt Luchie, I peeked at Tyrian to see that he was sitting in his swing asleep.

"That's good," she said. "You two do need to take it slow. But don't stop communicating. When the ear doesn't hear the news, it tends to make up the news."

"What?" I laughed at her saying.

"Well, if your husband isn't telling you what's going on, you'll make it up," she said firmly.

"You're right," I said remembering how Jamison's silence was what had put me off in the first place. "Oh, and I agreed to have Thanksgiving dinner here next week."

"Really?" Aunt Luchie looked stunned but happy. Jamison hadn't attempted to bring our families together completely since the wedding. That was over ten years ago now.

"He's always wanted to have a big Thanksgiving here in this house."

"Well, it's a house made for gathering family."

"I'm not excited about having to entertain his mother, but if it'll help us get through this, I'll do it."

"So, when are you going shopping?" she asked.

"For a dress?"

"For food, child."

"Oh, I don't cook. They'll bring food and Jamison is doing some of it," I said. "And I'm ordering some pies."

"What?" Aunt Luchie withdrew. "I know you're not going to let a bunch of women come into *your* house with food to feed your family. You aren't sick!"

"But I can't cook."

"Well, today you start."

"No, you have no idea how bad I am," I said, laughing. "And we don't have enough time."

"Nonsense." Aunt Luchie picked up a sheet of paper and a pen that was sitting by the phone. "I'm going to show you how to make your own pies. Sweet potato pies. And you'll make dressing on your own too."

"What? I can't!"

"You can try," she said, writing. "Can't you?"

It was a charge. A charge from my oldest aunt who never failed at being there to defend and take care of me—even when my mother was acting crazy.

"Fine," I said under my breath.

"Good. Now here's the list of things I'll need you to get from the store." She slid the paper over to me.

"Oh no, I'll have Isabella get the stuff for me. We can leave the list on the counter," I said, realizing Isabella had been a ghost all morning.

"Oh, she went home," Aunt Luchie said quickly.

"Home?"

"Yeah, I sent her home. There wasn't nothing for her to do. I got tired of watching her sit around here looking simple, so I told her to go home."

"For how long?"

"Until you call her and tell her she has her job back."

I wanted to believe she was faking or playing a joke, but I knew by her tone that Aunt Luchie was telling the truth. I couldn't believe it. How could she just send my maid home?

"Why would you do that?" I asked, trying to remain calm. Now it was clear that my mother and Aunt Luchie did indeed have the same parents. Only these two could pry into other people's lives without so much as a thought.

"I didn't get why that girl was here in the first place."

"I needed her to help me keep the house clean and cook. That's what she was doing here," I said.

"Keep the house clean while you do what?"

"I do a lot," I said, surprised Aunt Luchie was making me defend myself. She'd had a maid her entire life.

"Like what?"

"Help Jamison."

"He has an assistant. Two from what I can tell."

"Well, there are some things they don't know."

"Please," she said dismissively. "What else?"

"I also have to keep the house in order. I decorate and I have to take care of Tyrian."

"You have had that girl here for three years. Tyrian is a little baby. He doesn't need much. And it isn't like you're a working woman."

"So I need to be a working woman now?"

"Kerry, you need to be doing something. And from how it looks, you're doing nothing."

"You sound like Jamison now," I said. His words were still stinging me.

"What happened to your dreams? You were going to med school. What happened to that?" she asked.

"I don't know . . . I guess I just didn't go," I said simply. But I knew it wasn't that simple. Jamison was right. Something had happened to me, but I still wasn't sure what it was. "I guess I just didn't care about it anymore. I didn't want to do it."

"Well, what do you want to do?"

"I don't know. I just don't know." I was irritated now. Was this suddenly the question of the week or something? "Look, what I do has nothing to do with Isabella's work here. It's just how it is. And Jamison approves of it. He likes having her around."

"And that's exactly my point," Aunt Luchie said. "Why would you want some young girl walking around your house, taking care of all the things the lady of the house should do, right in her husband's face. That woman was feeding, looking after, and entertaining your husband, and you were walking around here like you didn't have anything to do."

"But she just makes things easier for us."

"She could make things really easy for you if she steals your husband."

"She couldn't." I laughed. "He doesn't see her like that."

"Hum . . ." She exhaled. "You can say what you will, but I know love and how to break it up. And a sure way to do it is to have another woman caring for your husband. Jamison works hard to give you all of these things you have and all you do is write a check for someone else to pay him back."

"My marriage isn't about favors. I don't have to earn Jamison's love," I said. "I don't have to pay him back for what he does for me."

"No, baby, you don't have to do anything in life. But that doesn't mean you shouldn't."

A couple of frowns later, I was walking around the supermarket looking for the things I needed to make sweet potato pie. I hadn't been in a grocery store in so long it was laughable. I wanted so badly to call Marcy and make her guess where I was, but I hadn't spoken with her since the party. She came over with Damien to see the baby when he came home, but I stayed upstairs. I didn't understand how she could do what she'd done. I'd always been there for her, and all I asked was that she be there for me in confidence. That confidence didn't include spreading my business. It hurt so much to be without her, to go through this whole thing with Jamison without a friend by my side, but I couldn't let her hurt me again.

A lot had changed since I'd walked the aisles at the grocery store; it seemed more like a night club now. Men and women were walking up and down the aisles, overly dressed and smiling at each other as they pretended to shop. But it was clear they were there to pick up people. No more elevator music; they were playing hip-hop and there were these little food sample stations where people stood and chatted as if they were at a cocktail party.

Without Tyrian for the first time since he was born, I was sad to be away from him, but happy to see that none of the men in the market could tell I was a new mother. They were giving me the eye and one guy even offered to push my cart. As usual, I simply flashed my wedding ring and said no. "He's a lucky man," he said, stepping back. "I sure do envy him. And I'm willing to share."

I was shocked by how forward this man was at implying that we have an affair. After that encounter I started looking more closely at all of the people I saw mingling at the food sample tables and I noticed that many of the women had on wedding rings, but the men didn't. But there they were, chatting and laughing as if they were hooking up at a single's club. Was that how it happened? Did people just know what the affair was before it even began? Marcy said the men she knew never even mentioned her marriage. It was just known and respected. I didn't want to start a situation like that. But I also wondered if I could. Could I have a discreet affair by the frozen peas?

Walking out of the grocery store with a cart full of some things on the list and a bunch of things that weren't—I'd forgotten all about the ice cream aisle . . . and the potato chip aisle too. I felt a bit more alive than I had in the past few weeks. It was great being a mother, and I missed Tyrian dearly—I wondered what he was doing every second—but it was also nice to see that the world was still going on around me. To breathe in a space as a woman alone with no attachments. No one who wanted anything from me. There was no one crying or needing to be fed. Now I fully understood why so many mothers wanted to go to the grocery store alone.

After placing the bags into the back of the car, I was about to push the shopping cart back to the store when a certain matted cocker spaniel I'd seen before was marching toward me. The only thing was that just like the first time, this little guy was stapled to a skull. It was McKenzie from the jail, pushing a row of shopping carts through the lot. My first instinct was to push the cart away and pretend I didn't see her, but she was heading right to me and a part of me just couldn't believe I was seeing her.

"I got that cart, mama," she said. She was obviously tired and while I hadn't noticed it at the jail, she was pregnant. Only now, her stomach was sticking out much farther.

"Oh, no . . ." I said, holding the cart.

What was she doing pushing carts in her condition? From the looks of it, she was at least seven months.

"I got to keep these carts out the lot," she said. "I ain't doing you no favor; I can push it myself. They pay me to."

"Oh, I know. . . . I need the exercise," I said.

"Suit yourself. But I asked."

She went on, pushing the rest of the carts to the store. It was obvious she didn't know who I was.

"McKenzie," I called after daring myself.

She stopped and turned, her stomach lightly brushing the cart in front of her. She looked like she was sure I was calling her name by mistake. Maybe I was talking to someone else.

"McKenzie," I said again.

"You calling me?" She pointed a broken nail toward her heart.

"Yeah, I'm Kerry. We know each other." I listened to how ridiculous I sounded and wished I'd just gotten into my car.

"We know each other?" She stepped toward me. "From where?"

"Well, we . . . Um . . ." Suddenly I was very aware of all of the things I had surrounding me: my Ferragamo bag, Vittadini shoes, the Benz, Chanel perfume. Yes, we were in jail together, but we didn't know each other. Not by a long shot.

"That's you girl?" she said suddenly, the cocker spaniel shaking from surprise with each syllable. "From the—"

"Jail," we said together.

"Oh my God," she said again. She looked like she wanted to hug me. I felt like I wanted to do the same, but there were things between us. "The mad sister that beat her husband's ass!"

"Yeah, that's me." I laughed at how she'd put it.

"So how you doing? Ya'll back tight now? You and your man?"

"Um . . . kind of," I replied. "I guess so." I felt bad for admitting that. Like I'd sold out on the "mad sister" she'd called me.

"Mama, please, you ain't got to apologize for being back with him," she said flatly. "Shit, I ain't never know a woman that went upside her man's head that didn't go back to him."

"I guess you're right," I said. "So how are you?" I looked at her stomach. "I hadn't noticed that you were pregnant."

"Yeah, I'm about to have a baby," she said proudly. "It's gonna be a girl. That's why I'm out here." She rubbed her stomach. "I got to make some changes before this one comes. I promised myself and my other kids that. No more out in the streets for me. I'm too old for that. I got to get clean and make some money so I can get a good doctor and a nice place to live."

"The state can't help you with that?" I asked. There were plenty of programs that could help her and get her out of the parking lot, pushing carts when she should have been somewhere off her feet.

"Please, the state don't do nothing," she said. "I'm tired of that shit—the lists and lines and folks that don't care nothing about you. See, you ain't got no money and the doctors and people with Section 8 know 'cause you working with the state. So they treat you like garbage. And ain't nobody in the welfare gonna stop them from doing it. Because they all got degrees and think they better than us. I ain't stupid. I know fake shit when I see it. I got to make my own way."

I couldn't say anything. These were all things I'd heard before, but never from someone who was directly affected.

"So there's no one who can help you?" I asked.

"Not no one I want to," she said. "There's my mother, but she got her own problems, and my child's father—I don't want nothing from him. That's how I was locked up before, fooling with him turning me out in the street . . . and he knew I was pregnant. No, I can't ask nobody for help. I think maybe it's time I help myself. I know this money ain't gonna be enough to get us by, but it's enough for me to make sure my baby is born in a nice hospital and not get no skin rash before she come home. Then after she come, I got to work harder."

"McKenzie," a man called from the front of the store.

"Damn, he getting on my nerves," she said, stomping her foot on the pavement. "I got to get back to work."

"Okay," I said, opening my wallet. I wasn't sure what I was doing. I didn't have any cash to give her and I had a feeling she wouldn't take it anyway. I pulled one of my old cards from when I used to work with Jamison and handed it to her. "You can contact me if you need to. I may, well, my husband might, have some work you can do for him."

"Really?" She took the card and a smile blossomed on her face. The spaniel shook accordingly.

"Yeah, I can't promise anything, but we may be able to help." I hoped what I was saying sounded as sincere as it felt. I didn't know how I would help McKenzie, but I wanted to.

She waved and turned, pushing the shopping carts along with her as I got into my cozy car and headed to my cozy house where everything was going to be exactly as it had been when I left it. I didn't have to worry about anyone taking care of me. Even if Jamison left me and I didn't work another day in my life, I didn't have to worry about anything.

Driving home, I couldn't help but think about how different things were for women like McKenzie. They'd made bad choices, but that didn't mean that they should have to fend in the world completely alone. Someone should be there to assist them when they really needed help. Someone who cared and did it not as a career move, but because of the kindness in their hearts.

TO: coreenissocute@yahoo.com
FROM: Jamison.Taylor@rakeitup.net
DATE: 10/23/07
TIME: 7:34 PM

I don't know how to respond to your letter. I wasn't going to write back, but I do think certain things need to be answered. I don't know what I said to make you think and believe some of what you wrote. I never said I didn't love Kerry and I never said I was going to leave her. We do have our problems and I did share some of that with you. Marriage isn't perfect and mine is hard sometimes, but just because I complained about it doesn't mean I was leaving. I apologize if I ever gave you that impression. What happened between us happened and as I pre-pare for my son to be born, I have to move on. You have to move on too, Coreen. And after I read your e-mail like three times, I kind of think that maybe you should see someone to talk to them about what's going on. Like a counselor. Don't hate me for say-ing that. I know it's a sore spot, but one person to another, I think that's best.

Jamison

TO: Jamison.Taylor@rakeitup.net
FROM: coreenissocute@yahoo.com
DATE: 10/25/07
TIME: 4:14 AM

You know what, fuck you Jamison for everything you just wrote. I can't believe you're going to try to act like I meant nothing to you.

So I was just some cheap fuck? Fuck you then. If that's how it's going to be, fuck you and fuck the world. I don't need anybody anymore. I'm tired of caring for a bunch of people that don't give a shit about me.

The Takeover

Kerry and I had been married for over seven years when I realized that not one night had gone by that I hadn't shared a bed with my wife. We'd traveled, but always together, and because of our families, we'd spent some holidays in different houses, but we always met at night in our bed. And it wasn't because we agreed to; it was just habit. I couldn't sleep without Kerry close to me. My true rest ultimately seemed to lie in the knowledge that she was nearby.

And in those seven years, my wife hadn't once bored me in bed, sent me to sleep on the couch or made me want to stay away from her. We'd had our problems just like the other couples I knew, and I did notice the other women who seemed to flock around me like pigeons since the day I'd gotten married, but I was happily sharing my bed with only one woman.

When Damien called and asked if I wanted to travel out of town with the fellas to an All-Star basketball weekend, I wanted to go, but I was sure it would be a stretch.

"Go," Kerry said easily when I mentioned it. "I think it'll be good." She was laying in bed beside me, reading a book.

"What?" I'd expected a bit more hostility, an argument.

"We haven't been apart. Go ahead and go. You have my full

support." She kissed me on the cheek and turned back to her book.

Now I know any other brother on earth would say I should've taken this quick approval and run with it all the way to floor seats at the game, but Kerry seeming not to care whether I was going to be leaving our bed was a bit of a jab at the old ego. See, it was one thing for me to kinda-sorta want to be out with the fellas, but for Kerry to want me to go out? That just went against the point of wanting to be out. I was a mature man, but I was a man who wanted to be wanted by his woman. I'd always felt that Kerry needed me there, really needed me there to protect her, but I was beginning to feel like that wasn't true anymore.

"You cheating on me?" I asked—half-joking after watching her read for a few seconds. "Hello . . ." She wasn't even looking at me. "Oh, now you're so into that Terry McMillan you can't hear me? Don't care if your husband lives or dies, huh?"

"What are you talking about?" She put down the book and slid off her glasses. "I do care if you go, but I do kind of need some time to myself. I have some things I need to do around here."

"Like what?" Kerry was still working with me as my first assistant, but we'd hired two more girls beneath her, so she didn't have much to do.

"Well, I need to start deciding what things we'll be taking to the new house, for example," she said, referring to the dream house I'd just bought her. I'd saved for three years and bought the house outright—no loans, no price haggling. It was one of the proudest days of my life.

"What you mean 'decide'?" I asked. "We're taking everything."

"Jamison, we can't take this old stuff to the new house," she said. "That's Cascade. We'll need all new things . . . well, a few of my antiques will be able to make the cut, but . . ."

"My green couch?"

"Oh, that's not even on the list," she said laughing.

"Kerry, that was my first couch!"

"And when you leave for the game, it will be the last time you'll see it."

We were both laughing together. I jumped on top of her in the bed and began tickling her.

"Stop, Jamison," Kerry cried.

"Not until you take that stuff back about my green couch."

"No, no, no," she cried. "That couch is out."

"Really?" I stopped tickling her and held her hands down above her head on the bedsheets.

"Yes, really . . ." she said.

"Really?" I bent down and kissed her on the cheeks.

"Yes, really."

"Really?" I kissed her on the lips and as I ran my tongue over her lips, I spread her legs apart with my knees.

"Really?" She took my line. Her body shuddered as my tongue went from her lips to her earlobes and then to the tips of her nipples, which I kissed through her shirt.

"Really, yes," I said, releasing her hands. She wrapped them around my neck and raised them around the backs of my ears as she looked into my eyes.

"Really?" she said. Her hands were on top of my head, gently pushing it down toward her breasts.

"Really, yes," I said.

I didn't bring up the green couch again. In fact, nothing green ever made it into the dream house.

E-MAIL TRANSMISSION

TO: coreenissocute@yahoo.com
FROM: Jamison.Taylor@rakeitup.net
DATE: 10/25/07
TIME: 11:22 AM

Coreen, where are you? I just called you. I don't like the way your e-mail sounded. I didn't mean to make you so upset. I don't know where your head is, but you're scaring me. Look, just call me when you get this.

E-MAIL TRANSMISSION

TO: coreenissocute@yahoo.com
FROM: Jamison.Taylor@rakeitup.net
DATE: 10/25/07
TIME: 8:15 PM

I've been calling you all day and I can't get you on the phone. I even tried your job and they said you didn't come in today. What's going on? Look, I'm going to come by later. I just want to check on you. Just answer the door if you're there. I don't know what else to do.

Giving Thanks

After spending most of the night making and remaking Aunt Luchie's sweet potato pie, I was up at 9:30 AM, walking into the church Jamison grew up. We were attending a prayer service the church held every Thanksgiving morning to send up prayers of thanks. It wasn't exactly my idea of a way to spend Thanksgiving morning—with Jamison and his mother in a church—but I did it as part of my agreement to try to communicate better with Jamison. We'd been doing great so far. Planning the dinner had actually given us something to focus on other than what we'd been going through. It also helped us to talk and communicate in ways we hadn't been able to for various reasons in years. We were laughing and singing, sitting up late at night chatting after Tyrian had gone to sleep.

"Don't mention what happened," Jamison said as we stood in the waiting area of the church, preparing to go. He was holding Tyrian in his arms and I was carrying the baby seat. "I didn't tell my mother."

"You didn't tell her?"

"Well, I just didn't want to give her another reason to . . . you know, be against you."

He had a point. It probably would actually make his mother happy to hear that he'd cheated.

"Fine," I said.

"Don't be mad," he whispered. "I was trying to protect you."

The choir stopped singing their opening hymn and an usher opened the door, so we could walk into the sanctuary. I hadn't been to church, or even out of the house much since Tyrian was born, so I was feeling a bit nervous about wearing what was once my favorite navy blue church suit, and how my less-than-fabulous after-the-baby body looked in a pre-baby-body outfit. It had been three weeks since my special delivery, so I was determined that I wasn't going to wear another maternity outfit, but my stomach—and oh GOD my thighs—weren't in agreement with this plan. I'd spread out in ways I didn't even realize in those nine months and nothing seemed to fit quite right.

I didn't expect the church to be packed; I figured most people would be at home preparing for company or be out of town, but this little church was near capacity. It almost looked like Sunday morning, the way folks were packed into the pews, piled on top of one another. The choir was up in the loft, the preacher was sitting in his seat at the altar, and someone was reading announcements. With all of this ritual, I wouldn't feel a need to go to church on Sunday. Jamison and I had been raised in very different churches. Or, should I say, had different church lives. While Jamison was a "holiday" churchgoer now, he attended the same small Baptist church for most of his young life. His uncle was the pastor and he'd spent nearly every night of the week sitting in the pews beside his mother. From Sunday service to Saturday Bible study, he said his mother kept him close to the good house. She seemed to blame me for Jamison's lack of attendance, but I never told him not to go to church; I just never made it part of my regular regimen. I'd been raised in the same church as my mother and grandmother. I went to service weekly as a child, but our attendance was more a matter of form. Not to say my mother wasn't a true Christian, but for her, church was an event, a social occasion where she got to see and say hello to old friends and need-to-know acquaintances. Our church was like an attendance sheet for lineage—no big hats, no holy ghosts, no tear-jerking gospel. Just an organ, spirituals, and lots of handshakes.

Jamison's mother was sitting toward the front of the church. I was sure the pews were about to go up in smoke at any moment with her there, but God saw fit not to kill us all because of one bad seed. In ten years, she'd proven to be the antagonist she'd threatened the day we met. Dottie knew not one kind word to say to me, and even when she came to see Tyrian in the hospital, she managed to rub me the wrong way. "He *does* look like Jamison did when he was born," she said, holding him. Only it wasn't the way most other people would connect a baby's looks with a parent's. She purposely emphasized the word "does," like I'd been cheating.

"Oh," she said surprised when Jamison tapped her on the shoulder. She slid down in the pew to make room for us, but I noticed that she kept her eye on me. "I didn't expect all of you," she whispered, with an uncomfortable smile.

"Yeah, Kerry wanted to come out," Jamison said, grabbing my hand as we sat down.

"Oh . . ." she said, looking around the church. She seemed rather nervous.

The service was quite moving, and I had to admit that I was glad I'd gone. As the preacher drew his prayer of thankfulness to a close, I sat, holding Jamison's hand, thinking of how thankful I was for everything I had. I thought of McKenzie and all of the things she didn't have—the basic things she probably had to worry about on a daily basis. I had the option as to whether I wanted to breast-feed. I didn't have to worry about where the formula would come from if I didn't. I wasn't exactly on great terms with my husband when Tyrian was born, but unlike

McKenzie, I knew he could and would take care of us and never even think of trying to make me have sex with another man for money. My life had been in turmoil, but I knew I was blessed anyway. And for that I was thankful to God. Jamison had hurt me. But I could try to forgive him in time. I was willing to move on and try to save my family. I did hear the things Jamison said about our marriage and that we needed to talk more. I was willing to give it everything I had to make it work.

When the prayer was over and the choir began to sing a soothing song, I was in tears.

"You okay?" Jamison whispered in my ear. Dottie was still holding Tyrian, who'd gone to sleep, even with all of the noise.

"Just thinking," I said, reaching into my purse for a tissue, but I'd left them in my other bag.

"Need something?" he asked.

"Yeah, I'm going to go to the bathroom," I said. "I'll meet you at the car."

"Okay," Jamison said. "Take your time. I'll get the baby in the car." He kissed me on the cheek and smiled reassuringly.

I got up from the pew and started walking down the aisle.

"Where she going?" I heard Jamison's mother ask.

I was still full of emotion as I stood in the bathroom, looking at myself in the mirror. I'd managed to get my eye makeup off with a wet tissue but inside I was still crying. Tears or joy, wonder, fear, anxiousness. It was all inside of me.

I opened my purse to get my lip gloss and when I raised my head to see my face in the mirror, there was a woman standing beside me. She had a short, strawberry blond bob and looked very familiar but I couldn't put my finger on it. I smiled and tossed my tissue into the trash can.

"Pastor got you all riled up?" she asked.

"I guess so," I said, closing my purse.

"Have a good day," she said.

"Happy Thanksgiving."

Walking across the back of the church, toward the parking lot, I remembered where I'd seen the girl in the bathroom before. She actually worked at the gym I used to go to before I was pregnant. She did the advanced step class.

"That's it," I recalled, closing my purse. Only, when I looked down, I realized that I'd left my lip gloss sitting on the counter in the bathroom. I tried to head back to pick it up, but when I turned, I stepped on someone's toes.

"I'm sorry," I said, sure it was the woman from the gym.

"It's okay," the woman said, looking down at her shoes to be sure no damage had been done. She stepped back and raised her head.

I was smiling, but this quickly changed. It wasn't the woman from the gym behind me. It was Coreen.

We stood there, face-to-face, in silence for a few seconds. I was stunned to see her, and by the look on her face I might as well have been a walking corpse.

"What are you here for?" I finally said. "Are you following us?"

"This is my church," she said tensely. "This is not what you think."

"Don't you tell me what I'm thinking." I stepped closer to her. "I just need you to know that you can stop whatever you think you're doing. I'm not going to let you ruin my marriage. So, whatever it was you thought you and Jamison had, it was nothing," I said angrily. "You were just a good-time girl for the moment. There's no way he'd ever leave me for you."

What I said must have stung Coreen just as much as I'd intended, because tears almost immediately began to fill her eyes.

"Really," she said, her voice shaking. "Well, I hope you know that his mother did all of this anyway. She hooked us up."

"What?"

"That's why I'm here. This is my church. No one was following you and Jamison," she cried. "This is my church."

The same alarm that was sounding in my heart the night I ended up at Coreen's house was rattling throughout my body at that moment. Either Coreen was telling the truth or she was really desperate enough to follow Jamison to his mother's church. While I had little trouble believing both takes on the situation, my heart just believed her.

"His mother?" I asked.

"She gave me Jamison's contact information . . . his e-mail, and told me to go after him. She begged me to. She said she didn't want you to be with him and that he needed," Coreen said, "someone like me . . ."

"Look," I said sharply, "I don't care what's going on. I just want you to stay the hell away from my husband."

"Well, you need to tell him to stay away from me," she said.

"Excuse me?"

"Check his e-mail."

"What?"

"He e-mailed me last night."

"Well, that hasn't been proven yet," I said, stepping to her. "Coreen, can't you find a man who isn't taken? What's wrong with you that you have to scrape and struggle to get at something that someone else already owns? I guess you thought that getting my husband to sleep with you somehow made you a stronger woman than me. No, it only makes you a trifling, low-life whore. Spreading your legs and you don't have a damn thing to show for it. Jamison isn't going anywhere. You were living a fantasy."

One of the ushers came over and tried to squeeze between the two of us as people walking by began to stop and stare.

"No, there's no need," I said to usher. "I'm so done with her." I stepped to walk away but then I turned back around and said, "Stay away from my family."

E-MAIL TRANSMISSION

TO: coreenissocute@yahoo.com
FROM: Jamison.Taylor@rakeitup.net
DATE: 11/21/07
TIME: 11:15 PM

Hey, it's the day before Thanksgiving. I just wanted to say hello and make sure everything is OK with you. I pray that if you need something, you'll call me.

Jamison

Black Enterprise

Success. Everyone seemed to be saying that word to me when Rake It Up celebrated its tenth anniversary. When our numbers were published in a story in the *Atlanta Journal Constitution*, the company that started with one truck and two hands, and had grown into a fifteen-truck, fifty-man operation servicing most major companies in Atlanta, people could only describe it as a success. I'd never thought about it. Maybe it was because I'd been there working and worrying since day one, but I hadn't had time to really assess my success. Yes, I'd done big things. I was far from the old neighborhood. I'd paid off three houses (including my mother's), completely funded both mine and Kerry's retirement, and had well over a million in assets and investments. I'd even set up a scholarship fund in my name at my high school for any young man seeking to attend Morehouse. I agreed to pay tuition if he promised to keep up his grades and do community service.

Everyone seemed so excited about the company. It was a unique idea that I'd stretched to its farthest potential, and not a day went by that I didn't get a pat on the back or a wave from a car window. While my mother still managed to mention medical school in between the compliments she gave me about Rake It Up, Kerry seemed to be coming around a bit too. She wasn't exactly the biggest supporter, but working with the business helped her see how much earning potential there was and she was good at what she did for Rake It Up. In addition to keeping me organized, she made all of our new contacts, and her mother helped us get big clients who ultimately changed the face of our company. Within three years of working with me, we'd gone from doing okay, to being invited to speak before the 100 Black Men, the Urban League, and Boule, and I was voted Man of the Year for my fraternity. For the first time, when we walked into those gatherings, Kerry was on my arm and I truly felt like she was honored to be with me. She'd cling to my elbow as we entered and while she never broke the rule of spending too much time with her husband at a public function, I often caught her looking at me from across the room.

When *Black Enterprise* called, saying they wanted to do a story and even take pictures of my house, I was ecstatic. Kerry had just left the company to focus on getting the house together and we were talking about having a baby. My life was like a picture and everything in it was in its place. I wanted to share this reality with the world; to show every little black boy in every 'hood that he could be everything I was and then some more on top of that. I'd come from the bottom and now I was at the top and they'd all know. Maybe someone would look at me and say, "I can do that too."

The day of the interview and shoot, Kerry and I were running around the house like cats on rollerblades. She was trying to get the house together; I was trying to make sure I had on the right tie. Nothing seemed to match and I'd seen so many bad tie pictures in *Black Enterprise* that I didn't want to make the wrong choice. I didn't want to be the man with the cheap tie, trying to look rich, or the dude with the tie that was way too expensive, looking like a complete wannabe. I was who I was and I wanted my tie to say that. I kept asking Kerry for help, but she seemed like she was in her own world. She hadn't really looked at me all morning and whenever I called her, she'd say she'd be right in. But she never came.

When the doorbell rang and Isabella let the interviewer in, Kerry and I found ourselves in the same room for the first time the entire day. We were in the foyer, arm in arm, smiling at the woman like we were completely at ease.

"Marial DeLouch," she said, shaking our hands.

"I'm Jamison," I said. "And this is my wife Kerry."

Kerry smiled pleasantly, but I could tell something was up.

"You two have a lovely home," Marial said as we headed to the reading room where Kerry had planned to have her take pictures.

"Thank you," I said as proud as a new father.

When we walked into the reading room, which Kerry had spent all week filling with books from an antique shop, the woman seemed excited, but then after a minute, she asked if there was somewhere else we could go. She said the lighting was poor and that she wanted to see a place that really defined me as a leader, "a powerful player," she said.

"Well the reading room is dignified and will show that he has a passion for culture," Kerry said.

"Yeah, but something tells me there's more to Jamison." She smiled. "I know you've come a long way. I want to show that in the picture."

Kerry crossed her hands over her chest.

"Well, there's the baby grand in the great room," I said. Kerry shot her eyes at me. She hated the piano. I'd always wanted a white baby grand, but Kerry thought it was gauche and in poor taste for the style of the house. She said it reeked of the nouveau riche, which I didn't know meant newly rich until I said it to Damien the next day. We fought about it for years and finally my mother bought it for me for my birthday (with money I'd placed in her savings). She had it delivered to the house with a note saying, "A baby for my baby," and Kerry said nothing else about the thing. She'd learned to play classical piano as a child, but I never once saw her sit down at the piano. And I couldn't play, so it just collected dust. But it sure looked good.

"That'll be great," Marial replied. When we walked into the room, she went on and on about how great the lighting was and how the piano added to the contemporary edge in the room. To this Kerry gave little more than a lifeless grin.

"So, before we take the pictures, let me do the interview," she went on. "I'll need some quotes from you first, Kerry."

Marial opened her bag and pulled out a little digital recorder, which she placed on top of the piano between her and Kerry.

"So, how do you feel about all of the attention Rake It Up is getting?" she asked.

"Oh," Kerry said, shifting her weight from one leg to the other. I listened just as intently as the little recorder. "It's kind of funny," she went on. A bead of sweat rolled down the back of her neck. "How so many people care about such a little company."

Marial and I must've recoiled at the same time. Her answer was clear and plain, but there was just something about the way she said "little" that made me feel like I was wearing the wrong tie. I was dressed like a big man, I'd gone with the black and gold jacquard print bowtie, but suddenly I felt small and my shoulders sank in a bit.

Kerry sounded as if she thought I was running some small-time, worthless company that only managed to bring home a few dollars. That couldn't be farther from the truth. She didn't have to want for anything. And it wasn't because of her parents' money. It was because of what I'd done. I'd made sure

that she could be independent and do whatever she wanted
without having her mother breathing down her back. Even if it
was just sitting in the house all day, having another woman do
the work she should've been doing. But I hadn't brought that
up. I didn't have the heart to do that. I only wanted to protect
Kerry, and I was beginning to see that I was the one who wasn't
being protected. I wasn't born a big shot and perhaps Kerry
would always see it that way—no matter how big or small my
company was.

"Well, it's not exactly a small company," Marial said, reading
off our numbers to Kerry as if she was a common housewife
who knew nothing of her husband's work. "It's a pretty big
deal. We have companies that are now modeling their business
plans on your husband's. A class at Wharton School of Business
is studying him right now."

"Really?" Kerry and I said at the same time.

The woman slid a stack of papers over to us that she'd been
holding in her hands. "Neither of you know?"

"Well, we just try to stay grounded," I said, but I was a bit
disappointed that she was now looking at me in the same surprised way she'd looked at Kerry. At first I'd been mad at
Kerry, but now I felt ashamed for not knowing. How could I
not know that? One of the top business schools in the nation
was studying my company and I didn't know? Why was I being
so indifferent to my own success? The pats? The waves? I
played it off during the interview, telling Marial that I was just
humble, but inside I was wondering if maybe part of my indif-
ference was coming from Kerry. Maybe if my only cheerleader
wasn't cheering me on, I simply couldn't see myself as the
MVP, making the winning shot.

Thanksgiving

"Girl, you look like you saw a ghost," Aunt Luchie said when I came in the kitchen door. I was steps ahead of Jamison and his mother, carrying Tyrian in my arms. "Did Jesus rise at that church?"

"And give me my grandbaby," my mother said, getting up from the table. I handed her Tyrian and headed out of the kitchen, toward the office where the computer was.

"Girl, you all right?" Aunt Luchie called behind me. I didn't say anything. I couldn't. I had to see it. I had to get to the computer to see if everything Coreen had said in the church was true. My heart was beating fast, my stomach was cramping, anger was boiling so hot within me that I couldn't even feel my hands. I didn't want anyone to say anything to me. I was tired of this. Just done. As I walked through the living room, I noticed that some of Jamison's family members had begun to arrive. Two of his cousins were sitting on the sofa in front of the television watching football, and his uncle was laid out on the chaise longue.

"Hey, Kerry," someone said.

I simply waved and walked into the office.

"Kerry," Jamison called from the kitchen. "Where did she go?"

"She seemed like she was in a rush," Aunt Luchie said to him. "Maybe she went to the bathroom."

I heard everyone exchange a barrage of greetings. My mother said hello to Jamison's mother. If only she knew what Coreen had told me. I was trying to hold it in, but I was about to crack.

"Oh, you should've seen Tyrian grinning at Pastor. He looked so cute," I heard Jamison's mother announce to everyone. "Pastor invited him back to the church to be the baby Jesus in the pageant next month."

I sat at the computer and tried, as I had many times since this whole thing started, to open Jamison's e-mail. I sat there, knowing I had to figure out the password this time. Numbers, names, dates all went through my head, none were right. And then, just like that, a word came to me that I'd been hearing for years, but had never tried. *T-Y-R-I-A-N* I typed, and after a prayer, I pressed the enter key. It worked.

My heart was pounding as I went through the e-mail. I heard talk coming from the living room and I could tell more people had shown up. It was a little after 12 PM and we were set to begin eating at 1 PM. Mostly Jamison's family agreed to come. We decided to keep it small, since it was our first time hosting. Only twelve people, enough to sit around the table in the dining room.

I wasn't nervous because of all of the people, though. I could not really care less about what anyone had to say or think at that point. My nervousness was stemming more from fear of what I was going to find. After Jamison and I talked, I reasoned that Coreen was just a fling. I'd been with Jamison for a long time and we'd never had anything like that. Coreen was nothing, I helped myself believe. And when he said it was over, I believed him. I trusted him. But now, here I was, stooping to breaking into my husband's e-mail, because the other woman had told me otherwise.

There was nothing in his "new" e-mail file. Just some stuff from work—employee's invoices, a request for service. I quickly scrolled down and opened the "sent" file. And there it was. The last e-mail he'd sent was to coreenissocute@yahoo.com.

In the outer world, the world my mind was no longer attached to, I heard people talking and the sound of the television in the family room. My mother was calling my name. Tyrian was crying. All of this was happening, but to my mind it was a haze, a soundtrack to a movie playing in another room, something someone else was watching. I was no longer a part of that world. I was in the office, reading e-mail after e-mail, dying and detaching along the way. My spirit sank deeper each time I clicked that mouse. How? Why? I almost wanted to believe it wasn't Jamison, my best friend, the person who knew me like no other, sending those e-mails, but there it was—his name at the end of each message, big and broad as the screen in front of me. I was falling to pieces again. And I wasn't sure I'd be able to get it together.

"Kerry." My mother scared me. She'd managed to walk into the office and make her way beside me at the computer without me even hearing her. "I've been calling you." She was carrying a receiving blanket in her hand. "Tyrian spit up on his clothes . . . do you have something you want . . ."

She trailed off, looking at the screen in front of me. My hands were at my sides. In my anger I had no energy to change the screen. I didn't want to hear her mouth, but the last thing I felt like doing was hiding anything anymore.

"What's this?" she asked, reading as she spoke. She dropped the blanket to the floor. "Kerry," she said, not even looking at me. It was my mother's serious voice. I hadn't heard it many times in my life, but when I did, I knew the woman meant what she was saying. She walked away and closed the door to the office, exhaling deeply as she turned back around to me. She came back to the desk and knelt down beside me in the chair. "Baby, I need you to hear me. I don't need you to say anything . . . I just need you to hear your mother right now. Can you do that?"

I was crying. I just nodded my head.

"I told you I'd be here for you right now. Didn't I?"

I nodded again. She'd called me after Aunt Luchie told her about the dinner and promised she'd come help me. That she wouldn't let me face Jamison's mother alone.

"And I am here," she added. "And your mother isn't going anywhere. And, Kerry, I need you to know this, because of what I need you to do for me." She swiveled the chair I was sitting in to face her and looked into my eyes.

"He lied to me," I said. "He lied."

"I know," she said, handing me the blanket from the floor to wipe my tears. "Take a deep breath," she went on. "Just let some of it out."

"I just don't understand, you know? After everything we talked about, how he could just do this to me," I said. "He's still in contact with her. Why?"

"I know, and you know your mother loves to say 'I told you so,' but now just isn't the time for all of that. Right now, we have to get you through this moment," she said. "And I know where your head is right now and what you must be feeling, but I also know that there's a house full of people out there. And your baby. I need you to . . ."

"I'm not going out there, Mother," I said. "I can't."

"Kerry, hear me out. This is your house and the first Thanksgiving you're having here. You have visitors and everyone is already getting ready to eat. They have all of this food everywhere. You can't just kick them all out, so you're just going to have to hold it together for a little while until people leave, then you and Jamison can handle what you need to handle."

"I can't, Mother," I cried.

"Yes, you can, baby," she said. "And I'll be there with you. I'll stay right with you. After everyone eats, we'll announce that you have a migraine and I'll get you upstairs and then start telling people to go."

I wiped my tears and tried to focus on what she was saying.

"But until we do that, I just need you to get yourself together and come outside and sit down. You don't even have to do anything. The food is ready and out and I'm going to change Tyrian's clothes. You can sit on the sofa and not speak to anyone. I'll tell people you're not feeling well. Okay?"

I nodded my head again.

"Baby, I know you're mad, but now is not the time. Not right now." She stood up and kissed me on the forehead the way my father used to do. "I'll get Luchie to help me get people to the table. Just get yourself together and come outside when you're ready."

When I finally got myself to a point where I thought I could last the forty minutes it would take to get through dinner, I made my way to the dining room where everyone was gathered, standing around a table full of food. Jamison was standing at the head of the table with his mother, aunt and uncle, cousins and their children beside him; my mother and aunt were on the the other side, leaving a chair for me there, directly opposite Jamison.

"There you are," Aunt Luchie said. "Thought we'd lost you."

"Yes she has a little headache," my mother said.

"Oh, baby, do you—" Jamison started, but when I looked at him, he stopped speaking, I guess noticing the lack of concern for anything he had to say on my face.

"Well, let's go on and bless the food so we can eat," his mother said as if it hadn't been announced that I was ill. If I was going to give anyone at the table a piece of my mind, it was her. I'd always known she was conniving and shady, but she'd just taken her drama to a new level. I looked in her direction to respond, but my mother caught me just before I tore into her.

"Okay, so I'll bless the food," my mother said sweetly.

"Um . . . no, I think that's the man of the house's job," his mother responded.

"Well, if we're going by tradition, it should be my sister Luchie because she's the oldest!"

"No," Aunt Luchie said, "it should be Jamison because it's his house."

Both my mother and I looked at Aunt Luchie with our eyes hot.

"What?" she asked.

"Look, I'll say the prayer. I can see everyone is very excited about this moment, so I don't want to prolong it," Jamison said smugly. He had no clue his little dream holiday was falling apart and about to punch the self-satisfied smile right off his face. "Let's join hands," he said as I balled up my fist. "Let every eye be closed."

"Lord, thank you for the food you have so generously provided my family. You have been good to me, better than I have been to myself." I didn't even bother to close my eyes. I just looked at Jamison as he spoke. "You have blessed me with a beautiful wife," he opened his eyes and looked at me. "Who I love very, very much. And a strong son who's growing every day. I'm so glad we could all come together, Lord, on this day, as it has been a dream of mine for years—to have my family together and be as one. We're thankful for all of these things and blessings to come. Amen."

Everyone else said Amen and opened their eyes, chatting as

they took their seat, but Jamison and I kept our eyes on one another.

"You okay?" he mouthed. I didn't respond. I just took my seat and nodded my head to Aunt Luchie when she told me that Tyrian was upstairs in his crib.

"So, as I was saying in the kitchen," Aunt Luchie went on, raising her voice so the rest of the people at the table could hear her, "we really need to support the city's efforts to keep Grady Hospital open. If it closes, where will all of those poor people go when they need good medical care? And where will our black doctors go to do their residencies?"

"Oh, please, Luchie," my mother said. "The problem is that the doctors from Morehouse Medical School have more choices of where they can do their residencies now. It's not like it was when we were coming up and they had limited options. Not every black person has to go through the old hospital."

"Well, I'm a Grady baby," Jamison's cousin said. "And I think it's important we keep the place open. We can't let it be shut down like the rest of everything that's black in the city. It seems like it's a part of that whole gentrification thing, if you ask me. They want the old, poor blacks out of the city, so they can bring some of the white money in."

"Exactly," Aunt Luchie said.

"Stop it. I get so tired of people always associating everything that's broken down and poor with black people. That's not a black hospital," my mother said. "It's an old, broken down building that was poorly managed and that's why it's being shut down, just like every other poorly run business in the ghetto."

"Oh, no," Aunt Luchie said.

"I mean that, Luchie. Black people need to stop making all these excuses and realize that if they don't run their businesses correctly, others will come in and get that money. That's the bottom line."

"Here we go," Dottie said. "Got to start putting down black people, like you're not black too."

"Excuse me?"

"Ladies," Jamison said, looking at me like I was supposed to stop the war that was brewing. I just looked straight at him as if I was deaf. If I even opened my mouth only one thing would come out. "Come on, we haven't even gotten through the first meal. Let's settle down. And we don't need to talk about black businesses failing because we have one that's doing very well right here in this house."

"That's right, baby," Dottie said, patting him on the back as she always did. "And that successful black business done bought this house and supports this family. And it's in no danger of breaking up. Right, baby?"

"Right, mama!"

She kissed him on the cheek.

"And it'll make sure it keeps my grandbaby good and healthy and only getting the best, so he can be the first doctor in the family," she said.

"Now that's a fine idea," Aunt Luchie said.

"No, we're not choosing his career for him," Jamison said. "We want him to be able to make that decision for himself. Right, Kerry?" He looked at me for a response. Everyone did.

"Um . . . hum . . ." I managed.

"Oh, he'll be a doctor. It's in his blood," Jamison's mother said. "Well from my side, anyway . . ."

"Excuse me?" my mother said.

"Well, Jamison is the only person 'round here bringing any money in," his mother went on, sipping the mimosa in front of her.

"Only person?" my mother said. "First, that business wouldn't be much of anything if it wasn't for my contacts and my daughter's work."

"Ladies," Jamison tried with his smug smile again, but it was too late.

"And if he's not a doctor, you can blame it on that silly name your son gave him. Tyrian? What kind of name is that. No one has ever had a doctor named Tyrian."

"No, you didn't!" Jamison's mother dropped her fork on the table.

"Yes, I did," my mother said. I couldn't believe her. She'd told me to keep my cool and she was clearly off her rocker. "If it wasn't for my daughter in this house, that boy would come just about as close to being a doctor as your son did."

"Well, he only stopped because your daughter didn't have the grades to do it. He was trying to protect her from you."

"Mama," Jamison said.

"You told her that?" I asked.

"No, Jamison," she started. "I'm tired of these people—"

"These people?" Aunt Luchie cut in.

"Coming in your house acting like they're doing you a favor by being here," his mother went on. "Like we ain't good enough."

"Oh, come on, let's stop it," Aunt Luchie said. "We have to get along for these two. We're family."

"Well, Lord help us if we're your family," his mother said. "I seen how you treat family."

"What's that supposed to mean?" my mother asked, getting up from her seat.

"Dropping your sick husband off in some home like you white or something. Whoever heard of black people just dropping people off to die with some folks they don't know? And it's only a walk and a stone's throw away from here. And you people only go see him once a year and spend the rest pretending he's dead."

"You take that back!" my mother cried.

"Mama," Jamison called to Dottie.

"No, I'm tired of keeping up this charade. That old man is sick and the only face he ever sees is one he don't even know."

"What's she talking about?" I asked, looking at Jamison.

"I—" Jamison tried, but she stepped in front of him at the head of the table.

"He been going to visit your father in the hospital every month. Taking him pictures of your selfish ass, but he can't even tell you because you're crazy."

"You what?" I asked. I got up. "You did what?" I stepped back from the table, feeling my knees turning to sand. "How? I never told you to . . ."

"Kerry, I just didn't know how to tell you," Jamison said, walking to me.

"Stay away from me," I said, stepping back farther.

"Kerry," Aunt Luchie called, but I turned and kept walking toward Tyrian's bedroom.

"Kerry, don't do this," Jamison said, following me up the steps. I could still hear the arguing going on in the kitchen.

"Don't say a thing to me, you jerk." I turned on the light in Tyrian's room and pulled his diaper bag from the door.

"I just wanted to keep him company. I was going to tell you."

"I'm leaving," I said. I wasn't even crying. I didn't know where I was going, but I was leaving and taking my child with me.

"Leaving? Because of this?"

"Yes." I picked up Tyrian's snowsuit and went to the crib.

"Kerry, you can't take him out. It's too cold." Jamison tried to get between me and the crib, but I pushed him out of the way and went and lifted Tyrian up to put the snowsuit on him.

"I can't let you," Jamison said.

"You touch me or my child, and one of us is going to the hospital and the other one is going to jail," I said sternly. I slid Tyrian into the snowsuit and picked him up.

"You're not in your right mind," he said.

I turned to the door and Aunt Luchie was standing in the doorway.

"Kerry, don't do this," she said, putting her hands out to take the baby.

"You don't know what's going on here." I started crying. Tyrian opened his eyes and looked up at me.

"He didn't mean to keep it from you; hear him out."

"Kerry, I—" Jamison touched my arm.

"Don't touch me!" I screamed. "Aunt Luchie, I'm asking you to move out of my way. I have to leave here now."

"Kerry," she tried again.

"I need to get out of here," I said furiously.

After she moved, I made my way down the stairs and found that most everyone, except for my mother and Jamison's mother, had left. And they were still arguing. I walked into the kitchen with everyone trailing behind me and picked up my car keys.

"Where's she going?" Jamison's mother asked. "It's too cold to take that baby out."

"Maybe we're going to Coreen's house," I said. And if words could cause a heart attack, I'd swear she was on her way to cardiac arrest. She didn't even respond. She just stood there with her mouth open, and her hand over her heart. "That's right," I added. "I know about her and what you tried to do, you old cow."

"What?" my mother said.

"What are you talking about?" Jamison asked.

"Oh, now you don't know? Your mother was the one who tried to hook you up with Coreen."

"Ridiculous," Jamison said. "She doesn't even know her."

I opened the kitchen door to head out to the car.

"She doesn't know about Coreen," Jamison said.

"I saw her." I slid Tyrian into his seat and closed the car door.

"Saw who?"

"Coreen. I saw her at the church today. And she told me everything, Jamison. About your fucking e-mails."

"It's over between us. I told you that."

"Really? Well, then why did you e-mail her yesterday?"

"Because she's sick. She really needs help."

"No, Jamison, I need your help. Your family needs your help." I climbed into the driver's seat. "And you weren't there for us. And then you go and see my father behind my back!"

"I was trying to protect you," he said.

"See, that's the thing you can't get, Jamison. I'm a grown woman. I don't need your protection anymore. I'm your wife. I'm your wife! How could you share all these things with your mother and not with me? Go behind my back for all these years? That's crazy. You're supposed to love me." I cried.

"That's what I've been doing all of these years, loving you."

"If you loved me you wouldn't have lied to me. I feel like a damn fool for trusting you and then going back to you only to have you do the same thing again. I feel so humiliated. I really resent you right now."

"You don't understand what's happening, Kerry," he said, holding on to the door.

"No, I don't care what's happening," I said. "The only thing I care about is my baby and my life, and that's it from now on."

"Jamison, I'm so sorry," his mother said, rushing up behind him. "I didn't know she was pregnant then. I thought I was doing what was best for us."

"*Us*, Mama?" Jamison said, turning away from me. "How could you even think of such a thing?"

"I'm sorry," she cried.

Jamison exhaled deeply and turned back to me.

"That's all you're going to do?" I asked. "She tried to ruin our marriage and all you can do is take a deep breath? God, Jamison, grow up."

I turned the ignition.

"Where are you going?" my mother said, running out of the house. Tyrian started crying in the backseat.

"Mother, stay out of it," I said. "I'm leaving."

"Leaving?" Jamison's mother said.

"Mama, just go in the house," Jamison said firmly. "I'll deal with you later."

She backed off, clearly surprised at Jamison's anger.

"I'm sorry, Kerry," Jamison said to me.

"I know you are. But it's not good enough anymore."

The Affair

When I was about seven, I remember my pastor saying in church one Sunday that the devil won't ever look like the devil when he comes into your life. And this was the perfect time to hear such a statement—at that time I'd heard my mother talk about the devil so many times as some evil, dark, floating man, that in my head he looked like a werewolf or something out of a horror flick. The devil had horns on his head, thick red skin, a tail, and razor sharp teeth that he'd use to cut into my stomach. But when pastor said that the devil had no one image, and that when he came it would likely be an attractive or familiar face, I went out looking for the devil in everything. Was my teacher a devil when she gave me a B? Was my mother a devil when she made me carry food stamps to the store?

As I grew, I realized that was an unlikely way of detecting and outing the devil. In fact, I realized that I seldom knew when I'd had a "close encounter" until the devil's deed had already been done. Now, I don't mean this to say that Coreen was or is the devil. The situation was quite the contrary. She was a beautiful woman who had little connection to the devil other than her human frailties, which I share. What I mean to bring up here instead is those situations, those evil situations

that seem wholly innocent as they are beginning or progress-
ing, but when you come out on the other end, you're left saying, "That wasn't nothing but the devil." Now whether you or
the devil is the person involved in the situation is entirely up
for question. Either way, something evil transpired.

When I got the e-mail, that first e-mail from Coreen, it was
just weeks after the *Black Enterprise* story ran in the magazine. I was feeling pretty good about my business and excited
by all of the accolades I was receiving from random people in
the street. I'd be out at lunch and someone would walk up to
me and say they'd seen me somewhere before and some people
would ask for my business card. I was sailing on top of the
world and wanted never to come down. When I did come down,
though, was when I'd get home. The first time Kerry saw the
article, she complained about the baby grand and how she'd
felt Marial dismissed her and pointed out that she didn't
include any of her quotes. She never once said how great it was
that I was in the magazine nor offered to have it framed, as I
thought she would. Instead, she complained and the only positive thing I heard from her was that my tie looked nice.

This, I tried to take without a bruised ego. I knew that
Kerry was having a hard time. She'd started putting on weight
and I was beginning to suspect that she was tired of simply sitting at home all day, waiting for me to come home. She seemed
unfulfilled and unhappy, but I honestly didn't know how to handle her in that way. I didn't want to make her angry by
suggesting that she go back to school, and I didn't want to
make her sad by pointing out all of the great things that were
happening to me. Instead, I chose to be silent to protect two
things: the quiet I enjoyed by not fighting with my wife, and
the sex I'd get by keeping the peace.

I thought this was fine. Not okay, but fine. We'd had rough
spots in the ten-plus years we'd been together and sometimes,

fine was all I'd get. Fine led to okay and then okay led to good.
But I never wanted to just be bad, and I was afraid that pointing out her flaws and my achievements would make things bad
on her part and the result—a bunch of arguments and no sex—
would be bad on my part. These two bads only led to one place
with my other friends—divorce court. And I never wanted to
be there. I wasn't in marital bliss, but I loved Kerry with every
piece of my being and I never wanted to change our relationship.

Then I got Coreen's e-mail. And the e-mail, which was so
innocent, turned to us linking up. Now, I'd been around attractive women before, but Coreen just had something about her—
the way she looked at me, the way she seemed to pay special
attention to herself when I was coming around. At first, I
thought I'd get over these things, and this was long before
anything really happened between us, but then the way she
spoke to me, always saying nice things and asking me for advice—hell, in my mind, that moved her from being cute to
being gorgeous, amazing, and in the face of Kerry's lack of reaction to me, everything I'd ever want in life. See, Coreen
never seemed to want much, and the little I gave her, she went
on and on about how great it was. If I found an hour in the day
to spend with her, she'd make me a meal and bring it out to
wherever I was. Then when she'd get there, she'd say how she
felt so special to be eating with me and was happy that I had
any time to spend with her. I hadn't had praise like this from
Kerry in years. Our Mexican fiestas had long turned into her
being afraid to stain the antique sofa she'd ordered from Paris.
And while she often came to eat lunch with me, she'd request
lunch at a fine restaurant or country club where we'd either
work to get connections or discuss the ones we had. Compared
to that, Coreen was a breath of fresh air.

I'm not stupid enough to believe that this made her a better mate for me than my wife. Or that I had a better relationship with her than I had with Kerry. I know that my main attraction to Coreen—other than that she was fine as hell—was that she was new. See, Kerry had been there for me from the time when I wore sneakers from Payless and ate Hamburger Helper every night for dinner. While both she and I enjoyed talking about those days and I loved her for sticking by my side, at times that seemed to get in the way of her being able to see the new me. She knew I had faults. She knew I worried about my company and sometimes didn't sleep at night. She'd been in my mother's house and had seen me cry more than ten times about how poor I'd grown up. Sometimes I felt that to Kerry I was a man, her man, but still a man with flaws and cracks. Coreen couldn't see any cracks. If I didn't know something, she'd laugh it off and bring up something else. And if I didn't want to talk about the next topic, she'd bring up something else or just sit there quiet until I started speaking. She depended completely on me. Now this wasn't exactly the kind of woman I wanted to spend the rest of my life with, but damn, it felt good to have her around after a hard day. Someone not connected. Not judgmental. Not wanting or expecting anything but me. It felt good.

"Nah, dog, don't do it," Damien said when I told him about Coreen over a beer. Damien had been involved with so many women since he'd married Marcy that we'd stopped memorizing their names—they'd have nicknames that described them: "Thick Ass," "Baby Mama," "Big Titties"—so I was very surprised at his reaction. I didn't even tell him about Coreen at first, but after we had sex, I felt really bad and thought that talking about it with the fellas would make me feel better. After ten years, I was finally in their club—married and dating. I wasn't ready for Damien to tell me to back down. I felt bad enough.

"I already did it," I said.

"Well, break it off now and never, ever tell Kerry. Just stop it now," Damien said, sipping his beer with a contemplative look in his eyes. "Once you start that shit in your marriage, there's no way to get rid of it. You know? Sometimes I think the only reason I been doing it all this time is because I did it that first time. Once Marcy found out, she became so angry and shut off from me that I had to go somewhere else to find comfort. Shit, a brother needed a hug."

"Well, why didn't you go to Marcy?"

"She'd hug me, and then sometimes even kiss me, but the shit wasn't the same. I could see in her eyes that she resented me for what happened. And that shit hurt because I knew I couldn't fix it. And I couldn't talk about it with her, so I went and talked to someone else. Then Marcy got so mad that she started cheating. Then I did it again to get back at her for that. And here we are now."

"Well, if you know it won't ever be fixed, why not just leave?" I asked. I was surprised. Damien was my dog, but we never really spoke about his feelings about his wife and the only reason I knew Marcy had other men was because Kerry let little stuff slip every now and again.

"Shit, I ain't leaving that woman," Damien chuckled. "That's my wife. And I ain't breaking up my family either. Have some other man raising my daughter? All up in my crib. Hell no." He paused and took another sip of his beer. "Marcy and I was just made for each other. I can't leave her."

"Can't live with her; can't live without her."

"Exactly," he said. "And I know if I feel that way about Marcy, you'd be messed up if Kerry left you. You been drinking her tittie juice since I introduced you two at that Valentine's dance."

"Kiss my ass." I took a playful swing at him.

"Brother been whiiiipppeed!" He laughed and took a swing back at me. "But really, man. I'm telling you this because I know what's out here. Just leave that shit alone. I don't even want to hear about this broad. Go home tonight and tell her to leave you alone."

"What if I can't?"

"No such thing. You're a Morehouse man."

We gave each other dap and just like that, I was in my car and on my way home to end things with Coreen. Damien was a lot of things, but he wasn't stupid. He was one of the smartest people I knew and I had to respect his opinion. And it didn't help that the little voice inside me was saying the same thing. "Run like hell, brother," the voice kept saying. And now Damien had put it on full blast. He was right. The whole thing was exciting and the sex felt good, but that feeling of emptiness I felt inside from lying to and cheating on my wife when she hadn't done anything made me want to vomit.

Kerry was sitting on the couch in the living room when I walked in. The lights were all off and when I switched a lamp on, she turned to me and I could see that her eyes were red. I knew she'd found out then. She'd been suspicious and asking me all kinds of crazy questions for weeks, and now she'd found out. Had Coreen called the house? Had she called? Was she waiting in the bathroom?

"Kerry, I can explain," I said, rushing over to her.

"No, I want to go first," she said.

"But it's nothing you did," I said.

"No, it's what we both did." She opened her arms and wrapped them around me tight. "We're pregnant," she whispered in my ear.

"What?"

"A baby," she cried. "We're pregnant."

"What!"

She hugged me tighter and even in my disbelief I started crying too. We'd been talking about it, but Kerry and I hadn't had sex in weeks. She'd been cranky, had some kind of flu and was feeling bloated, so I had to take up residence on the other side of the bed. We weren't exactly working on a baby. But damn if the news didn't sound and feel good. I was going to be a daddy. This was just what I needed.

"What is it?" I asked.

"We don't know yet, silly," Kerry laughed and kissed me on the cheek and I swear it was the softest kiss she'd given me in months. It was so soft and real that we caught eyes and kissed each other hard on the lips.

"I love you," she said.

"I love you too, Kerry."

After we called our mothers, we sat down in bed together and Kerry was moving full speed ahead as usual with her planning. I tuned out somewhere when she was talking about ordering a crib from some store in Los Angeles. Something about a valance and a celebrity stroller and I was sitting there nodding, but not really listening. While I was still excited about the baby, my mind had gone back to remembering what I was doing and where I was headed when I walked in the door. I was going to break it off with Coreen to save my marriage and now I had more reason. I needed to save my family.

When Kerry got up to take her nightly shower, I went into the office to call Coreen. I picked up the phone, but every time I did, I realized that I had nothing to say that would sound right. Any way I said it, I would sound like a heartless jerk. One thing I knew was that women always claimed they wanted to hear the truth, but when it came out and it wasn't in their favor, they hated it and usually flipped out. Now Coreen hadn't shown me that side of her personality just yet, but some of the stories she told me about her husband and her past suggested that she was a bit more of a firecracker than Kerry. Coreen was a sweet girl, but she was also very emotional and had a temper. But I had to do what I had to do. Call me a punk; call me a buster, but sitting in that office alone with the sound of Kerry singing "Rock-a-Bye-Baby" in the shower in the background, I decided there was only one way out. I had to end the thing quick and clean. I decided to write her an e-mail. I knew it was wrong, but shit, she wasn't my wife. I didn't owe her anything. We both agreed that there'd be no strings attached. She said she was a big girl.

Coreen wasn't exactly okay with the news about the baby, but I figured she'd get over it. In fact, I forwarded most of her e-mails to Damien and he said they were all pretty normal for a breakup. He said not to respond and just let it go. I listened to him, but the messages kept going. Every day. Every night. There was either a phone message or e-mail from Coreen. And then they started getting sadder and sometimes just dark. She accused me of lying to her. Said we were meant to be together and that Kerry was no good for me. That she would wait for me didn't even care that I was married. It sounded so crazy. I mean, I liked her, but love was a big word I reserved for one person. And her feelings for me just sounded too deep. I didn't know what they were based on. We'd had laughs and sex less than a handful of times. I hadn't given her any romantic gifts or claimed I was doing anything with her other than what was happening. I did complain about Kerry from time to time, but I never said I was going to leave her. Sometimes I felt like maybe Coreen's feelings for me, or what she'd claimed she'd had for me, were from somewhere else. That maybe she was struggling with losing her husband or the fact that her life wasn't at the point where it needed to be. I actually e-mailed her that one time, breaking my rule of silence, but Coreen ignored it. She just kept saying I was lying and that I really wanted to be with her but I was scared to leave Kerry and wanted to be there for my son. Damien laughed and said he had so many girls claiming he was a liar when he said he didn't want to be with them that it was pitiful. He said to stand my ground and not contact her.

But then, one late night I got an e-mail from Coreen that scared the shit out of me. It was maybe two, three, or four nights before Tyrian was born and she sounded like she'd just given up hope on life. This both worried and frightened me. I didn't want anything to happen to her, and I was afraid she was going to do something to herself. I didn't even want to mention the word *suicidal*, but damn if the letters didn't sound that way. Her anger had gone from me to the world. And she was talking about checking out altogether.

I read the e-mail a few times. I didn't want to respond. Kerry was acting very erratic with her hormones and I didn't want to do anything to piss her off. But then I kept having these visions of Coreen hanging from a rope in her kitchen with some note about me leaving her on the table and I knew I couldn't just sit back and do nothing. I didn't know much about Coreen. I had no way of knowing how to handle her emotions, but I knew I couldn't let something happen to her when I was a part of her pain.

I called. But she didn't answer. I called again. No answer. Then I decided to write. I figured she would at least respond to that. But nothing. The silence was killing me. And walking around the house all day, all I could think of was that body swinging in the kitchen. Her giving up and my being involved.

It was after 7 PM on Thursday when I decided to roll over to Coreen's house. I hadn't heard anything from her and I had to make sure everything was okay. When I got there, her car was in the driveway, but the house was dark. It was late, and every other house on the block had a light on but hers. I tried her cell from the driveway, but there was no answer. Then I went to the door and peeked inside. I couldn't see anything, but I knocked anyway. I stood there for five minutes knocking, then

I decided that maybe I was overreacting. The girl could've been on vacation for all I knew. Maybe she'd moved on to another man. Good for her. I headed back to my car, ready to leave. But then I heard her voice.

"Jamison," she said. I turned to find her standing in the doorway naked. I ran over to Coreen to block her from the street and push her into the house.

"What are you doing?" I asked, noticing that her eyes were red, her face was sunken in and her skin was ashy. She looked like she hadn't eaten in days. "Get in the house. I've been calling you. I was worried."

"I've been here," she said weakly. "I've just been thinking about things."

"Are you okay?" I sat her on the couch and headed into the bedroom to get a sheet or something to wrap around her. When I pulled it from the bed, a bottle of pills rolled from beneath the pillow. It fell to the floor and pills scattered everywhere. I walked over to see that they were sleeping pills.

When I came back into the room, Coreen was crying and rocking herself on the couch.

"I love you, Jamison, and I can't let you go," she cried.

"Coreen," I said, sitting down beside her. I didn't know exactly what I was going to say next, but I knew I had to say something. Something to comfort her. "I told you how I feel. But I don't want you to be like this. I want more for you."

"There's no more for me," she said. "I can't seem to do anything right. Duane died and now you left me. I can't get anything right. I'm just going to die. That's it. Just stay here in this house and die." Her crying turned to a sad grieving. She fell into my arms and I began to rock her back and forth.

"There's much more to life," I said. "Your career. What about school? You seemed so excited about that."

"I'll just fuck it up."

"You won't know until you try."

She was quiet. I wiped her tears with a piece of the bed sheet. "Coreen, you're a beautiful woman. You can have and be anything."

"But not you," she said.

"Not me."

We sat there on the couch talking like that until the last bit of sun in the sky set and the evening turned to night. Every time I seemed to lift her spirits, she'd turn another emotional corner and start crying again and ask why we couldn't be together. I wanted so badly to look at the time. I knew Kerry had to be looking for me. But I was dealing with life and death. I didn't want to risk one for the other. And I didn't know what else to do. Every time I asked Coreen if there was someone I could call, she'd get mad and start crying again.

I finally got her to agree to take a shower and get some clothes on. I thought this, along with some soup, would at least make her feel good enough to get back into bed. And then I could talk to her reasonably and get her to a hospital or something. But when she stood up, it was clear she wouldn't make it in the shower alone. The girl was weak.

I carried her into the bathroom and stood there in the shower with her, fully dressed, washing her body with my hands as she cried. It was one of the most sobering moments in my life. I realized at that moment that what I had done in my selfishness was ruin a piece of someone else's life. I didn't know if most of what Coreen was going through was about me, but I'd gotten her to that place somehow. Damien was right that the affair would ruin my marriage, but he'd forgotten to mention what it would do to the other woman.

When I got Coreen into the bed, I took off my shirt and pants and went into the kitchen to make her some soup. I looked at my cell phone. It was already 12 AM.

I carried the soup into the room and fed Coreen myself. She seemed to brighten in the face immediately as that heat hit her.

"You're a good man," she said. I was sitting beside her on the bed in my boxers and a T-shirt.

"Thank you," I said, handing her the bowl. As she ate, I cleaned up the pills from the floor and stashed them in my jacket pocket, so I could take them with me when I left. I brought up the topic of counseling, saying I would find someone, and she finally sounded as if she was willing to give it a try. She admitted that she did actually miss Duane and that she'd never dealt with his death. She'd gone to all of the memorial services and accepted the calls and concerns from everyone, but in all that time, she felt like she just had to be strong. She had to put her best foot forward because with all the attention, she felt like all eyes were on her. When she was finally ready to talk to someone, she turned around and realized that there was no one there. Just her and the house she'd bought with the money from Duane's death.

"I know you're going to leave," she said. "But I just want you to hold me a little while before you go, until I fall asleep."

"Coreen—" I tried, but she cut me off.

"I just need someone to hold me," she said. "Just for right now. I promise it's nothing."

It had to have been at least 2 AM by then, but her request was so simple. So easy. I could see that she could get better, and she'd already opened up and agreed to get help. I couldn't turn her down. I climbed into the bed and rocked Coreen to sleep. It was peaceful and quiet. And I knew in my heart that while my part in her life was over, she was beginning something else. Soon, I drifted off to sleep as well, but I was awakened by a knock at the door. Kerry.

PART THREE

Death

*"For I [Paul] am now ready to be offered,
and the time of my departure is at hand."*

—Paul,
2 Timothy 4:6

E-MAIL TRANSMISSION

TO: coreenissocute@yahoo.com
FROM: dablackannanicole@yahoo.com
DATE: 11/27/07
TIME: 8:09 AM

Coco! Where are you? I've been calling you all weekend and when I came in this morning I noticed that your stuff was cleared out of your desk. Lori said you resigned last week. Why didn't you tell me you were leaving? I hope everything is OK. Just give me a call when you can and know that I'm here for you.

Anna

What Lies Can Do

Cheating is bad. Cheating is really bad. But, in the beginning, I think what was worse about Jamison's cheating wasn't the actual act, it was the lying.

Jamison, who championed himself for being a hardened man from southwest Atlanta, was mostly a creature of habit. He did things in a certain way and was no fan of change from his normal schedule. I fell in love with him for that. In college, Jamison microwaved Hamburger Helper, saying it was the best meal in town on Friday night and I only needed to try it. I protested, but Jamison ate this meal every Friday night. And even after we graduated he still craved the mushy treat. So, on cold Fridays when I knew we'd be sitting at home in front of the television, I learned to make Hamburger Helper and have it waiting for him when he got in from work. Now, one Friday night, just days before Jamison was supposed to be beefing up a proposal for a big contract that would take our services to a string of law offices throughout Tennessee, I had a pot of Hamburger Helper (made with ground sirloin and extra cheese) waiting on the stove for Jamison.

"Oh, I'm going out with Damien tonight," he said when I offered to make him a plate. "I'll be back later."

"Damien?"

"Yeah, we're going to have some beers," he replied.

"Well, then you need to put something in your stomach," I said, getting up from the table to get the plate.

"No." He stopped me. "We'll eat too. Just put the food in the refrigerator and I'll get some when I get back."

He kissed me on the forehead and left the room.

Now we'd been married for a long time, and not once had Jamison been caught in a lie or cheated on me, so I had no reason to worry or be suspicious. But in those years, I'd also "learned" my husband. He never turned down food. Not even if I'd made it. So, while suspicion was the farthest thing from my mind, when he nonchalantly rejected that plate, my ears immediately raised. Not only was it strange for Jamison, but I'd been to Pilates with Marcy earlier that afternoon and I knew that Milicent had her first fencing class on Saturday at 8 AM. Damien was so excited about the class because he'd fenced as a boy and he'd broken out all of his old gear on Thursday night, claiming he was going to "teach Mili the basics" on Friday night before the first practice. Now this could've changed, but the odds were small.

These kinds of questionable exchanges occurred in our kitchen for weeks. And after a while, Jamison seemed tired of my constant interrogation and actually tried to turn the thing around on me. He said I needed to be more trusting and made it seem as if I was going crazy with my suspicions. Now I was going a bit crazy; I can admit that. He'd been lying to me and I just knew. I didn't need him to admit anything.

The lie was beginning to pull us apart. I didn't want Jamison to even touch me. I stopped having sex with him, claiming I was sick and feeling bloated. Then, the funny thing was that I actually did start feeling sick and bloated. I was vomiting during the day and my stomach felt queasy all night. I might've thought I was pregnant, but we hadn't had sex in a while and vomiting after lunch didn't qualify as "morning sickness"—I'd later be proven wrong.

Things got serious when I finally told Marcy about my suspicions and she volunteered to help me follow Jamison during one of his nights out, which were now a part of his regular routine. We decided to rent a car and follow him one night. I felt bad for doing it, but Marcy kept telling me that if I didn't do something I'd really go crazy. And there was no need accusing a man of doing something when he was doing nothing. "He could be doing nothing," she'd said. "But he could be doing something. You need to know either way." I said maybe I could just ask him again and she frowned. "When most men cheat, they lack the ability to tell the truth," she said. "And not because they don't want to—but because they don't want to risk hurting and losing you. The only time they'll tell the truth is when you catch them in the act, and even then, they might claim the woman in the bed is their aunt."

So, there we were, in a rented car, driving behind Jamison, on our first stakeout. It was exciting and dramatic. And the whole time I was nervous and scared, but also, like Marcy had said, ready to confirm what I already knew. But this changed when we ended up outside Coreen's house. I'd pat Jamison on the back ten million more times, kiss him more, have sex with him every night, even make nice with his mother, to make this go away. But there it was, in front of my eyes, my worst nightmare, a reality. It wasn't a lie. It was true. True indeed. How would I ever be able to come back to loving Jamison from that? That was a Hamburger Helper recipe I simply didn't have.

Refugee Camp

From the antique mahogany-encased Victrola in the living room, to the dramatic magenta French lace curtains hanging from ceiling to floor in the formal dining room, every day in Aunt Luchie's house was like living on the set of an old '30s movie. It was beautiful and timeless, unchanged in a world that seemed to always look for change.

When I was a child, my father brought me to Aunt Luchie's house most Saturdays. She had a great blues record collection, and he'd sit in her den listening to records most of the afternoon as Aunt Luchie let me play with her makeup and jewelry at the vanity in her bedroom. It was a great weekly journey for both of us. My mother hated the blues and constantly came into the room to turn down the music whenever my father listened to records at home, and I wasn't even allowed in her bedroom, let alone to sit at her vanity and play with her jewelry and makeup.

Tyrian and I moved in with Aunt Luchie after two days of staying at a hotel where he'd gotten his first cold. I swore that nothing had changed in that woman's house since the last time my father took me there. From the over-red lipstick lying on the right-hand side of the vanity top to my grandmother's pearls sitting in a tightly spun circle on her dresser, everything was in its place. It was as if Aunt Luchie wanted time to stand still inside that place. And this was a surprise, coming from a woman who was so full of life.

After putting Tyrian down for his afternoon nap, I went into the living room to find Aunt Luchie reading a book, as she sipped on a tall glass of brandy. We'd been staying there for about two weeks and I'd come to realize that whenever Aunt Luchie wasn't out trying to save the world and my mother with her bare hands, this was her afternoon routine.

"Whew," she said when I walked into the room. She slammed the book closed and slid it on the coffee table sitting beside the sofa. "That was a good book."

"You were done with it?" I asked. "You seemed like you were at the beginning. No more than halfway through."

"I know, but the story was over for me, so it's done."

"You're funny," I laughed. "You don't have to stop reading because I came in; I can go to my bedroom and watch television."

"Please. Who needs to read the entire story? I've read enough of them and seen enough of life to know how stories end."

"And how is that?"

"The big gamble is taken and the protagonist either gets what she wants or not," she said, sipping on her brandy.

"But don't you want to know what she gets?" I asked.

"I prefer to make that up for myself," she said. "I don't like other people choosing fate for me. Sometimes I want a sad ending; sometimes I want a happy ending."

"I know what you mean." I walked over to the window and looked outside to see two children playing in the street. Aunt Luchie's house was just down the street from the Atlanta University Center. It was a gorgeous Queen Anne–style home with magnificent fireplaces and hardwood floors throughout. She'd bought it with her inheritance after she graduated from Spelman. My mother wasn't exactly excited that she'd used the money for that. She had enough money to buy a home right beside my mother. But Aunt Luchie's love with Red blossomed on the campus of the AUC, as he was a senior at Clark Atlanta when they started dating her freshman year. He was in the jazz band and caught her eye the first week of school. She was in love and felt that she'd always be tied to that place.

"So how will your story end?" Aunt Luchie asked.

"What?" I turned and looked at her.

"Your story with Jamison."

"I guess I don't know," I said, walking over to sit on the sofa beside her. I'd been trying not to think about it. It just hurt too much to consider my marriage being over.

"Well, there are only two options—either you stay or you go. You just have to decide if you will take the gamble."

"Well, it's the gamble that I'm worried about. Taking Jamison back after this. . . . I don't know."

"So, you're just going to walk away?" she asked.

"I didn't say that."

"You know, there was a time when folks didn't just get up and leave over things like this. They stayed and figured it out— worked it out, no matter what. It was a disgrace for a black family to fall apart," she said. "We'd fought so hard to stay together during slavery, only to have people pull us apart, so when we were free, being with family was a sign of strength."

"Well, times have changed," I said.

"Just because times have changed doesn't mean they should've. You know that boy loves you. He's done wrong, yes, but he still loves you and I know you love him. Whatever happened with that woman may not be what you think. You never know what all was going on."

"Please, Aunt Luchie," I said. "I don't want to think about them right now." I sat back on the sofa, afraid I'd hurt her feelings. "And since we're talking about the past not changing, what about this place? Why haven't you changed anything here in like twenty years?"

"I don't know," she said before swallowing the rest of the brandy. "I just kind of like these things here . . . the way they are. The way they were when my Red was here."

"Do you think he'll ever come back?"

"Oh, he sends me flowers—"

"Flowers?" I recoiled. "I thought he was off in Paris living it up in love with some French white woman."

"Yeah, he is," she smiled. "But he still sends me flowers for my birthday every year. White lilies." Her eyes went off to an old place. "The flower he bought me when we were together."

"Well, do you think he'll come back?" I asked excitedly. "Maybe that's why you keep your place the same . . . like a part of the romance when he returns."

"Oh, he's a grandfather now. Been married a long time. He's not going anywhere. That's done now," she said. "I've accepted that ending."

"Oh," I sighed. "That's so sad."

"Yeah, it's amazing how love will make you either accept the stone cold reality or run away from it," she said. "Now, I just accepted that my only love was gone. I have never looked at another man like I looked at Red and that's fine by me. That's just the way love used to be back in the day. You didn't try to fill someone's shoes with someone else who clearly couldn't fit them. But your mother . . ."

"What about her? You think she's still upset about my father being sick?"

"You ever wonder why your mother is so hateful when it comes to your relationship with Jamison?" she asked. "Your mother can't accept the love you have until she finds her way back to her own," she said as I poured her another glass of brandy. "Now, she never wanted your father to go away to that war. She told

him not to go, said she'd heard they were killing men over there—
poisoning their minds with gas and the government was sending them back home and not telling the families what happened."

"I know," I said, getting back up from the couch to go look
out the window. I'd heard this in bits and pieces in the past
whenever my mother got upset during the holidays or after our
annual trip to see my father. She'd cry and retell how she'd told
him not to go, but he was too stubborn.

"Your mother, she loved that man more than you could ever
understand—even as their child. If ever the sun did rise and set
on a man's temples, it did the day your mother met Eldridge
that afternoon when our mother introduced him as her escort
for the debutante ball. Lord, all Janie could talk about was Eldridge this and Eldridge that," she said laughing. "And it wasn't
so funny back then because my bed was only three feet away
from hers and I had to hear her talk about him. Now, we had a
big old house and plenty of rooms, but your grandfather was so
old school, he'd always say the only privacy we'd ever see was
when we got our own houses—that's how old folks back in the
day would keep young people from getting beneath the sheets
together—if you know what I mean."

She winked and we both started laughing.

"Anyway, Eldridge promised Thirjane that he'd come back
to her in one piece from Desert Storm. He wasn't going there for
combat or anything. He was too old for that and his rank would
keep him far from much combat. But when he came back . . . he
just was never the same. And your poor mother had to watch
his mind slip away from him one day at a time. I was there with
her in that house every day, watching him forget and forget and
get angry and lash out, until finally he just lost it altogether
and your mother had to let him go. And when he left, when she
had to send him away, I think she also lost a piece of herself. You
both did."

"Both of us?" I asked, turning from the window.

"I don't see you running to visit your father. Maybe it's just as hard for you as it is for Thirjane."

"I go with my mother every year," I said.

"Child, it's not like visiting a grave. He isn't dead. Just gone from his mind. And that's why he shouldn't be alone. Maybe if you went more, he'd find his way back," she said. "Maybe that's why Jamison goes over there to see him."

"Oh, don't defend him now. That's just more of his bull."

"Is it? Or is it just him being the man you married? Trying to protect you and the people you love?"

I looked down at the slippers I was wearing and kicked at the floor.

"He had no right," I said. "That's my father. If he wanted to see him, he could've asked me."

"You don't think I want Thirjane to go see him? Eldridge was my friend too," she said. "But if both she and you are acting like he's dead and standing on it, what can we do but accept it and let you live? I don't want to hurt your mother's heart no more than it's already been hurting. She's my baby sister and I just want to protect her. Maybe Jamison was just doing the same for you."

The Color of My Parachute

"**Y**ou need to have an appointment for that. Take a number and have a seat."

Those were the two sentences the woman sitting at the front desk at the Department of Social Services seemed to say to everyone who approached. She never changed her indifferent tone, no matter what they said, and always responded with one of those two rehearsed lines I'd imagined she'd been saying for years. When it was my turn, I was determined to break the pattern, but also afraid to appear uncooperative. She wasn't exactly a peaceful-looking woman.

After Aunt Luchie and I spoke about my father, I told her about the effect seeing McKenzie had on me and how I'd thought about opening a facility to help women like her. She thought it was a fantastic idea and immediately went through her mental Rolodex of all of the people who could help me get it started. I took her suggestions but I kept imagining McKenzie in my mind, standing there with those shopping carts, and something in me said I needed to do this on my own. No connections, no tea and crumpets, making this another rich-people-doing-something-for-poor-people thing. I wanted to do more. To really get involved. I was pumped up and ready to act. Together, we decided that it might be a good idea for me to go over to Social Services to see if there was even a need for the outreach program I was talking about. Aunt Luchie volunteered to watch Tyrian and I set out to find answers.

Standing in line, listening to the lack of commitment the front desk woman was exuding, I was sure it wouldn't be that easy.

"I'm here to get information about the—" I started, but she cut me off. I just knew she was about to tell me to make an appointment or take a piece of paper and sit my behind down for five hours.

"Internship?" she said, looking me up and down as if I wasn't even supposed to be there.

"Internship?" I asked.

"Here's the application," she handed me an old clipboard with a piece of paper on it. "Fill it out and bring it back. Mr. Duncan, the director, will call you in to meet with him."

Afraid to say another word, I took the clipboard and went to find a seat in the packed waiting area.

I sat down and looked over the application. Trying to concentrate above the growing pitch of screaming children seemingly running only around my seat, I learned that the department was looking for interns to volunteer to assist them during the new year. The internship was for students and professionals interested in a career in social services. It wouldn't pay, but it would give participants the opportunity to see what social services was all about and actually assist in certain cases. It was a part-time commitment that would last five months. It seemed like the perfect opportunity had fallen and was sitting right in my lap on top of a clipboard that someone had apparently chewed on. It was just what I was looking for—well, not exactly, but it seemed like a great first step to get where I needed to be. It would be a good thing to actually have some experience in the field before I put any money behind my project. In the meantime, I could see what other special services were offered and decide how mine would be different. I was so excited, I wanted to jump up and hug one of the screaming children passing by. It was the very first time in a long time that I felt like I had the potential to be a part of something that was of my own making. I filled out the application and anxiously handed it back to the woman. Even she looked more friendly with my new attitude.

"Have a seat," she said. "Mr. Duncan is seeing someone right now. So, he'll probably call you in a minute."

The minute turned to forty, and like most of the other women in the waiting area, I was sitting there looking weary and worn out. The noise was too loud, the air was too stifling, and the seat was so hard I thought it was becoming a part of my own behind. In a minute I would have to create a social service project to get myself out of this seat. I was trying my best to keep my mind on my goal and not lose my excitement, but I was sinking fast. I was about to break my diet and get a bag of potato chips out of the snack machine when someone called my name.

Mr. Duncan was an old, bald Irish man whose years tackling issues facing the poor seemed to leave him a bit battered but wiser for his journey. Instead of asking me a bunch of questions about my intentions for working in social services (which was a good thing, because I hadn't intended on anything before I'd gotten the application an hour ago), he told me what I might face being employed there and informed me that this was no job for someone simply interested in pushing papers and even wishing to save the world. "It's hard work," he said. "And you have to know when to pull back or it'll go home with you. Many of us do take it home, thinking we can save everyone, but then we only lose ourselves and burn out. We have good people here, but we all have to learn where to draw the line." He then looked over my application, saying he'd had many Spelman graduates come through the office and knew I'd be a quality intern because of this. "Now you're a bit older than the other applicants. Any reason why you've decided to come here right now? I see your last position was in administration," he said eyeing me.

"Well," I started, "I just had a baby and . . ." I was nervous and had to stop to catch my breath. All I could hear in my head was Jamison asking why I hadn't gone back to med school, visualize in my mind the stack of envelopes, the rejections, the look of disappointment on my mother's face. I was frozen. I couldn't fail again. I couldn't lose another thing I cared about.

"Take your time," I heard Mr. Duncan say and I knew I must've looked like I was about to cry but I couldn't. I took a deep breath and imagined in my mind Tyrian's face. The little smile he'd recently learned to flash whenever I kissed his nose or whenever Jamison walked into the room. I looked back at Mr. Duncan and tried to start again. "He's almost two months now and I can't lie, I've had a very easy time with him. I haven't had to worry about anything. He's taken care of and all of his needs are met—just like that." I snapped my finger. "Now he's beautiful and deserves everything the world has to offer, but the more I look at him, I realize that other children deserve the same. Other families deserve to know where their next meal is coming from. Mothers need to know how they can provide it. And if I could just be a part of that, it would be great."

Mr. Duncan looked like he was about to cry too. He sat back in his seat and held up my application.

"I guess this is one we'll have to keep," he said, smiling. "So, we'll have a way to call you to let you know when your first day is."

"I got it?" I asked.

"You got it," he said, putting the sheet down on his desk. "We'll see you in the new year."

* * *

It was December and freezing outside, but I was floating on air. The screaming children turned to singing angels as I headed out of the office. I felt like a new woman. A woman of purpose. Not Kerry Jackson, the black Barbie doll, but Kerry Jackson who was about to do some hard work and make some hard changes in the world. It sounded crazy, but in that moment, with each step I took, I felt like the old me was dying. And I didn't know what it was that I was stepping away from or why I needed to go. But there was a spring in my step that I felt from the inside. Walking down the street with other women who were working hard and facing probably the same things I was facing, I felt a rush of life I had never felt. I knew it was a little premature, but I was a person on a mission.

I smiled at every face I passed, wondering who they were and where they were going. What they did. How they added to the world. I wanted to run home and kiss Tyrian's nose, to hold him and tell him what his mother was about to do. I wanted to tell the world. I wanted to tell . . . Jamison. This need flashed into my mind in the worst way. I'd never had or achieved anything in my adult life without sharing it with that man. He was a part of who I was. I wondered if this was the feeling Jamison had when he started Rake It Up. Like he was about to build something and the possibilities were limitless. How could I have missed that for so long? What had I been doing? Suddenly, the idea of working through this without him, without a listening ear at bedtime, scared me to death. He was my husband. A sinking feeling fell over me and then I really wanted to go home. My step became less peppy, my smile was fading. My opportunity seemed like less of an opportunity without my partner by my side. I had missed Jamison. Each day without him was unbearable. He came by most afternoons to see the baby and bring us things, but in my anger I was keeping my distance. I still had nothing to say to him. But deep in my heart I was unsure of how much longer I could go on. But still, I had to stand my ground. He'd hurt me, and while I wanted so badly for that to just go away, it couldn't.

"Barbie Doll?" I heard someone call from behind me. I was sure they weren't talking to me. I hadn't had anyone call me that since college. "I know that chocolate syrup skin anywhere. Is that you?"

I turned to see a familiar face looking at me. Only it seemed older and much more mature than it had been the last time I'd seen it, so I couldn't quite place it.

"Kerry, you're going to act like you don't know me?" he said.

"I'm sorry," I said, trying to place him. It was someone I'd dated. . . . Gone out with.

"Preston, Preston Allcott," he said, opening his arms to hug me.

It was *the* Preston Allcott that grabbed my crotch during our date in undergrad. I hadn't seen him in over ten years. He was local, of course, had gone to the Morehouse School of Medicine just like the other men in his family, but he'd fallen off the radar a long time ago. He pretty much looked the same, only he was more handsome. His olive skin had darkened a bit and now the sun, even in the cold December breeze, seemed to catch each curve on his face.

"Wow," I said, hugging him.

"Don't act like you don't know me," he said, laughing.

"I just haven't seen you in so long," I said, wanting to say that I knew him *too* well after he'd grabbed my crotch.

"Well, I kind of left the whole scene after graduation. I needed to get myself together. Get away from all of that stuff. You know?"

I nodded my head, but I wasn't sure exactly what he was talking about. Preston was a true blue Atlantan man of society.

His family pretty much made the scene from its beginning, and from what I recall of slick Preston in college, he'd embraced it.

"You look amazing," he added. "Like the wife I should've had."

"Stop it," I said.

"No, really, I was too much of a jerk to recognize it back then, too caught up in a bunch of bullshit, but now I see that I missed out."

"Thank you," I said. "So, what are you doing downtown?"

"I own a health clinic down here," he said, poking out his chest. "We service people with HIV/AIDS who have trouble getting good healthcare and insurance."

"Really?" I asked. It didn't sound like the Preston I'd known. I was sure he was a surgeon or something. His father was a cardiothoracic surgeon. A free clinic? Working with the poor? That wasn't the Allcott way.

"Yeah, it's real," he said. "Before I went to med school, my father insisted that I go to Europe to vacation for a month, but when I got there, a guy I met invited me to travel with him to Kenya. He was a doctor and said I could assist him and learn some things about ground work before I went to school. I'd never even thought about it, but I went—without my father's blessings—and seeing the HIV/AIDS epidemic there, my life was forever changed. I just wanted to come here and work to make sure the disease didn't continue to ravage our people."

"That's amazing," I said. I hadn't at all expected any of this to come from Preston. Not the crotch grabber! He seemed so changed. So much more mature.

"So, what about you?" he asked. "Career? Married? Children?"

"Oh," I struggled. "I just had a baby and . . . I'm—"

"Married," he grabbed my left hand. "Oh, yes, you married um . . . Jamison. Right?"

"Yes," I said, trying to hide my uncertainty.

"And you just had a baby?" He stepped back and looked at me. "You do mean a year ago or something, because you don't look a pound over a size two."

"Stop it," I said.

"So, what about your career? How is that? Where are you practicing?"

"Practicing?"

"Yeah, you're a doctor, right? You were going to med school."

"Oh, no," I said. Now I'd have to explain that to another person. "I just decided—"

"Stop," he said, cutting me off. "You don't need to explain your life path to me. I'm just some dude you used to date. No need to explain."

We both stood there laughing for a minute.

"But I can tell you're coming from somewhere." He looked me over again.

"Well, if you must know," I said, "I just got an internship with the Department of Social Services. I start helping them next month." I was so proud to hear those words coming from my mouth. Now I'd have something to say when people asked me what I was doing. I wouldn't have to appear "made busy" by things around me—not Jamison, not the house. I had a job.

"Wow, that's cool," he said. "Sounds like you're on your way to my side of the game. Service!" He held up his hand and I gave him a high five. "That was weak! You just got a job. You better slap this hand again." He put his hand up again and I jumped up to slap it like I'd just made a winning touchdown. "That's right, woman!"

"Yeah," I said playfully.

"Now, the only thing you need to do next to make the celebration complete is to meet me for dinner."

"Dinner?" I asked. I hadn't had dinner with any man but my husband since . . . since . . . ever.

"Yes, a meal to celebrate your new job. I insist," he said. "Now, I know you're married. But this is strictly me trying to catch up with an old college acquaintance and make up for grabbing your crotch."

"You're crazy," I said.

"But I'm serious." The smile left his face. "I'm not that man anymore. I'm a new person. I want to show you and do a little bit of celebrating. Strictly platonic. Nothing to tell your husband."

"You promise?" I asked before realizing that I was accepting. Was I accepting? Hell, I needed to get out for one night. Without Marcy around I needed someone to talk to. I was tired of cleaning up vomit and changing diapers. I wanted to feel like a real adult for just an hour or so. I was still young and sexy and if Preston could see it, so be it. I had no intentions of sleeping with him or even seeing him again after that evening.

"I promise," he said. "Look, I'll be waiting at the Four Season in midtown at 7 PM. If you come, you come. If not," he reached into his pocket, "you have my card, and you can call me if you ever need anything. Sound fair?"

"Yes," I said, taking the card.

"Great." He took my left hand and kissed it softly. "See you later," he said.

TO: Kerry.Taylor@rakeitup.net
FROM: Jamison.Taylor@rakeitup.net
DATE: 12/16/07
TIME: 7:15 AM

So, it's been a few weeks since I've heard your voice. Well, I have heard you speak when I visit Tyrian or when I call to say I'm on my way, but you're not really speaking to me, as much as you are tolerating my existence. I know that you have every right to be angry with me, but not hearing your voice or speaking to you is killing me slowly. Not having my wife and baby in the house just hurts. And I'm man enough to say that I cried and I even drove past the hotel you were staying at a few times. I don't even feel like I have a right to complain to you, but I have to say something. I have to do something to fix this. The only thing I could think to do right now, at least to begin to open the lines of communication, was to write to you. The funny thing, though, is that this is your old work e-mail and I don't know if you check it anymore. I don't even know if you have another e-mail address. Either way, I hope this reaches you and I want you to know that I miss you and Tyrian so much. Please come home.

TO: Jamison.Taylor@rakeitup.net
FROM: Kerry.Taylor@rakeitup.net
DATE: 12/16/07
TIME: 11:22 AM

I find it entertaining that you should decide to contact me in the very fashion that you used to contact Coreen. Don't you get tired of e-mailing people? Let's hope you don't mistakenly send me a message that was meant for her. Maybe you should've been writing your wife all along. And as far as me coming home, I need you to know that's going to take a lot more than some text on a computer screen. I'm really, really upset right now. Your betrayal of our family was unacceptable. And I resent you more than I could've imagined. WHAT DID I DO TO DESERVE ANY OF THIS? I was nothing but a good wife to you. And to add to that, you went behind my back to visit my father, claiming I "was too weak to take it." No, you're weak and if I was, as my husband, it was your job to build me up. NOT sneak around behind my back. That hurts and it's a slap in the face. So, I really can't be concerned with your feelings right now. You can save them. What'll bring me home?

TRY A MIRACLE.

The No-Tell Motel

It was an hour before I was supposed to meet Preston at the Four Seasons for dinner. I hadn't even decided if I was going. In fact, I was leaning against it, but then I got the e-mail from Jamison and with my blood steadily boiling, I decided that I had to get away. I couldn't believe he thought some sad e-mail was going to bring me home.

I didn't know what I was doing by going out with Preston, but I knew I had to get away from Jamison's mess to avoid getting any more angry at the world. The only problem was that Tyrian wouldn't take his eyes off me. He wasn't even two months yet, but that boy had the eye coordination of a tennis player. From his baby swing, his eyes followed me around the room as I got dressed. Most parents would've been excited that their child was showing such strong motor skills at an early age, but the circumstances and the fact that he was beginning to look more and more like Jamison every day was making me feel a little guilty. But guilty about what? Yes, Preston was fine. Yes, Preston was rich and smart and clearly a changed man. But we were just going out for dinner. I didn't owe him anything; he didn't owe me anything. But . . . Why was I so nervous? Why was I getting so dressed up? Why had I lied to Aunt Luchie and told her I was going out for drinks with Marcy? Why wouldn't Tyrian stop watching me?

"Mama is coming back," I said, trying to calm him before he started crying.

He looked at me and I swear that baby narrowed his eyes and then rolled them in disgust.

"You're looking mighty fancy," Aunt Luchie said from the bedroom door. "I guess you girls need some excitement. Nothing wrong with that."

"Yeah, we're just eating though, so there will be no excitement."

"I'm sure," she said with a hint of speculation in her voice. After staying with her for two weeks, I came to the realization that Aunt Luchie was so much like my mother in her constant desire to investigate the lives of others. The only difference was that my mother had a problem holding her tongue when it came to her inquisitions. She ruled with cutting questions and biting advice. Well, Aunt Luchie's style was much more subtle. She chose the question-without-a-question route. It was all about polite suggestions and silence. Even in the politeness and silence, she was working her magic. But I was on to her now and determined not to crack under the pressure. She wanted me to break down and come clean about where I was going. But there would be no breaking down here. The last thing I wanted or needed was more advice.

"Great," I said, kissing her on the cheek before slipping on my coat. "There's plenty of milk downstairs and after his next bottle he'll be out like a light for the rest of the night."

"I know how to care for this boy," she said. "I know when he eats and sleeps, don't I?" She looked over at Tyrian for an answer and that little boy nodded his still-soft-on-the-top head.

"Wonderful," I said. "One big happy family. I'll be back no later than eleven."

*   *   *

When you're married and have children, you forget just how busy the rest of the world is outside of your circle. Other than dinner with Marcy and Damien, annual parties, must-be-seen-at events, and business functions, Jamison and I seldom got out of the house. But driving to the Four Seasons, I realized that apparently, everyone else was. Peachtree was packed with cars carrying people here and there, smiling faces peeking out of car windows, excited about what was waiting for them inside the growing city. No matter that it was a weeknight; no matter that it was an unusually frigid night. They were out for a night on the town. Every day, the small city where a single name was once able to open many closed doors was seeming bigger and bigger. It was considered progress to many people, but to my people, it felt more like an invasion. No one knew who anyone else was anymore. The old special names were fading fast as more money and more lineage came in from other cities. "It started with that Coretta," I heard a woman say once at one of my mother's book parties. They'd sit and talk for hours, gossiping about who wanted in and who would never be in. Coretta Scott was one of their favorite topics. As nice and sweet as she was, these women, who were her age, seemed hell-bent on keeping her at an arm's distance just because she wasn't a true Atlantan. "She came here thinking she'd already be inside because she was married to Daddy King's son," she added. "Ha!"

Driving through the traffic, and thinking about this old practice, I thought of just how ridiculous it was. The city was growing and changing and while I was taught to disdain the growth, it seemed unreasonable to believe that we could keep the secrets of Atlanta to ourselves. Yes, after Coretta, more blacks from outside of Atlanta did come into the city, but why not? Why shouldn't the city grow and change? There were some bad things about the city, but there were also some wonderful things. Maybe

the old way wasn't the only way. What were we protecting anyway? Access? This was the kind of thinking that had troubled
Jamison and added to the stress in our marriage for so long. Even
with my name attached, it kept him out of certain contracts.
Constantly made him feel like he wasn't enough. And while I
tried my best to chalk it up to "the way things were," that way
was wrong. I could admit that now.

"I was about to leave," Preston said when the hostess led me
to the table where he was waiting. He stood up immediately to
pull out my chair and I could see that he was dressed hand-
somely in a navy blue suit and white shirt. I also noticed that
he'd gotten a haircut and was freshly shaven. He looked like
he'd just walked off a movie set, and I had to admit that he
made me look rather undressed. I'd decided to wear a pair of
black slacks and a fitted, red sweater. My hair was curled loose
and pushed back behind my ears. It was attractive, yet not
overdone. I didn't want to send the wrong message.

"I am not that late," I replied. It was just ten or so after seven.

"Well, I guess I'll have to forgive you anyway. You look
lovely," he kissed me on the cheek and went back to his seat.

"That's an overstatement," I said, laughing.

"Why do you always do that?" he asked.

"Do what?"

"Not take compliments," he said. "You did that this morning
when I said you looked nice."

"You know, I don't know," I said, trying to remember if I'd
actually been doing that. The baby did have me feeling a bit less
attractive, but I'd never thought about it.

"You're a beautiful and desirable woman, Kerry. And your
husband is a lucky man for it."

"Thank you," I said. "So what's good on the menu this season?" I picked up the menu to avoid talking about Jamison.

"I asked the chef if he would make us a little something special," he said grinning.

"What?" I asked. He looked like he was planning something.

"Well, I do recall one beautiful black woman tearing through a meal on a date I'd taken her on. She even broke her rule of etiquette, eating the last bite and saying it was the best quail she'd ever had."

"I did not," I lied. I could feel myself smiling. I didn't even remember that until he brought it up. The moment had been eclipsed by the infamous crotch grab.

"Well, we'll put that in the history books, but we both know how it went down that night," he said jokingly.

"So you ordered the quail?" I asked, half-excited he remembered what I ordered that night and a bit peeved that he'd ordered for me. That was a bit presumptuous. Was this how folks dated nowadays? No, no, no! I wasn't on a date.

"Now, I know that might seem a bit forward and old school of me to order food for you, but I have a reason," he said, looking into my eyes. "Right now in my life, I'm all about moving forward and letting go of the past."

"Okay," I said.

"And I know I was a complete jerk when we went out . . . what was it, ten years ago?"

"Longer."

"Well, I'm asking you for a friendly do-over. So, call me superstitious, but I thought having the same meal might get me some luck in becoming your friend again."

"That's very kind of you," I said, but what I was thinking was that it was downright charming.

"And it's not just any quail that I had to call the chef personally to convince him to make—because it's not on the menu. It's roasted quail flambéed in—"

"Cognac," I said, with my mouth watering.

"Glad you remembered," he said.

"I honestly hadn't known I did."

The quail was better than I'd remembered and Preston was an even better dining partner. His work with HIV/AIDS had taken him all over Africa and he seemed so committed, so fervent about what he did that it was inspiring. I could listen to him talk all day about the people he'd met, the things he'd seen, and even though it was sad and enough to make anyone cry, it was also heartwarming and I could see how it had changed him. I'd traveled throughout most of Europe and even took a cruise with my mother once that stopped in South Africa, but we never went away from the tours or resorts. This place, this Africa that Preston was talking about, was beautiful and exotic and unforgiving in a way that made me feel more alive just for hearing about it.

"There's no way I could have done anything to save her," Preston said, looking just as lost in the story he was telling me as I felt. "The outdated drugs we'd given her to treat the virus were not as effective as they could have been. People have been speculating for years that the drugs that companies send to Africa as charity when they are out of date are less active and perhaps poisonous. But it was all we had. We could either watch her die fast without the drugs or give her the stuff we weren't even sure was working."

"Awful," I said.

"Yeah . . ." He paused and took one of perhaps three remaining bites on his plate. My food was looking low as well. It was just too good to leave sitting on the plate. "But I don't mean to bore you. I know I can get carried away about this stuff."

"No, it's fine," I said. "It's great to know you've experienced so much."

"Try telling that to the women who refuse to date me," he said.

I couldn't imagine anyone turning him down for anything. I hadn't had one drink and I couldn't help but wonder what he looked like with no clothes on.

"Really?"

"Please, me and love don't get along," he said. "Once women realize how committed I am to my work and that most of my money goes into the clinic and not a fancy car and big house, they run for the border."

"So, you haven't had any luck? No marriages? No kids?"

"None . . . Well, I was about to get engaged once, but it didn't pan out."

"What happened?"

"A few years back, I was dating this model I'd met when I was doing research in France. She's a Ralph Lauren model from Alabama, of all places. We just hit it off. I guess it was the whole Southern thing."

"You mean Chan?" I asked. Chan was one of the prettiest black models in the business. I didn't follow the industry, but you couldn't see a Lauren ad without noticing the delicate almond sister and how she commanded the camera's attention with her dark brown eyes. She was graceful and soft, yet she also seemed to have an air of sophistication.

"Yes," he said, but a smile didn't appear on his face in the way I'd expected from a man who'd dated her. "We dated for a while. Even did a little long distance thing between Europe and the States when I had to come home. I was a good boy. This was when I was like thirty-one and she was just twenty, so it wasn't easy."

"Twenty?" I plucked his hand playfully.

"Please, you try finding a working model over twenty-five and I'll buy you an airplane."

"Very funny," I said.

"Things were amazing. I think maybe because she was so young and had less limitations, it was just fun. And with what I do, things can get very frustrating, so I just need a little outlet sometimes. I fell for her quickly. And I went out and bought this rock to put on her hand that could have fed a village in Kenya for eight months."

"You're crazy," I said laughing.

"No, really," he said without laughing. "I had the ring and she came here to visit for a weekend. I was so nervous that the entire weekend went by without me saying anything. I missed every opportunity. And then I decided that I'd just ask her when we got to the airport. I'd walk inside with her and ask the question right there in front of all of those people. She was young, so she liked stuff like that. The time came, and we were sitting in the lobby of the airport, talking before she was supposed to walk through security. I had the ring in my pocket and I was about to pull it out and get down on one knee."

"What happened?"

"She started talking . . ." He paused. "She asked me if I loved her."

"And, you said, 'yes'?"

"No, I was too nervous. I just stood there. I knew I loved the girl and what I was about to do, but I just couldn't. Something was holding me back. The surprising thing was that she didn't even look sad that I wasn't saying anything. She just kept smiling. 'Well, I don't know if I love you either,' she said."

"What? Do you think she was mad?"

"No, she was dead serious," he said as the waiter came over and poured more water into our glasses. "Then she wrapped her arms around my waist and said, 'But I know we're good for each other and that I could learn to love you, Pres . . .' I was so confused. It was like she'd practiced everything she was saying. I dropped the ring down into the bottom of my pocket. 'I think we should get married,' she added. 'Would you marry me?' she asked me as if she was ordering extra cheese on her pizza."

"What?" My mouth fell open. "She told you she didn't love you and then asked if you would marry her?"

"Imagine how I felt. I was about to ask this woman to marry me. I told her that didn't sound like a good idea since she didn't love me."

"Exactly."

"Then she went into this whole speech about how we were both good for each other—a great team," he said. "And said she knew she could be a good wife for me. That I could pick the weight I wanted her to be and that she wouldn't go a pound over that weight and that she wouldn't even need to have children if I didn't want them."

"If *you* didn't want them!"

"It was nuts. I felt like I was talking to some crazy Stepford wife," he said. "This was most men's dream deal, but I couldn't believe a woman actually supported it. The girl said she'd 'stay out of' my business."

"Wow."

"I don't even need to say it, but my love faded just as quickly as it had come, right there in the airport lobby. I wanted to get away from her fast. I was actually embarrassed."

"What did you do?"

"I told her I needed to go," he said. "But then she was saying she meant what she was saying and that she wouldn't get on the plane if I said yes. I said no and walked out."

"That's awful."

"Yeah, that was the height of my venture toward marriage. The ring is in a safe deposit box. I just never seem to have any luck."

"Tell me about it," I said as the waitress cleared our plates and handed out dessert menus. There was no way I had any room for anything else. I'd repeated my break in etiquette and had eaten the last bite of quail.

"Dinner's over," a voice said as a hand grabbed my shoulder. I turned to find Marcy standing behind my chair.

"Excuse me?" Preston said.

"Don't say anything to me," she said to him firmly. "Kerry, let's go." She began pulling at my chair.

"Marcy, I'm having dinner with a friend," I said, trying to resist, but people were beginning to look.

"You come with me right now," she said, grabbing my purse.

I got up as she was walking out of the dining room.

"I'll be right back," I said to Preston. "She's just . . . I'll be right back."

"What are you doing here?" Marcy said when I made it to the lobby where she was standing.

"I'm having dinner with a friend," I said, snatching back my purse. "Which is none of your business. The last I checked, we weren't friends anymore."

"Look, I told you I had nothing to do with the thing with Piper. She admitted that she found out at work."

"Work?"

"Coreen works at her firm. Piper saw her having lunch with Jamison and had her assistant pry into Coreen's e-mail to see if she could find something."

"Oh, no," I said with my heart sinking. "I can't believe this. Now everyone knows."

"Piper promised not to tell another soul."

"A promise from Piper? That's got to be worth about a penny on a good day."

"It's worth a bit more when she had to come to your best

friend to get a Viagra prescription for a man who isn't her husband." Marcy paused. "Kerry, it was all one big misunderstanding. I would never hurt you."

"I'm sorry. I should've listened to you," I said with the news about Piper still coming together in my mind. I felt like such a fool for having cut Marcy out of my life for so long. I missed her.

Without hesitating, she opened her arms and embraced me.

"Look, everything's fine with us," she said, backing up and looking into my eyes. "I'm your girl. I'm not going anywhere. You know how we do . . . pick up right where we left off."

"Right."

"And since we left off with me all up in your business, I might as well get all up in your business right now. What's up with you and Preston?"

"We're just here for dinner," I said. "It's not what you think. He's just a friend."

"Then why are you having dinner at a hotel?"

"Plenty of people have dinner here."

"Not married women without their husbands."

"Well, you're here," I said, looking around. "And I don't see Damien anywhere."

"Exactly," she said with her eyes narrowing. "This isn't the place for you, Kerry. I know you're upset about what's happening with Jamison, but this really isn't for you. Stop now before it goes to far."

"How can you tell me what not to do to a man that cheated on me?"

"Because I know what you're going through," she whispered to me.

"Marcy," a handsome man that I'd never seen called from behind her.

"And I don't want your marriage to end up like mine. Your

husband loves you. He just fucked up. You can work it out and come back from that. But if you do this, there is no coming back," she rattled off.

The man walked up and handed Marcy her coat.

"I'm just having dinner," I said. "Preston is my friend."

"Go home," Marcy said, walking away with the man. "Just go home."

I felt like everyone in the dining room was watching me when I walked back inside. I lowered my head and walked quickly to the table.

"I'm sorry about that," I said as I took my seat. "She's just upset."

"About what?" he asked.

"Well," I laughed playfully, "she seems to think we're on a date . . . that you're trying to sleep with me."

"Hum," he said as if this was something he'd thought of. "Well . . ."

"Well, what?" I looked at him, sure he was joking. This was Preston Alcott—a changed man. He was here to celebrate my internship, talk about Africa and Chan, and that woman he couldn't save. This was no date. We weren't seeing any other parts of the hotel.

"I mean, she's not wholly wrong for that," he said with his eyes turning from friendly to dreamy. He was looking *at me . . . into me . . . through my shirt* . . . and he wasn't doing a medical examination with his eyes. The man was flirting. "I don't mean to be forward, but when I saw you today, I just knew how good you were—that I'd missed out. I don't want to miss out again." He reached across the table and tried to grab my hand, but I retreated quickly.

"Preston," I said. "I'm a married woman." I looked around

the room to be sure no one had seen him. I felt silly and ridiculous for being there. Marcy was right.

"Kerry, don't be shy. I can tell something is going on between us. And that things at home aren't okay. You didn't exactly seem happy to say Jamison's name."

"That's none of your business," I said, getting up.

"There's no need to leave," he said. "I'm just saying, if he's not doing his job correctly, I volunteer myself."

"My marriage is fine," I said getting up. "And you're still a jerk."

EMAIL TRANSMISSION

TO: Jamison.Taylor@rakeitup.net
FROM: Kerry.Taylor@rakeitup.net
DATE: 12/16/07
TIME: 10:27 PM

Apparently, Dottie came by my aunt's house this evening without calling or letting anyone know. I don't have a problem with your mother seeing Tyrian. I have made constant arrangements for everyone to be able to see him, but at this point I want nothing to do with her and it is best that you arrange for her to see your son. As I told you the other day, what she did was unacceptable and YOU need to speak to her about it. As far as I'm concerned, a huge part of our problem is outside people placing stress on our relationship. And I admit that my mother is no saint, but your mother has been running wild, constantly putting me down and not RESPECTING our relationship since day one and you have done NOTHING to stop it. The only way she could've thought hooking you up with Coreen was a good idea and that you wouldn't do anything about it was that you never ever stand up to her about anything she says. That entire situation was crazy. She created unrest in your household and compromised your marriage, even though you were having a child. Who does that? I wanted nothing more than to curse your mother out, but, you know what, that's not my job. It's yours.

EMAIL TRANSMISSION

TO: Jamison.Taylor@rakeitup.net
FROM: Kerry.Taylor@rakeitup.net
DATE: 12/16/07
TIME: 10:33 PM

I need you to know that I lied earlier in my e-mail. I am hurting, Jamison, and I do miss you. But I can't be anyone's fool and I have to love myself right now. A lot of what you said last month about my not focusing on my career and supporting you was true. And I started doing things to change that. I feel like I am being reborn and finally in love with something I can do. Something huge happened to me today and to be very honest, I did want you to be there. I DIDN'T WANT ANYONE ELSE THERE. But I also know that I can't always have what I want and I can't continue to build myself and my marriage if every time I lay down one brick, your mother is there to tear it down and no one does anything. I have been trying to do my part. You asked me to come home last time. And I did. Look what happened. And I even began to distance myself from my mother. Not because I don't love her, not because I don't want to communicate with her, but because, right now, I need someone by my side who is ONLY going to nurture me and what I am trying to do. My mother is who and what she is. She's been that way for a long time and I know I can't change her. But what I can change is the way I once allowed her to control my life and how much access she has to it. Can you say the same about your mother? If not, what are you willing to do to change it in order to save your marriage?

E-MAIL TRANSMISSION

TO: Kerry.Taylor@rakeitup.net
FROM: Jamison.Taylor@rakeitup.net
DATE: 12/16/07
TIME: 10:43 PM

First, I think it would be best if we spoke in person about this because I don't want anything that I am saying to be taken out of context. But I know that's not going to happen right now, so I will respond.

I am very happy that you have found new interests and I really want to know everything that's going on with that. I have always known that you can achieve anything you put your mind to. You are a hard worker and a strong woman. My opinion, as you already stated in some ways, was that the only thing holding you back was your mother. Now, I know it's not cool to talk about someone's parent—especially a mother, but for years I have had to sit back and watch that woman constantly put you down and let you down. The crazy thing to me was always that sometimes the things she did actually worked to get you going, but most times it just left you with hurt feelings that I felt a need to try to repair in some way. That's the real reason I didn't go to med school. I didn't want her to continue to control you and the thought of leaving you alone in Georgia with her there tearing you down made me feel like I needed to take charge. RIGHT now I am very aware of the damage my mother has done in our relationship, but you need to know that your mother has also had an effect on our marriage. Her judgments and how they affect you have caused me to often feel out of place in my own home. So many times I felt like you were perfectly fine with how things were going, but as soon as your mother showed up, you'd change your mind and leave me out there looking like a fool. Sometimes I think the only reason you left your job to come work at Rake It Up was because your mother wanted you to come and make sure the business didn't fold and ruin her name. It was like all of your hard work wasn't because you believed in what I was doing, but because you didn't want to be embarrassed if it didn't work. I am not blaming you for this. I know the way she influences you. But when we got married, I always thought it would stop.

I also know that I have had a problem standing up to my mother. After my dad died we were all each other had and I have always tried my best to make her happy. The two times I did anything that she disagreed with in my entire life were not going to med school and marrying you. You have always known that she blamed you for my not going to med school, but the truth is that I'm glad I didn't go. You were the reason then, but really, I think that inside, I knew I had a higher calling in my life and it was in Georgia with you. The funny thing is that while those two things caused my mother so much pain, they were the only two things in my life that I was completely sure I wanted to do. And I knew then and I know now that no matter how she feels about it, I am happy I did them. She won't have a son she can call "doctor," but I have a great business that I love and a beautiful wife that I adore. Being with you is what I want and she is going to have to accept that. I really didn't believe that she did what she did, but she admitted it after you left the house on Thanksgiving and we've since spoken about it on several occasions. For some reason she thought that she could replace you with a woman who was more like her and I'd be happier. But, as I told her, I didn't want a woman like her because I didn't want to marry my mother. I married you. I told her she'd have to accept that but I think the damage she did really didn't hit her until she saw the impact it had on my life. After you left this time, I've been even more depressed and I've even lost some accounts. She's come by to clean and cook for me, but I can't eat anything and when I do, I feel sick to my stomach. My house isn't right without you and Tyrian there and she is seeing that now. I realize that I have to stop going to my mother for advice and letting her know every little thing that's going on in our relationship. I can't promise that she will change, but I do know that she has learned her lesson and we are finally speaking about it.

I hope we can speak more about this in person soon.

Jamison

_____

Finding His Way Back

Only a few months ago, whenever I got into my car, it was to go to the store to buy something for the house, my closet, or even Jamison's closet. No doubt about it, I had to have my pocketbook and wallet with me every time, because plastic would be needed to complete the exchange. These things I'd buy made my world look nice and made me feel good. All of that changed in October when I left the house at five in the morning without my purse for the first time. Now I went where my needs, my dreams, my desires, my heart carried me, and with each new destination, I felt closer to touching who I really was. While my life had been steadily pulled apart since that drive to Coreen's, a new one was being built up, and while it was scary and not yet what I completely wanted, I already felt better for the journey. And I hadn't bought anything!

I woke up with my mind fixed on one thing. I'd always heard people in church say they'd woken up with their minds "stayed on Jesus." Well, my mind was "stayed" on a man, but not Jesus; it was my father. Since I was young, I'd often thought of him in the morning, especially after having a dream from my childhood where he was either present or noticeably not present, but the thoughts would usually fade by the time I got to the breakfast table. So instead of sitting and thinking about my father, I decided to try to let it go by following my morning ritual: I showered and dressed myself quickly before Tyrian woke up, bathed and dressed him, and then headed down to the kitchen to meet Aunt Luchie for coffee and these homemade biscuits she made that were wreaking havoc on my hips. But there, at the table, my mind was still on my father. I kept remembering times we'd shared—when he insisted on putting together my first bicycle and it fell apart the moment I sat on it, the way he'd hugged me that afternoon, picking me up off the driveway and saying it would be okay. I also wondered what it was like to be in his mind, closed in from all sides. Earlier that year when I went to see him with my mother for his birthday, he didn't even look at us. He just kept grunting and saying something about a deer in the woods he needed to find. He looked completely lost, worse that year than he'd been the year before, but then that was how it always was.

"You okay?" Aunt Luchie asked, putting another biscuit on my saucer that I didn't need. "You seem upset."

"I just had this dream about my dad. Can't seem to get it out of my head."

"I see," she started. "He's been on your mind then?"

"Yes. After the whole thing with Jamison, he's been on my mind a lot."

"Well, your brain must be calling on your body to do something."

"What?"

"Only your know that. It's not my brain that's speaking."

"It's probably just me being upset about Jamison," I said dismissively.

"Seems to me that if your brain was upset about Jamison, then you'd dream about him and not your father."

"Fine," I said, rolling my eyes at her game. "So you're saying I had a dream about my father, because my brain wants me to go see him?"

"Well, if you think your brain said all that, then it's fine with me," she said innocently. "But if you do decide to do so I'll—"

". . . watch the baby for you," we finished together.

"I know," I said. "I know."

He'd been staying in the same room, down the same dark hallway at the back of the Day Star Nursing Home. It was a lovely place really. While most of the residents were suffering from some form of Alzheimer's or dementia and there was a clinic on-site, the place had a chic resort-feel with fresh flowers in vases, newly polished marble floors, and chrome nurse stations that resembled minibars. There were other nursing homes in the area, but my mother wanted no expense spared when she was selecting a place where she'd thought my father would stay only for a while until he somehow magically awoke and called her name to come pick him up. She hoped he'd see how much she cared when he found his mind, but that hope only lasted about nine months until it was clear that he wouldn't be coming home anytime soon.

"Ms. Taylor?" a nurse called as I approached the station closest to his room. She was a short and round, middle-aged woman, who had a head full of dirty blond hair that was unfortunately showing at least two inches of black at the roots. I couldn't remember her name, although I'd seen her many times as I walked down this hallway. She hadn't looked as confused as I'd thought she would; in fact, she looked as if she'd been expecting me.

"Yes," I said, holding the daisies I'd purchased to put in his room.

"I'm glad you finally got here," she said. She came from around the station and began walking with me. "He's much better now, but this morning—"

"What are you talking about?" I felt my heart beating.

"We've been calling your mother."

"Something happened?" I began walking faster, nearly running.

"No, he just, well, he had a seizure," she said, walking quickly beside me. "We left a message. I thought you knew."

"No, no," I said, counting the doors as I walked to be sure I went into the right one. I'd been doing this since I was a child. I hated walking into the wrong room, seeing some sick man I didn't know connected to a bunch of machines, lonely and lost.

"But he's okay now," she went on. "Back to normal. We have it under control."

I turned into the room to find my father sitting in a chair beside his bed, facing the window. I stopped on the threshold frozen in my tracks and put my hand over my heart in relief.

"See," the nurse said nervously. I could tell she'd felt bad that I'd gotten the news from her.

"Oh, I just . . . I just thought," I said.

"It's okay," she put her hand on my shoulder and I could see her nametag: PAT. "We just had to inform you."

We were talking loud enough for him to hear; he was maybe only ten paces from the doorway, but he didn't move. He simply kept his eyes on the window.

"What happened?" I whispered, looking at him. His chestnut skin had developed a permanent pale ash over it. He was thin, as thin as a man who'd spent his life on the streets begging for food. His cheeks were sunken and his hair had begun to fall out in patches on the top.

"We really don't know. He's never had a seizure before. But last night when Emma and I tried to put him to bed, he resisted and then he started seizing. The doctors don't know what it means or why it happened. They're still running tests."

"Will he be alright?"

"We have no reason to believe otherwise," she said. "He

woke up this morning like it was any other morning. Put on his robe and went to sit by the window."

I took a step toward him and placed the flowers on a table by the bed.

"I'll be at my station in case you need me," Pat said behind me.

"Thank you," I said, walking closer.

"Oh," she said, although I thought she was gone. "There was one thing."

I turned to look at her.

"And it was the oddest thing. Emma and I didn't even make much of it until the seizure."

"What happened?"

"When we were getting him to bed, he looked Emma right in her eyes and called her Jane or Janie. Is that what he called your mother? I noticed when I called that her name is Thirjane."

"Yes," I said. I hadn't heard him call my mother's nickname in over fifteen years.

"Well, we didn't make much of it then. He says things a lot, you know," she said. "But never really anything specific. And he never looks us in the eye. Not once in all these years. But yesterday he did."

She nodded and turned to walk out of the room, leaving me there alone with my father for the first time. I didn't know what to say. Where to go. I kept thinking of being rude or overstepping my bounds. It was an odd feeling. Like I was visiting someone I'd always known but had never met. I decided to sit on the bed, facing his chair.

"Dad," I said. I tried to see if he would look at me when I said it. But he just kept his eyes on a shaking tree bark that was tapping at the window. How could he see that, hear that, but not see or hear me? I exhaled and felt tears coming. Earlier, I'd wanted so badly to be there, like I'd change something, but I already felt like I was failing. I caught a tear with my thumb as it rolled down my cheek. "I'm sorry," I said. "I just wanted to come see you. And I bought you flowers. Daisies. They're right over there. You can see them . . ." I sounded like a fool. What was I saying? What was I there to say? I bent over and rested my face in my hands. Here beside me was the man who gave me life. And now that everything in my life was changing, I needed to hear something from him. I didn't need to hear that it would all be okay, but that I was making the right decisions and that this was all a part of life . . . that it was going somewhere, leading me somewhere that I needed to be.

"Christmas is the season for miracles," I heard. I looked up to see that his face hadn't changed. He hadn't said a word. "I'm here," I heard and turned to find Jamison standing in the doorway.

I turned back to my father.

"What are you doing here?"

"Tuesday," he said. "Watermelon jello. It's his favorite."

I wiped a tear from my eye.

"So this is the day you come?" I asked dryly.

"Well, not every week, but mostly I come on Tuesday, when I get to see him eat that jello." He came over and sat next to me on the bed. "Now, he doesn't even look at Keisha, the nurse that brings the food, but when she places the jello on his tray and steps back, he digs in like he'd been waiting on that jello all week." He looked at my father. "It's great to see . . . see him react to something like that."

"Great," I said, moving away from Jamison on the bed.

"I'm sorry," he said without looking at me. "I didn't know how to tell you about this."

"You could've tried words."

"I came for the first time before I asked you to marry me," he continued. "I was so nervous and I just wanted someone to talk to, so I remembered where you said he was and I came over here and lied and said we were already married." He paused and turned to me. "I asked him for permission to marry you and he said nothing. Not a word. So I just sat there and sat there and pretty soon the sun went down. Then I realized that I'd sat here all day thinking. Just like him, I was in my mind, thinking about everything that was going on in my life. I was so unsure about everything. The business. Going to med school. But when I left that night, everything was clear. I was focused. I tried to tell you I'd been here when I got home that night, but when I brought him up, you said you didn't want to talk about it. I left it alone, but then every time I wanted to think or needed to think, I came here."

"How do you deal with it? I mean, that he doesn't say anything back."

"I don't think I come for that. I think he knows I'm here, and that means a lot to me. With my father being dead and never having had the chance to just sit and be in his presence, it's nice to have that . . ." he stopped talking, obviously choked up, "support you need."

I wanted so badly to hold him and hug him, but something in me wouldn't let that happen. I just looked back at my father and we sat there in silence, all three of us, together for about thirty minutes. It was one of those moments where I couldn't, didn't, want to say anything. I was tired of being sad and angry and just done with everything that was going on. Jamison. My father. There was nothing else to be said. I just needed more time to think. I wondered what I'd done wrong in all these years. I was just now realizing that I'd abandoned my father, denied my true feelings about being without him for so long. What else was I hiding from myself?

Jamison and I left the nursing home together. I kissed my fa-

ther and promised I'd be back the next day for what Jamison
called Granola Wednesday. Then, he said, it was funny to watch
my father refuse to eat granola. He'd put it in his mouth himself
and then spit it out.

"Can I come see Tyrian tonight?" Jamison asked after walking me to my car.

"Sure," I replied. "I don't think he has any plans."

"Great."

"And can you bring my thick bathrobe from the bathroom," I
asked. It was getting colder outside and Aunt Luchie's old
house had an icy draft.

"No," he said surprising me.

"Excuse me?" I asked, getting into the car.

"I said, 'No.'"

"Jamison," I said, "I don't have time to play games with you."
I tried to close the car door but he wouldn't let me.

"I need you to understand that I fully intend on getting you
back, Kerry," he said. "Whatever you want. Whatever you
need. I'm going to give it to you. But I want you back. I want
you home."

"You can't have that. You already made your decision."

"Yeah," he said, "and it was on a cold February morning
when I agreed to distract a girl at a Spelman dance for my best
friend.

"Stop it," I said, pulling at the car door.

"I fucked it up. I know I fucked it up, but I didn't do this all
by myself," he said. And then we were both crying. I still had
my hands on the door, but my fingers unraveled slowly.

"There's so much shit we deal with every day . . . from everyone around us that sometimes it seems impossible for us to just
be. To just be in love." He pulled me out of the car and into his
arms. "I wonder sometimes, Kerry, that if we'd met in another
lifetime without all of the stuff would we be okay. If I could love

you as much as I could and you could do the same and no one could come between us. You know what I'm talking about?"

I nodded my head and rested it on his shoulder, wetting his coat with my tears.

"I know I can't protect you from the world," he said. "But I can't give up on us. I can't do this without you. You're my wife."

We stood there in the parking lot crying. I could hear everything he was saying so clearly, and now while I'd hated what we'd been through, I needed to hear those words long before Coreen ever came into either of our lives. I knew I wasn't ready to go home just yet, but something in my soul told me that our love, our marriage was worth fighting for.

Hell No, We Won't Go

Now the March on Washington was in August and even Farrakhan was smart enough to hold the Million Man March in October, so why did Aunt Luchie and her crew decide to hold a rally to protest changes at the hospital in the middle of a very cold and windy December? And why in the world was I with them? We'd been standing out there in the cold in front of the hospital chanting and walking in a circle and every inch of my body—from my baby toes to my ear lobes—was completely frozen. And that wasn't even the bad part. The bad part was that I had to be the youngest person out there protesting and I was sure that at any moment one of those feisty seniors would faint from the cold and need to be rushed into the very hospital we were protesting.

We were out there because a board had voted for a nonprofit to take over Grady's operations. I thought it was a great idea and that the shift was just in time. The hospital had recently failed an inspection and was running out of money fast. The change would bring millions of dollars from public and private groups. At the very least it would be saved from shutting down, which was their initial goal and now it seemed the place would be better. But Aunt Luchie said the plan wasn't enough. It would take dollars out of the community where they helped poor people and put them into a bunch of silk-lined, executive pockets. Unlike the old board, the new board wouldn't have to answer to the public or help the uninsured and the poor. That's the position Grady used to hold. Where would those people go now?

With my new outlook, I got so fired up about this I sent Tyrian to my mother's house for the day and set out to be heard. While I was freezing, I admit that the whole thing was pretty exciting. There were only about fifteen of us—a few church leaders, a man from a local radio show, and seniors from the civic organization Aunt Luchie belonged to—but we were being heard. Aunt Luchie had a bullhorn and was leading us in an off-key medley of chants from "No Justice, No Peace" to "The New Grady Is Shady." A few doctors gave us a thumbs up as they walked by and even some of the people driving by in their cars honked to show support. One man came back with a few cups of coffee and a basket of doughnuts. To warm my frozen fingers, I volunteered to hand out the stuff. As I looked into the faces of each of the protestors, I felt more confident that what I was doing was right and that even if the hospital didn't change its course, people needed to know that the poor were important to us. My heart warmed my entire body as I thought of the possibility of the women I would someday help, women who probably had been touched by Grady in some way and would surely need its services again. If I was going to assist them, I had to protect the hospital and its mission to provide services for them. Grady wasn't perfect, but I had to make sure they had somewhere to go, somewhere to take their children.

"If your father could see you now!" Aunt Luchie whispered in my ear as I walked by. "He'd be so proud."

I smiled and kissed her on the cheek. Since my first visit alone, I'd been spending most afternoons at my father's side. I just felt like I needed to be there with him. No one knew if he'd ever be okay, but I decided for myself that I didn't want him to be alone again. If he was going to die, he'd know somehow that his family was there for him. My mother's refusal to come with me to the hospital let me know that she was incapable of being there and I didn't have time to force her. I couldn't ignore him anymore. I had to focus on my dad and getting him better.

We didn't speak much when I was there. He still hadn't made eye contact with me and as far as I knew he didn't even know I was in the room. But I still sat there and sometimes talked about Tyrian and my mother's antics. And he'd get real quiet sometimes, almost like he was listening. The nurses couldn't say if it was a sign or anything, but it was enough to suggest that maybe he was making a connection. And even though I kept telling myself I was there to help him, in the silence in that hospital room, I was also helping myself. I was thinking and planning and freeing my mind from all of the garbage and rules I'd let fill my head. If my father was all of the things my aunt said he was, I needed his strength, his vision to really figure out who I was. I wondered what my life might have been like if he'd always been there. If he'd kept my mother happy. I didn't resent him for not being there. But I did know that I had to stop pretending that I was okay with it. That it hadn't affected me.

"You think they can hear your bullhorn in the hospital?" I asked Aunt Luchie. "That we're really making noise?"

"Oh, that's not the point," she said. "Protesting isn't only about upsetting the perpetrators; it's also about making the public more aware and getting the word out about what's going on through the media. That's what makes the change—awareness and national embarrassment." She switched the bullhorn back on and turned to the group shouting, "The New Grady Is Shady."

And we replied with the same words. I kept circulating through the crowd, making sure everyone was warm.

"Excuse me," a woman said, tapping my shoulder.

I turned to find a familiar face holding a microphone in front of me. It was a local black reporter who had a short, bright blond head of curls you couldn't miss in any crowd.

"Monica McPherson?" I said, noticing that there was a man holding a camera behind her. "Fron the news?"

"Yes, it's me," she said, smiling and pulling me away from the crowd. "I was wondering if you had anything you wanted to share about the recent changes at Grady with our viewers."

"Me?" I asked, looking at the camera and wondering why in the world she'd selected me out of all the other people out there. I didn't know anything but what Aunt Luchie had told me. Surely there was someone else out there who would be a better representative than me. "Well," I said into the microphone, "I'm sure there are other people who can add a bit more information."

"We're not on camera yet," she said. "But we're looking for someone like you—someone who's involved but really representing the voice of an everyday Atlantan."

"Really?" I asked, trying to recall if I'd put on lipstick before I left the house.

"Great," she said quickly.

"Great what?" I was reaching into my purse for my compact.

"We're on live in," the camera man said, and I was wondering what he was talking about, "three, two, one."

"This is Monica McPherson reporting to you live from outside Grady Memorial Hospital," I heard Monica say.

I looked back up from my purse to see that she was speaking to the camera.

"Community members are here protesting the recent decision for the century-old hospital to turn into a 501(c)(3) nonprofit," she went on. "I have here with me—" she put the microphone in front of me.

"Me?" I asked, knowing I must look like a crazy person. Now

I knew how they got so many people to look completely insane on the news. She nodded. "Oh, I'm Kerry Jackson."

"Tell us how you feel about the recent decision."

"I think it's bad," I said. "And that the new plan would make it so that more people without adequate health care will suffer. These people didn't do anything wrong and we can't accept any plan that might even allow them to be displaced and left without a safety net."

Monica nodded and a few protestors gathered behind me, clapping their hands in support. I was amazed at how good I sounded. Surprising both Monica and myself, I snatched the microphone and looked directly into the camera.

"Rich or poor," I said. "We must protect one another and that has to start with making sure each American has access to health care. We won't stop until Grady hears that."

The crowd clapped and Aunt Luchie came over and gave me a hug right in front of the camera.

"You heard it here first," Monica said after taking the microphone back. "More news on this story later. Maybe we'll get Kerry to share more."

"That was great," Aunt Luchie said.

"Thank you," I replied. I felt my phone ringing in my pocket and I was sure it was my mother calling because she couldn't stop Tyrian from crying. I took it out of my pocket, and of course, her name was on the screen.

"Mother, guess what, I was just—" I said excitedly.

"Kerry, get to the hospital right now," she cried. "It's your father."

PART FOUR

Resurrection

"I really need to confess a love I knew from a past life. . . .
Love was so strong, I had to find this woman twice . . ."

—Abyss in "God Sent"
(Courtesy of Team Abyss, LLC)

Daddy

For so long, somehow in my head I'd managed to accept the fact that my father was dead. Well, at the time, he wasn't really dead, but my anger over his illness and fear of facing it left me and my mother with no choice, emotionally, but to bury the love we had for him deep down inside. So, while his body was alive, to my heart, he was dead. But after moving beyond that hurt and developing a new love for my father, even with his illness still controlling his mind, the thought of really losing him was unimaginable. Running into the hospital with Aunt Luchie at my side, all I kept thinking was that my father had died. My father had died and he'd never gotten to really see who I was, what I'd become and the life I'd made for myself. My son, his grandson, who was only a baby, but growing stronger each day, had never known my father to be the strong man he was when I was a child. The man who could hold me up with one hand when I was five years old and spin me around the room, calling me Super Girl. Tyrian would never know that man, and now he would never have a grandfather.

When we got off the elevator at the floor where they'd been keeping him, I saw doctors encircling the doorway and heard my mother's cries. Like me, she must have been feeling now, for the first time, the reality of losing him again.

"Hurry," Aunt Luchie said.

We ran down the hall to see my father for the last time. The doctors turned toward me as I got closer and I saw a look of compassion in their eyes. Tears began to fall as my feet carried me closer to the place where my father had spent so many days alone, so many days thinking the world had forgotten about him. I wanted to scream that I had not forgotten and I was here now to comfort him, for whatever it was worth.

When I stepped into the room, Jamison came toward me. There were tears in his eyes,.

"You made it," he said. "They don't know how long he's going to be like this."

"What?" I asked.

"Baby," my mother cried again, looking away from my father lying on the bed. "Kerry, come here. He's asking for you."

I can hardly describe the flooding of emotion that engulfed my body in those two seconds as I realized what my mother was saying. My heart went from sinking to flying as it thumped into action. What was my mother saying? Why was Jamison smiling, his tears now obviously happy? Was my father alive? Really alive?

"Daddy?" I called, dashing around the bed to stand next to my mother. His head was turned toward her and she had his hand in hers.

"Daddy?" I called again desperately. I didn't expect anything. This was the same man who I'd left at the hospital the day before. His mind had left him. There was no response that he could give me then to even let me know that he knew who I was. I had no reason to believe in my mind that there'd be anything different today. But this desperate call wasn't coming from my reasoning mind; rather, it came from my heart.

Then he moved. He turned his head just one inch away from a focus on my mother and his eyes, just as glossed and tired as

Tyrian's the day he was born, as if he'd just come off a long journey, set on me as if I was the miracle in the room.

"Kerry Ann?" He reached to me with his other hand.

I hadn't heard that voice in so long. It was scratchy and faint, but it was my father's, not doubt. And the weight it carried inside of me, the mere sound of my father calling my name pushed me to my knees. I fell to the side of the bed and buried my face in his hand.

"Yes, it's me, Daddy," I cried. "It's me."

He looked confused; I guessed it was because I wasn't the little girl he was expecting. But he smiled at me and moved his frail hand to the top of my hand.

"Super Girl," he said, running his hand through my hair. "I missed you."

"I missed you too, Daddy." I looked at Jamison, who was standing on the other side of the room holding Tyrian. He was still crying, but he had a smile on his face that I hadn't seen in so long.

He nodded at me and winked his eye.

"A miracle," he whispered.

Husband

That night, the night my father woke up from fifteen years of darkness, I felt like I was dreaming. It wasn't just that he'd woken up. The miracle was nothing like the one Jamison had predicted. My father was weak and still fading in and out of consciousness. One minute he'd be awake and crying, asking for someone or something he'd been thinking about. The funniest request was for a root beer float. Apparently, he and my mother used to split floats when they'd first started dating. But then he'd fade out and sit there not speaking for minutes at a time. The doctor said it would take months, maybe years before his mind fully pulled itself together, and then, he still might not return to being the man he once was.

So my father's waking was certainly a wondrous miracle, but the dream I was having was truly a combination of many things that were taking shape in my life. My mother. My husband. My child. My father. Myself. Pieces that I never even knew had been shattered were becoming whole again and the cloud I'd found myself floating on because of it seemed nothing short of the stuff that dreams were made of.

That night I rode home in the car with my husband in the driver's seat and my son in the back seat. I felt so secure, so complete in that position I couldn't stop crying.

Jamison kept telling me that if I kept crying my father would think he'd done something wrong by waking up and go back to sleep. I laughed, but it was more than that. I was crying for all of us. For the love we had between us and the future ahead.

Jamison and I said nothing to each other about the separation. And it wasn't because we couldn't face it. It was because, as Aunt Luchie said when she handed me the key to my house and said she would not be returning, it was "time to go home." What we were doing was right, and after talking to Aunt Luchie, I knew that while I'd been hurt by Jamison's affair, I was ready to move on . . . with my husband. And he was my husband. The man I loved. The man I missed. The man whose feelings I now knew I had to protect. Just as he'd done for me. We'd shared a covenant, an agreement that said that we'd grow together and forsake all others for one another. I believed that and I was ready to move on and do just that. And while I didn't care to hear the name Coreen or read an e-mail ever again, I knew that I could trust my husband. With my new clear heart and open ear, I knew that I could trust my husband to talk to me, and more importantly, trust myself to listen.

After Jamison put Tyrian to bed, he returned to a bedroom that was shining with the light of white pillar candles, and a bed that was covered in purple rose petals, and a wife who was sitting in the center of the bed wearing the same nightgown she'd worn on their wedding night.

"What's all this?" he asked, his eyes as wide as a child's on Christmas morning.

"It doesn't look familiar?" I asked in return.

He looked around the room and smiled.

"Our engagement . . ."

"Yes," I replied. "You filled a pool with rose petals and floating candles and asked me to marry you."

"Yes, I did." He came and sat on the side of the bed.

"And on that day you handed me a scroll that said that you had decided that you didn't want to live with the memory of me in your mind. . . . That you didn't want to spend another minute having to be a magician and recall me in your mind," I said. "Do you remember that?"

"Yeah, but I didn't know you did."

"I did and I want to let you know that I want you here by my side forever," I said, repeating the last words he'd written. "I love you and I don't want to go another day without being your wife. I don't want this separation. I might be your first wife, but I'm also going to be your last."

"Baby, you don't need to say this." Jamison took my hands into his. "What I did was wrong. What I did to my family was wrong. Do you understand that?"

"Yes," I said.

"So, I can't let you apologize to me or ask me to stop the separation. Neither of us were completely innocent in this," he said, "but as a man, I have to take responsibility for the fact that my actions caused this. It was unacceptable and if I have to spend every day of my life apologizing to you and my son to make it better, I'll do that, because that's just how much you mean to me. And if you take me back, I promise that I'll always come to you first with my feelings."

He stood up and pulled me to sit on the edge of the bed.

"So," he started, kneeling beside the bed. "Will you, Kerry Ann Jackson, have me as your husband, to love, protect, and cherish you all the days of your life? Will you be my wife again?"

"Yes," I cried, scooping him into my arms.

That night I made passionate, new love to my husband. It was as if we were together for the first time but already knew what the other needed. It was a first wife's wedding dance that I somehow knew would result in a second child. And the baby in the other room slept through the night . . . finally.

Son

Tyrian must have known he was going to be the baby Jesus on Christmas Eve, because he would not go to sleep. Jamison and I had finally gotten him on a regular sleep schedule, but his regular bedtime of 7 PM had come and gone and that little baby was wide awake when we were getting ready to head over to church.

Just after my father woke up, my mother and Aunt Luchie had arrived to decorate the house for the holidays. Suddenly, my mother was in the holiday spirit again. She kept talking about wanting everything to be just right for her grandbaby's first Christmas. And with the news that my father was going to be able to come home, with a nurse of course, she was beside herself. She came bearing boxes of trinkets and stockings that I hadn't seen in years. By the time they finished unloading everything, my house was transformed into the Christmases I once knew growing up. Tyrian's wide eyes bounced from one strange thing to the next as he waited in his carrier in the living room for his big day on stage.

"Jamison, we're going to be late," I called, picking up Tyrian. "Your mother said we needed to be there by eight or so."

"I know, I know." Jamison came running down the stairs way overdressed for the event, but I figured people would understand—his son was the baby Jesus. "I just didn't want to forget the camera."

He slid the camera into his pocket.

"We got everything?" he asked.

"Yeah, you, me, and the baby," I said, laughing at his nervousness. "That's all we need."

"Woman, you're playing and it's my boy's big day!" he joked. "Trying to make us all late."

"I was not the one dragging behind."

"I know, baby, but I'm excited," Jamison said. "Now, give me some sugar, Sugar." He kissed me softly on the lips. "And you too, baby Jesus."

He kissed Tyrian on the cheek and we stood there in the foyer of our home laughing.

Between mine and Jamison's family, the evening may as well have been called a family reunion, rather than a Christmas pageant. We were packed into the rows. While my father couldn't be there, both my mother and Aunt Luchie came out. Marcy and Damien brought Milicent. Even Ms. Edith and Isabella were there. Of course, Jamison's mother occupied two rows with her clan.

While I was nervous when I handed Tyrian off to be placed in the manger, the show went on without a snag. The children knew their lines and the pastor even got a band that was visiting from France to play music in between their acts. The audience loved the show and the music. And Tyrian didn't cry at all. In fact, at one point, he cooed so loud that we all started laughing.

When it was over, I had to go get Tyrian from behind the altar where they held the children for the pagent. While Jamison insisted on coming with me, I told him to stay with his mother. I wanted to walk to the back of the church alone, the same way I had when I ran into Coreen. Really, a part of me wondered if she'd be there again. If she was in the audience watching. My competitive side wanted her to see me happy and have a huge slice of humble pie, but I knew she wouldn't be there. And if she was, I had nothing to say to her. While I hadn't forgiven her for what she'd done, I'd moved on from Jamison's mother's drama and forgiven my husband. Nothing Coreen could say could or would break my spirit. There would be no fighting. I would not lose control of myself again like I had before. I was exactly where I was supposed to be, and so was she. I was stronger. Thanks to her.

"OK, here he is," Aunt Luchie said when I walked back into the sanctuary with Tyrian in my arms. "Now let's all get together and take this family picture. We need Kerry and Jamison in the middle with the baby." We began to find our places on the altar as others shuffled out.

Aunt Luchie stood guard, telling everyone where to stand.

"Let's hurry up; we got good food to eat at home," I heard someone holler and we all laughed.

"Oh, look at my godson," Marcy said, smiling at Tyrian as she, Damien and Milicent squeezed into a space behind Jamison and me.

"They ain't family," Jamison's mother murmured.

"Mama!" Jamison shot her a hard glare.

"Okay . . . Okay." She quickly snapped back into her place next to Jamison as he and I grinned at each other.

When we were all assembled and in place, only Aunt Luchie was standing alone in front of us.

"We look lovely," she said. "A family."

"Where are you going to stand?" my mother asked.

We began moving in to make space.

"Well, someone has to take the picture," Aunt Luchie reasoned, reaching for her camera.

"No, no, no," I protested. I couldn't have a picture without her in it.

"I can take the picture," a handsome, older man I recognized from the visiting band said, walking up behind Aunt Luchie.

"Oh, thank you." Aunt Luchie said, turning to hand him the camera.

She stopped almost immediately.

"Is that—?" my mother started as she squinted with her eyes set on the gray-haired man.

"Red," Aunt Luchie said, her voice heavy.

"Oh, my God," my mother said, leaning into me.

"I come all this way and you only got one word for me, Luchie May?" he asked.

"Oh, I got some more." Aunt Luchie dropped the camera just in time for Jamison to catch it.

"Who's that?" I heard people whispering behind me as tears filled my eyes.

Aunt Luchie jumped into Red's arms like she was still 19 and sneaking around the AUC. He laughed and held her up as she ran her fingers through his now gray hair, making sure, it seemed, that it was him.

"What happened to your red hair?" she asked, crying.

"Time, Luchie May. A lot of time."

E-MAIL TRANSMISSION

TO: dablackannanicole@yahoo.com
FROM: coreenissocute@yahoo.com
DATE: 1/1/08
TIME: 12:17 AM

I know this e-mail might be a little late, but I figured I'd wait until the right time to respond to your heartfelt message. And now, as I begin my new life, in a new year, I think it's good to let you know that I am fine. I was going through so much last year that I needed to pull back and really get myself together before I could reach out to anyone. I hope I didn't scare you, but I had to do this for myself. I've been running from my feelings for so long and I finally realized that I had to face myself and the pain I felt after losing Duane in such a violent way. I do miss him, but I didn't allow myself to feel that. I hid it with a bunch of other drama and I'm tired. I sold the house and moved to Oakland with a cousin and I am now seeing a therapist who specializes in helping victims of 9/11.

I am not sad about this. I am excited and ready for a change and prepared to let go of the pain. I am sorry for hurting people and I can only pray that God forgives me for what I did.

This will be the last e-mail you receive from me. I don't feel a need to carry on any relationships from the past. I am seeking to build new, healthy ones that match my new attitude. I hope you understand and know that this is not about you; it's about my recovery.

I wish you all the best in the New Year and pray for you and your family.

Coreen

HIS FIRST WIFE

Grace Octavia

ABOUT THIS GUIDE

The following questions are intended to
enhance your group's reading of
HIS FIRST WIFE.

Discussion Questions

Point of View

Making light use of the *Rashomon* effect, where various characters provide differing perspectives of the same event, *His First Wife* takes advantage of the idea that there are "three sides to every" *affair*. It evolves around three major points of view— the wife, the husband, and the mistress. In fact, secondary to their points of view, others provide their opinions of characters' actions. For example, as "girlfriends," both Anna Nicole and Marcy explain Jamison's actions based on their perspectives. How do these shifts add to the unraveling story? Is it necessary for Jamison to have his say and to also hear what might be going through the mistress's mind? Have you ever been in a situation where you wished you could be a "fly on the wall"?

Family and Marital Issues

Kerry and Jamison face many issues in their marriage. While they agree at the beginning of their courtship that family won't be one of these issues, the fact that both mothers are against the union eventually takes its toll on the intimacy the two share. In fact, Jamison's mother provides the veritable "pea" beneath Kerry's pillow. How do the mothers directly influence the issues between Kerry and Jamison? While they vow to remain strong and cut their mothers from matters surrounding their marriage at the close of the novel, can their marriage work if both families aren't on board? How else could Jamison have handled his issues with his mother?

Relationship Abuse

From the acceptance of infidelity to forced prostitution, mistreatment, and exploitation in relationships is discussed in the novel. Several issues are communicated through the choruses of women at the jail when Kerry is arrested and the sorority sisters she encounters at Marcy's party. What kinds of issues do these women face? How do they differ by economic class? How do both groups of women deal with their issues?

Brotherhood—Male Influence

It is said that if you want to know what someone is about, look at his/her friends. In Jamison's case, his best friend Damien is a successful man whose marriage suffers from issues of mistrust and infidelity, all stemming from his first affair. In fact, Jamison admits that most of his friends cheat on their wives. Was it only a matter of time before Jamison cheated, because his friends also live such lifestyles? How does Damien's opinion of Jamison's affair surprise and affect Jamison? How else do these black men influence one another?

Infidelity

Like other couples in the book who frequent grocery stores and hotels, Damien and Marcy seem to have accepted infidelity in their relationship and use it to grow seeds of mistrust and to allow for indiscretions; however, both partners agree that their marriage will never end and Damien claims he couldn't live without Marcy. Can their marriage survive in this way? Is it healthy? How does cheating affect the psyches of Jamison and Kerry? How does it affect Coreen? Do you believe Kerry and Jamison's relationship can survive infidelity?

Beauty

Kerry believes that others—including her mother, men she has dated, and other women—take issue with her dark skin and adore her long hair. While this is an old community topic, Kerry reveals that Eurocentric beliefs about skin color and hair continue to be an issue, even pointing to people's reactions to Milicent's color and hair as implication that it will affect another generation of black women. What examples does Kerry provide to highlight her own experience? How do adults influence Milicent to color her face white? How does the lifestyle her parents provide add to Milicent's issues?

Social Class

While lines are beginning to blur, Kerry admits that her elite social class in Atlanta discriminates against others based upon lineage—not wealth, education, or even social status. This is the biggest issue affecting Jamison and Kerry's marriage. While Jamison later makes more money than he did during their college years, he still feels Kerry sees him as a poor man who will never be accepted in her social class. How does this affect Jamison and create the conditions that might have led to his affair? According to Jamison, how does the way Coreen treats him differ from Kerry? Does it excuse his behavior?

Friends and Bad Advice

When Kerry tells Aunt Luchie that she waited to confront Jamison about the affair because of something Marcy told her, Aunt Luchie says Kerry needs to follow her own mind when making decisions about her own marriage. While well-meaning, the friends of both Kerry and Coreen offer what could be considered bad advice. Is there any truth, though, in their statements? Were the women right to seek support from their friends? How else could the women have handled the situations?

Career Success

While Kerry and Jamison were to go to medical school, for different reasons, neither did. Why is this? How does Jamison feel about the fact that he didn't go? How does Kerry feel about his not going? Switch the names around. Can Kerry ever truly be happy for Jamison's success if she doesn't find her own? Does she really want to be a doctor? Is she sincere in her desire to help poor women? Does this matter if it leads her someplace else career-wise? Does a woman have to have a career for her marriage to be successful?

Mental Issues

While there are small signs at the beginning of the novel, as time progresses, it becomes clear that Coreen is suffering from depression and loneliness. How does this heighten her attraction to Jamison and the affair? Does it excuse her actions? How is Jamison responsible for adding to her issues? Should he have paid better attention to the signs that something was wrong? Does Coreen get off too easily in the end?

Lost Loves

Aunt Luchie explains that Thirjane can not accept the love Kerry has for Jamison because she has not dealt with the possibility of losing her own true love to mental illness. She implies that a loss of love can lead to unexpected psychological issues—both good and bad. This is true for most of the characters in the novel—Aunt Luchie, Jamison's mother, Thirjane, Coreen, Kerry, and Jamison. What kinds of loss are these characters facing? How do they deal with the loss and how does it affect others around them?